■ SCHOLASTIC

BROKEN STRINGS

Maria
Farrer

First published in the UK in 2014 by Scholastic Children's Books
An imprint of Scholastic Ltd
Euston House, 24 Eversholt Street
London, NW1 1DB, UK

Registered office: Westfield Road, Southam, Warwickshire, CV47 0RA
SCHOLASTIC and associated logos are trademarks and/
or registered trademarks of Scholastic Inc.

Text copyright © Maria Farrer, 2014

The right of Maria Farrer to be identified as the author
of this work has been asserted by her.

ISBN 978 1407 13816 9

A CIP catalogue record for this book
is available from the British Library.

Printed and bound by CPI Group (UK) Ltd, Croydon, CR0 4YY
Papers used by Scholastic Children's Books
are made from wood grown in sustainable forests.

1 3 5 7 9 10 8 6 4 2

This is a work of fiction. Names, characters, places,
incidents and dialogues are products of the author's imagination
or are used fictitiously. Any resemblance to actual people,
living or dead, events or locales is entirely coincidental.

www.scholastic.co.uk/zone

For Beatrice, Katie, Tara and Rosanna

Chapter 1

I slump back in my chair, push the table leg with the bottom of my shoe. It grates across the floor and puts my teeth on edge. My head's hurting; pounding between my eyes. I shudder – full of hope, full of dread. Sometimes I wish I'd never started this crazy dream. It all seems so stupid now it's come down to this.

One performance.

I stare around the whitewashed room; gaze at a dirty smudge on the wall. After eight years of violin lessons, exams, competitions and trophies. After eight years of working my arse off, I get half an hour. Just half an hour to show the judges that I'm worth it. And I'm scared: scared like I've never been before.

I push the table again, then set about removing

my nose ring. Better try to look the part. And where the hell is Stefan? I'm not going to be able to do this without an accompanist. Why does he always have to be late?

My violin teacher comes in, stares at me and sighs.

"What are you doing, Jess?"

He means what aren't I doing. I should be well into my warm-ups. I lean forward, put the rosin on my bow and pick up my violin.

"Where's Stefan?"

"On his way. I've told him there's no piano in here. He'll warm up down the other end."

I don't want him down the other end. I want him with me. I check the tuning of my violin and start my exercises.

Mr Noble watches, leaning against the table, his face a mixture of smile and frown.

I hear snatches of music from down the corridor. Other candidates: three of them, and all younger than me. They're talented — that's a given — but I bet they're not skint, not desperate like I am. For them, getting this scholarship will just mean another certificate on the wall. For me, it's my whole future.

I stand up straighter, play over some tricky

phrases. My fingers don't feel like my own and I stop, put down my violin and shake out my hands. Mr Noble hands me a glass of water and orders me to drink. I grip the glass tightly, watch the surface of the water skitter and spill, then take a sip.

"It's OK, Jess," he says. "This is no different from any other performance. You'll be fine when you get out there."

I nod. But he's wrong. It *is* different. If I don't get this scholarship to get me through the next year then I'll never get to music college. I've begged from every charity. The grants are all used up. The money's run out and that's all there is to it. I'm done. I wipe my hand down my dress and pick up my bow again.

There's a knock and a lady puts her head round the door.

"Twenty minutes," she says.

My heartbeat rockets. I need another day; another few hours. Sickness swims through my stomach. Mum and Dad are in the audience, stressed out like me, most likely. If I fail today, I'll be flushing eight years of hard-earned lessons down the toilet. I can't do that to them. Not after they've given up so much.

I play some more. I'm making silly mistakes —
mistakes I'd never normally make. I wipe my hand
again. This is stupid. I've performed this piece
enough times before. I need to get a grip — and fast.

"I think that's enough now." Mr Noble smiles.
"Just keep it steady in the opening section. Don't
rush Stefan."

"Rush? Stefan? Have you ever known Stefan to
rush?"

"Calm down, Jess. I'm simply saying that you
need to pace the opening carefully. If you press
forward, Stefan will be forced to keep up with
you."

Stefan — my brilliant accompanist. He'll get me
through. He understands what this means to me.
And if I get this scholarship, then maybe. . .

"Jess, are you listening to a word I'm saying?"

I'm not, but I nod. I want to make Mr Noble
proud because this means a lot to him too. He's
given me hundreds of extra hours and only accepted
half payment — sometimes none at all.

"Thanks, Mr N." I give him a hug. "I'd never have
got here without you. I owe you."

"You can pay me back when you're famous," he
says, smiling.

"*If* I'm famous. . ."

"*When*. This is just the start, Jessica."

Another knock at the door.

"Five minutes," says the woman.

Five? My stomach swims. I take some short, quick breaths and windmill my arms round and round, trying to get rid of the adrenaline. I check the tuning of my violin one final time, then walk with Mr Noble to the wings. We don't speak. I can't speak.

Stefan's waiting for me, silhouetted in the light from the stage. I'm already a mess, but seeing him makes my heart charge off in some wild direction that I don't need right now. I stop for a moment and take in his tall straight back, his dark curly hair, while I try to pull myself together. I work to slow my breathing before joining him. He jumps when I touch his shoulder. So he's on edge too. I shiver.

"Hi," he mouths and gives my arm a quick squeeze. His touch is like an electric current and I close my eyes, letting the sensation run through my body. "OK?" he whispers, frowning.

I shrug. I've never felt this *not* OK in my life. "Left it a bit late to arrive, didn't you?"

He puts his warm hand on my shoulder and

massages it gently. The thin strap of my dress presses into my skin. If he's trying to reassure me, it's not working.

It can only be moments now. Stefan starts rubbing his hands together to keep his fingers warm and flexible. I know this ritual inside out: stretching those long, beautiful fingers, circling the wrists, pulling at his shirt cuffs. His eyes are fixed on the stage, focused on the piano, and I know he is mentally preparing his performance. I should be doing the same but the adrenaline is pumping out: too much, too soon. I swallow and force myself to concentrate.

The trombonist reaches the end of his performance with a flourish. I blow out my cheeks and puff out the air, as if I've been playing with him.

"He's good," I whisper to Stefan.

"Not as good as you."

The audience applauds enthusiastically; too enthusiastically for my liking. I tip back my head, stare at the ceiling. Eventually the trombonist walks off the stage and gives me a triumphant look.

Dickhead.

Only seconds away. I wait for the announcement. My legs are shaking so hard it's almost visible through my long green dress. I hope no one can see. I have to get this scholarship. I have to. I try to focus.

"Our second candidate is sixteen-year-old Jessica Cooke. . ."

Oh God, that's me. It's time.

"Ready to do it?" says Stefan, interlinking his fingers and stretching his arms in front of him. He gives me a too-big grin and we high five each other. I watch him walk out on to the stage, seat himself at the piano and make the final adjustments to the piano stool. A blackness settles in my body.

It's quiet now. The audience waits. I breathe in and exhale slowly. I push back my shoulders, prepare myself, and begin the lonely walk to the centre of the stage. It's exactly eleven steps. I know. I've played here before. I've counted. The audience claps. I wait until I'm in position, then turn and smile. The grey faces pin me in their gaze and the applause dies away, leaving a shuffling silence.

The body of my violin rests against my hip. I'm gripping my bow a little too tightly and I loosen my fingers. Every nerve-end in my body tingles and the seconds stretch out as I focus my muscles and my mind. I have to get this scholarship. I have to.

The auditorium lights fade to darkness, and I'm isolated in the white heat of the spotlight. I tilt my chin up a little and turn to Stefan. I nod.

Someone coughs.

The introductory bars of Wieniawski's *Légende* fill the auditorium. The notes are haunting, and I wait for that magic shift when the music carries me away from the moment and into a separate world of performance. It's not happening. I force myself to raise the violin to my shoulder, to lift the bow. The music rushes towards me and my fingers hover over the strings, searching for the first notes.

What are they? I can't see them, can't feel them. I grope around, try to start, but nothing happens. I can hear the violin in my head but my fingers are frozen, my arm held like wood in a vice. My chest is squeezing up. I try to gulp but the air sticks in my throat.

Stefan plays on, barely falters as he repeats part of the introduction, and I know he's giving me a second chance. I fight to clear my mind, to find the music. But it's gone.

In the silence that follows, the audience swims into focus, and I see them shifting awkwardly, whispering to one another. Embarrassed laughter, then hushed voices that rise to loud exclamations of shock and disbelief.

This isn't happening – none of this is happening. I flee to the darkness of the wings. But I can still hear the audience. Desperation explodes inside me. I lay my precious violin carefully in its case, take one last look at it, then head for the emergency exit and run.

I'm dead.

Chapter 2

I curl up in a tight ball under my duvet, my arms wrapped round my aching stomach. The volume on my iPod is turned up as loud as I can bear and I focus on the music pounding through my head. It doesn't work. Nothing can blank out what happened this afternoon. Failure floods over me again and again. Failure and humiliation and desperation.

And Stefan? What's going through his head? He must hate me. I embarrassed him, made him look like an idiot, then left him stranded. What did he do after I'd gone? All those people watching him. How could I do that to him? News travels fast in the music world and I'm not the only one trying to get a place at music college.

His image is huge in my head, as if he's here in the room. His eyes, his chaotic hair, his incredible hands. I know every tiny detail of those hands. I've dreamt about them. About him. But I've always known I'm kidding myself. Boys like Stefan don't go for girls from the wrong part of Manchester. Except I'd hoped – stupidly hoped – that if I could prove how good I was, if I'd got this scholarship . . . but that's all over now.

Oh God, I think I'll go mad if I don't see him. I fling myself on to my back and let the music throb in my ears. He wound me up so badly when I first started working with him. I thought he was a drip; just another posh public schoolboy. I never thought it would work, but things changed the day I pulled the piano stool out from under him as he went to sit down. I thought it'd be funny and I wanted to see what he'd do. I can still see the shock on his face, the anger, then the way he smiled and held out his hand for me to pull him up. I felt a bit guilty, so I took it, and before I knew it, he'd whipped my feet from under me and I landed with a smack on the floor beside him. One look at his huge grin and I started laughing.

"Truce?" he'd said.

It was only later he fronted up and told me he was terrified of me – my piercings, my big boots, my black eye make-up.

Since then it's been brilliant. Two whole brilliant years of working together. OK, I have a crazy, impossible crush on him, but I can live with that, because rehearsing with Stefan is the only time I don't have to pretend to be normal. He's never teased me or tried to steal my violin or told me I'm boring or weird. My friends — not that I have many — have no idea. I've been the odd one out since primary school and it's hard. I pretend it's not, but it is. And in my head I can't separate Stefan from my music because he's almost as important to me as my violin. He's part of everything I do and he's the only thing that keeps me sane half the time. Stefan just gets it. He understands — or understood. Now he'll think I'm useless. He'll never want to see me again and he'll find another musician to work with — probably some beautiful girl with lots of money who can afford to make mistakes. I just need one more chance to prove to him that I can do it: a chance I'll never get because it's all over for music, Stefan and me.

I stuff the corner of the duvet in my mouth and bite on it hard to stop myself from screaming. Misery hurts, physically hurts. It squeezes and pulls; it rips and tears.

I don't want to give up the violin; it's all I know how to do and it's all I want to do. I don't want to give up Stefan either.

The ache in the pit of my stomach gets worse. It's a strange sensation and I let myself dream that it's Stefan trying to pull me towards him – pulling me to where it's just us and the music and. . .

The doorbell rings and it jolts me back to the real world. What if it's him? Please let it be him. I stumble down the stairs too fast.

It rings again, longer this time.

"Get the door, can't you," yells Dad.

"I'm cooking tea," says Mum. "You get it."

"Stay where you are," I shout. "I'm getting it."

I hate to think what I look like. I run my fingers through my hair and try to spike it up. Then I open the door.

It's not him. Of course it's not. Instead I'm face to face with an old lady and the last glimmer of hope is squeezed out of my body.

"Jessica?"

I nod. Should I know her? She's got silver-grey hair set in perfect waves around her face. The rest of her head is covered by a headscarf. Brown leather boots, an old-person tweedy skirt, red sweater, jacket and three neat rows of pearls. She stares at me and I stare at her. At first I think there's something a bit familiar about her, but I'm wrong. She's way too fancy for round here.

"Does it always take you this long to answer the door?" Her voice is sharp. Accusing.

"Sorry? Can I help?"

"Is your mother in?"

Mum's voice comes from the kitchen. "Who is it, Jess?"

I raise my eyebrows and wait for an answer. Maybe she's hard of hearing.

"What's your name?" I say, a bit louder than normal.

"My name is Tara Chamberlain." She looks at me as if I'm supposed to curtsy or something. She sounds like the Queen too. "I'm your grandmother."

"Sorry?" She has me for a moment. She must be having a laugh. "I think you've got the wrong house."

I try to shut the door but she's got her foot in the way, which is pretty savvy for an old biddy.

"I don't believe so. Is this where Susan Cooke lives?"

"Yeah. Why?"

It must be one of the old ladies from the care

home where Mum works. It's not far away and Mum's always telling us how they get confused and go off wandering. I feel bad for her now.

"She says she's called Mrs Chamberlain," I shout to Mum, then smile at the old lady. She doesn't look senile. It's lucky Mum's on shift tonight so she can take her back.

I hear the TV go off and I jiggle from foot to foot. What's taking Mum so long? When she appears, she's wiping her hands down her skirt, her lips pressed together so hard they've almost gone white.

"You'd better come in," Mum says as she pushes me back out of the way and opens the door.

"She's a bit confused," I whisper to Mum. "She thinks she's my gran."

A look of panic streaks across Mum's face. Dad's in the hall now and he's not looking too happy either.

"You'd better *not* come in, I'd say." Dad's voice is cold, almost threatening. "You're not welcome in my house."

"Dad!" I can't help myself. "You can't just throw her out. She's lost."

"Dave, please," says Mum.

I look from one to the other. And I realize. She's not lost. She's not senile. They both know her.

"Good evening, David. I see you are still as charming as ever," says the old woman.

David? No one calls my dad David. She slowly removes her gloves and unclips her small handbag, dropping them inside. Her hands are elegant. There's a huge diamond on one finger.

I shuffle closer to Mum. "Who *is* it?" I whisper.

Mum ignores me – stares at the floor.

"Please leave now," says Dad, and he looks ready to pick her up and throw her into the road.

"Wait, Dave." Mum has her hand on Dad's arm. "I want to know what she's doing here."

"What do you mean, what I'm doing here? You're the one who wrote to me about Jessica's concert. I came to hear her play. I thought that's what you wanted." The old woman looks at me now.

"My concert? What the hell has this got to do with my concert?"

"What do you mean Susan wrote to you?" says Dad. "Why on earth would she do a thing like that? She hasn't heard from you for nearly seventeen years."

"Seventeen years? Can someone fill me in here?" I'm feeling pushed out of this not-very-cosy little circle. "Who are you?"

"This is my mother," says Mum. "Your

grandmother." Mum's voice is flat. I struggle to take in what she's telling me.

"But I don't have a gran." I stare at Mum.

"*Grandmother*," says the old lady.

"Sorry?" I say.

"I am not your *gran*, I am your *grandmother*."

I turn to Mum, who is looking at the floor. "I thought you told me my gran was dead."

Mum doesn't answer, but I know I'm not wrong. She told me her dad died before she was born and then her mum passed away before I was born. I've always felt sad for Mum about that.

"I have no idea what your mother has told you," says the old lady, "but I can assure you I am very much alive."

Her face is pinched. Unreadable. I look at Mum. Look at Dad. Nobody speaks. I switch my gaze to the old lady. Her eyes are like grey stones and she seems to be staring at some distant point.

"Can someone please tell me what is going on here?" I say.

Silence.

"Oh come *on*, everybody!" I raise my eyes to the ceiling and cross my arms, drumming my fingers against my upper arms as I wait and wait. Finally

17

my patience runs out, but I have so many questions I don't know where to begin.

"So you came back from the dead to watch my performance today?" I say to the old lady. "Lucky you."

"Not your best performance, I take it?" She raises one eyebrow and smiles condescendingly.

How dare she. I boil up and fight to hold it in.

"It's not funny and it's none of your business," I say.

"I see you have your father's temperament, and I agree, there was nothing funny at all about your performance today."

Dad takes my hand, squeezes it, pressing me to keep calm. I pull my hand away.

"Standing here is ridiculous," says Mum. "I think we should discuss this inside like sensible human beings."

"Sensible?" I laugh. "Who are you kidding?"

The old woman gives a short, satisfied little sigh as she steps inside the house. I kick the door shut and follow behind her into the living room. She perches on the edge of a chair, her feet neatly crossed at the ankles. Her eyes wander around the room. I keep looking and looking at her. Can she really be my grandmother? The atmosphere feels explosive – one match and boom. Or is that just me?

"Well, you'd better tell us what you want," says Dad. "I presume this isn't a social call."

"I have come to make you an offer."

"We don't want it," says Dad.

"More specifically, I have come to make Jessica an offer."

"It's Jess," I say. But I'm listening carefully. I'm curious about the word *offer*.

"I happen to have a keen interest in music," she says. "I believe young musicians should be supported. I hoped to be excited about your performance today, Jessica. I hoped you would get your scholarship. You did not."

"Thanks for reminding me."

She puts up her hand. "Wait until you have heard what I have to say. I have reason to think that you may be deserving of another chance. So I have decided to give you that chance."

"What right have *you* got to decide anything?" says Dad.

I ignore Dad. So does she. "What do you mean? What sort of chance?" I say. I don't care who she is, I want to know more.

19

"In the absence of your scholarship, I am offering to pay for all your music studies for the next six months."

I'm all ears now. Did I hear right? This is the kind of grandmother I could get to like.

"After that we should have a good idea of whether or not you can make it to the next level – to a level where you can confidently audition for music college."

"*We?*" says Dad. "You've never even acknowledged that Jess was born and now all of a sudden it's *we?*"

I wish Dad would shut up. How could she acknowledge I was born if Mum's been telling everyone she's dead?

"I can," I say to her. "I can make it to the next level. I promise. I'm good. Normally. Today was just. . ." I need this woman to believe me.

The old lady waves my words away as if she couldn't care less. I wonder what I can say to convince her.

"I understand, Jessica. However, that doesn't change the fact that you have to learn to perform, even under extreme pressure."

"But usually . . . I mean, it's never happened before and I've done, like, hundreds of performances."

I look to Mum and Dad for support. Immediately I see the doubt in their eyes. "Tell her," I say to them. They say nothing.

"There are, of course, some conditions attached to my offer," she says.

"Here we go," says Dad, folding his arms.

She ignores him and speaks to me and I'm concentrating hard. "You will move to London to live with me for six months."

"She will not," says Dad.

"I will be responsible for all your living costs and any educational costs, whether they be music or academic. You will, of course, need to continue to study music A-level, and we may need to discuss your other subjects. I will make the rules. You will abide by them. I will not tolerate any interference from anyone else. If any of these conditions are not met, my offer will be withdrawn immediately and you will return home."

I try to take it all in. It sounds more like an arrest than an offer, but all I know is that if she's going to pay for everything, for six months, then I'm up for it.

"Six months!" Dad's standing and shouting now. "You think we'd let our daughter go and stay with you for six months after what you did to Susan?

You've got a nerve coming in here and making your demands. This is my house and I make the rules here."

"Hang on, Dad. . ." I say, but no one's listening to me.

"So you'd rather keep Jessica here with you and see all that talent go to waste? See her dreams destroyed?" The old lady's eyes are blazing.

"What do you know about her talent — or her dreams, come to that? You'd never met her before today."

"I think you'll find I know more about her dreams than you think."

"How dare you!" Dad's hands are clenched.

"I think I'm the only one who knows. . ." I begin again, but it's pointless and my voice is drowned out by Dad's. My eyes begin to fill with tears and I blink them back and try to focus on what is being said. I can't even begin to make sense of what's happening, but I know that this lady is the only one who seems to understand. She's the only one offering to help.

"You've not been in touch with us for seventeen years. Nothing. Not a single word. Now you come waltzing back in here and try to tell us what's best for

Jess. If you're so keen to support her, what's wrong with paying for her studies here in Manchester?" With each sentence, Dad slams his fist down on the arm of the chair. The wooden frame is poking through the foam. It must hurt.

"I believe this is a decision only Jessica can make," says the old lady. Her voice is quiet and calm. She turns to Mum. "You know I can provide her with the right environment in London. She'll never get that here." She looks around our living room. "Will she?"

"She's managed all right up to now," whispers Mum.

"Up to now. Exactly. But what happens next? I suggest you talk some sense into this husband of yours. I give you my word I will look after her."

"Like you did Susan?" asks Dad, and his voice is full of sarcasm now. "The answer is no."

"I don't think you understand, David. Do you want to wreck your daughter's life?"

"That's rich – coming from you."

I look at Mum. She's like a statue. I wish I knew what they were talking about.

"I'm leaving now," says the old lady. She's removed the gloves from her bag and she's putting them on. "I have put my offer in writing and I will expect Jessica's answer within the week. There's no time to waste."

She fixes me with her grey-brown eyes and places an envelope on the shelf.

"You can't go," I say. "Not just like that."

"Oh yes she can," says Dad. "And she needn't come back either."

The old lady ties her headscarf as she walks out.

I jump up and follow her. Dad tries to stop me but I shake him off, open the front door for her and follow her out. She looks out of place on the streets of our housing estate and I hope the neighbours aren't watching or they'll be poking their noses in as usual. She heads for a taxi waiting on the far side of the road.

"Where are you going now?" I ask as I match my steps to hers.

"Back to London." She opens the door and climbs in.

"Are you really my grandmother?"

"It's hardly something I would lie about."

"Mum lied about it."

The old lady shrugs but says nothing.

"And will you really pay for everything – all my lessons – everything?" I continue.

"I don't make empty promises."

"Why did you decide to come to listen to me today? You have to tell me that much, at least."

"I don't *have* to tell you anything."

"But Mum says she wrote. I mean, why couldn't you help me before? Why now?"

"You ready?" asks the driver. "You'll miss your train unless we get going."

The old lady pulls the door shut.

"Wait," I say, rapping on the window. She winds it down a little. "I can't understand why you would do this. You don't know anything about me."

"No one should have to give up on the basis of one performance. That's all I need to know."

I'm holding on to the door handle of the taxi as it starts to move.

"What's up with you and Mum, anyway? What happened?"

"Let's just say we've had our differences. Think about my offer carefully, Jessica. It's your choice – your life."

"But I want to know about you and Mum." I jog for a few steps but it's hopeless and the taxi pulls away.

"What differences?" I yell after it and kick the edge of the kerb. Ouch. I hop around on one foot holding my toe. I hobble back to the house. The door's closed but Mum and Dad's voices are loud.

". . .and I'm not having it," says Dad.

"But what about Jess?" says Mum.

Yeah, what about me? I bang on the door.

"I'm not letting her go," I hear Dad say. "What are you thinking of, Susan? Are you out of your mind?"

I rap on the window, ring the doorbell long and hard.

"Mum! Dad! It's freezing out here."

Their voices stop.

"Sorry, love," Dad says as he opens the door and pulls me inside.

I square up to him straight away. "Well, thanks a million. That woman —" I jab my thumb towards the outside "— that woman — my grandmother — who you told me was dead — comes here offering to pay for all my music tuition and what do you do? You tell her to go away!"

"Now just one moment, young lady."

"How could you do that? You don't give a shit about me, do you?"

"You mind your mouth, Jess. I know you're

upset, but you don't understand who you're dealing with here. Trust me."

"Trust you? After you and Mum have lied to me for all these years? I don't care who I'm dealing with. If she's giving me the chance to keep studying, then I'm going to take it, and I don't care what you and Mum think."

"That's enough. The answer is no. You simmer down and we'll talk about all this later."

Mum's yanking her coat over her shoulders and tying the belt with a too-tight knot. She picks up her work bag and walks out of the door without saying goodbye.

Dad watches her leave, and then he and I stare at each other for a moment. His nostrils flare in and out as he breathes. That only happens when he's properly angry, but I'm not giving in now.

"She said it's my decision. I'm sixteen — nearly seventeen. I'm old enough to decide for myself and I've decided I'm going."

"And I've decided you're not."

Dad heads for the door.

"Where are you going?"

"To the pub. Don't wait up."

The door slams and I'm alone in the house.

I walk back to the living room, sit down, close my eyes and try to make sense of everything – of *anything* – but I'm left with more questions than answers. I take Grandmother's letter from the shelf and slide it backwards and forwards between my thumb and first finger before easing up the flap carefully. The paper feels thick and heavy, the address and phone number printed in the centre at the top. She's written in bright blue ink and her handwriting is spiky and tall. A letter from my grandmother. A grandmother who wants to help me. My hands are unsteady as I read.

Dear Jessica,

I am writing this after your concert, at which I was present, following the invitation from your mother. I thought it better to come anonymously, for reasons which I suspect will become clear.

Your performance was not what I had hoped for and, I dare say, not what you had hoped for. However, I am inclined to believe that you deserve another chance. I propose that you come to live with me in London for a period of six months. You will continue with your musical studies and may also be schooled in other areas as I see fit. I will personally

*fund all your living and education expenses. You
must obey my rules at all times. Failure to do so will
result in a total withdrawal of my offer.*

*At the end of six months we will evaluate your
progress and make appropriate plans for your future.*

*I will expect your answer within the next few
days. If I do not hear from you, I will assume that
you do not wish to take up my offer.*

Regards,

Grandmother

There's no time to waste. I don't stop to think.
With my hands shaking, I pick up my phone and
punch in the old lady's number. I still can't believe
she's my grandmother. When she answers, the line
is faint. She must still be on the train. I can hardly
speak.

"I'd like to accept your offer," I stutter out.

"I'm sorry? You'll have to speak up."

"I'd like to accept your offer." I make my voice
strong. "I'd like to come to London."

"And your parents are in agreement?"

"Yes," I lie. Why shouldn't I? They've lied to me.

"Good. I will book you on to the 14.15
tomorrow and I will arrange for your train ticket

to be ready for collection at the ticket office at Manchester station. Just give my name. We will meet you at Euston."

"Tomorrow? As in . . . tomorrow?"

"We have no time to waste, Jessica."

"But that doesn't give me much time to. . ."

And the phone goes dead. Did she hang up? I have no idea. Tomorrow? I sit silently for a moment, feel the blood racing round my body. I check my surroundings to make sure this is for real.

Then I text Stefan. It seems the natural thing to do and it's the perfect excuse to make contact with him.

You'll never guess what's happened. I'm going to London to study for six months. Call me. X

My thumb hovers over the send button. I take out the kiss, then put it back in again. What the hell. I press send.

There's a long pause, then "message sending failed" comes up.

I try again.

Same thing.

Perhaps he's blocked my number. Can you do

that? Refuse access to someone who's trying to contact you? Surely he can't hate me that much?

I haven't got much credit left but I decide to dial his number.

Nothing.

I need to talk to him. If Stefan hears about what's happened, it will all be all right. I know it will. I'm bursting with excitement and I have to tell him. No one else can know.

I try one last time, double-checking every digit . . . work, please work.

It doesn't.

I shriek and hurl my phone across the room. It hits the table on the far side and falls apart. Swearing, I kneel on the floor, gather up the pieces and try to put them back together. When I try to switch it on again, it's dead. I'm such an idiot.

I'm glad I'm leaving Manchester. There's nothing for me to hang around for now. No music, no Stefan, nothing. I'm ready to go. Right this minute.

Chapter 3

No one was home to witness my escape. Now I struggle along Platform 9 at Manchester Piccadilly station with only seven minutes until the train leaves.

People rush past, rolling suitcases, carrying bags. For about the hundredth time, I check my ticket. *"The train on Platform Nine is the fourteen fifteen for London Euston calling at. . ."* People hurry towards it.

I get on and look around for somewhere to sit. I see a woman who looks about Mum's age. She's close to the doors and there's space for my bag. I stretch up and put my violin on the rack above, then yank down my skirt and sit down. Her eyes are on me all the time, making me uneasy.

I don't sit by the window. I don't want to risk being spotted. What if Mum and Dad have found out? Right this minute they could be rushing towards the station to pull me off the train and take me home. I turn my body so my back is facing the window.

The whistle blows and a few stragglers rush for the train. The doors hiss shut. The train judders forward and begins rolling out of the station. I chew my nails and feel my fingers shaking against my lips. I slide across into the seat next to the window and watch as my hometown disappears into the distance.

The train's almost full. A youngish man eyes the seat next to me.

"This free?" he asks.

I nod. His dark, curly hair reminds me of Stefan. If only it was Stefan. Imagine if we'd run away together? I tell myself to shut up.

What will Mum and Dad do? I picture them reading my letter.

Dear Mum and Dad,

I am writing to tell you that I have gone to London. Please don't be angry. I know I should have told you but I knew you would only say no. I didn't want us to argue any more.

I can't stop playing the violin. Not while I still

33

have a chance. And my grandmother is giving me
that chance. I hope you understand.

Please don't try to come and get me. I have made
my decision. And DON'T WORRY. I'll be fine and
it's only for six months.

I love you both.

I'm sorry.

Love, Jess

I swallow hard. Blink. But it's no good. The tears overflow and run down my cheeks. I never normally cry but since yesterday it's all I've done. The man next to me turns away a little and plays a game on his iPad. My nose is streaming again. The lady opposite holds out a tissue and gives me a little smile. I take it and blow my nose loudly.

"You all right?" she asks.

I nod and stare out of the window. The buildings of the city thin out and green fields take over. The gentle rhythm of the train is soothing. There's music in everything if you listen. I close my eyes and try to relax, but I'd be kidding myself if I said I wasn't terrified. I've no idea what's waiting for me in London. I wish I knew more about whatever happened in the past – between my mum and my grandmother. It can't have been good. I'll find out all in good time, no doubt. Still . . . I wonder.

I must've fallen asleep because next thing I know, I'm awake with a jolt, my neck aching. Snippets of strange dreams flick through my thoughts. Stefan and Dad are screaming down a long tunnel and I try to hold on to them but I can't. The woman opposite is smiling. I check my watch. Still forty minutes to go. I rub my neck.

"Good sleep?" asks the woman.

I nod. The man beside me has gone.

"Off somewhere nice?" she continues.

Nosy old bat. She reminds me of my teacher in primary school.

"I'm going to stay with my gran." As soon as it's out of my mouth, I know I shouldn't have said anything. What if someone's heard? Of course no one has. Or no one that matters. Nobody on this train knows me. Nobody in London knows me.

"You lucky girl, how lovely. Nice week with Granny in London. Splendid."

"Six months, actually."

The woman looks surprised.

"How old are you?" she asks.

I hate that question. I can't see what difference it

makes. "Seventeen." I'm not seventeen until August, but seventeen sounds better than sixteen.

She shuts up for a while, which is a relief. Then she starts off again.

"So what're you off to do in London for six months?"

I can't just ignore her. "Play the violin, mostly."

"That's interesting. Nice instrument. My daughter used to play. Got to Grade 5. She was very good. Have you done any grades?"

"I did Grade 8 when I was thirteen." It slithers out sounding mean, condescending.

"Goodness. You must have started playing when you were a baby." She stops talking then, goes back to her magazine.

She's wrong. I wasn't born wanting to play the violin and I didn't start until I was eight. I'll never forget that day when the *Make Music* people turned up at school. I wouldn't have been able to tell you what a violin looked like. I remember walking in pairs to the school hall. I was with my friend Beth – as usual. We plonked ourselves down, cross-legged, on the dusty floor. I put my elbows on my knees and my chin in my hands. That's what I did when I wanted to look uninterested, which was most of the time. I wasn't really naughty, just bored.

I glared at the music people as they showed off their instruments and invited the good children to go up. And then the violin lady started to play. I stopped my wriggling. Listened. I couldn't believe so much sound could come out of one small wooden thing. It was magical. The music pulled me up and down and round and round. I remember closing my eyes and letting my body sway – Beth nudging me and giggling.

"You," said the violin lady, pointing in my direction with her violin bow. "Would you like to have a go?"

I looked around to check it was me she was talking to. Beth gave me a push and I scuffed my way to the front.

The lady put the violin in my hands and I knew I never, ever wanted to let go.

That's how it was. That's how it is. That's why I'm on this train.

I press my face against the window of the train. Think about Beth. If only her dad hadn't got that job in Dubai. I still miss her. She'd understand why I'm doing this.

The scenery is changing again. We must be getting closer to London because we're back into streets and houses. The train's slowed down and we're gliding through the buildings at a steady pace, past blackened walls with no windows. A train flies past in the opposite direction and suddenly I'm travelling at the speed of light. Then it goes quiet again.

It's stop-start into the station until the train shudders to a halt and everyone gets up at once. I put my bag over my shoulder, my ticket between my teeth, my violin in one hand and my case in the other. I struggle out of the door and follow the crowd towards the barrier. I'm about as far away from it as I could be.

On the far side of the exit there are hundreds of people milling around. I try to spot my grandmother but I can't see anyone who looks like her at all. What do I do if she doesn't turn up? I check my watch. Mum and Dad still won't know. I wish I had my phone.

I scan the faces again. A young fair-haired guy looks as if he's checking me out and I give him the evils. I'm pushed in his direction by the river of people leaving the platform and I cling on to my violin and my suitcase. Next thing I know, he steps forward, almost blocking my path. Suit, tie, scar by his eye. He's good-looking, but I'm not stupid. I veer to the left to avoid him and bash into a buggy with my violin. The baby's already crying.

"Hey, watch what you're doing," says the woman. She's all aggression and I mumble an apology.

"Jessica Cooke?" It's the same guy, I'm sure. He's right behind me and when I turn I'm face to face with him. He's looking down at my violin case. How does he know my name? There's no name on the case. In a rush of panic, I turn and keep walking. *Police* is my first thought. Mum and Dad have sent someone to fetch me home.

"Jessica?"

"Yeah?" I say, still moving.

A hand on my shoulder. "Don't worry. I'm Charlie, Mrs Chamberlain's driver. I've come to collect you."

I don't know if I'm more relieved or embarrassed.

"Driver? How was I supposed to know she had a driver? She never told me you'd be picking me up."

"Check your phone," he says. "Mrs Chamberlain left you a message."

"My phone's died. Or I killed it, to be more specific."

Charlie grins. "That sucks."

"Where is she, anyway?"

I like his smile. He's fit. Doesn't look that much older than me. What's he doing driving for an old lady?

"She – Mrs Chamberlain, that is – is having tea with a friend."

"I thought she'd be here to meet me."

"You'll see her soon enough."

"How did you know it was me?"

He glances at my violin case. "Not too difficult. Mrs Chamberlain told me to look out for a scruffy girl with a violin. Couldn't miss you!"

"Thanks a lot."

"Only joking," he says. "Don't take it to heart."

Now I feel silly. He takes my case and I follow him through the station and out the back. It's way busier than home. The air is different. Heavy. There's solid traffic as far as I can see. We stop by a small black car.

"Is this it?" I ask. Somehow, I guess because my grandmother employed a driver, I expected something bigger.

"Yeah, sorry. The Rolls-Royce is in the garage at home."

"Really?"

"No," he laughs. "Mrs Chamberlain doesn't believe in gas-guzzling cars. Do you want to hold on to your violin or shall I put it here with your case?" He's got the back of the car open.

"I'll hold on to it."

"Front or back?"

"Sorry?"

"Do you want to sit in the front or back?"

"Front – if that's OK."

"Fine with me." He opens my door and stands waiting, like I'm royalty or something. I get in quick and he shuts the door, then goes round and swings into the driver's seat.

"First time in London?" he asks.

"Yep."

"It's a great place, you'll love it." He leans forward as if he's trying to get a better view. His eyes are the palest blue.

"Do you come from London, then?" I ask. "I mean, were you born here?"

"Yes. East End boy, through and through. You can probably tell from my accent. Mind you, it's nothing compared to what it used to be." He puts on a posh voice. "The influence of Mrs Chamberlain."

I laugh. He's got Gran's accent completely sorted.

He drives with one hand on the steering wheel. With the other he points out streets and buildings, telling me their names, giving me a bit of history. He knows everything.

"One day I'll drive a black cab," he tells me.

"Why – what's wrong with working for Gran – sorry, Grandmother?"

"Nothing at all. But she won't be around for ever."

"Have you worked for her for long?"

"Three years – give or take."

"She can't be that bad, then."

He gives me a funny look, but it's good to know that he's stuck with her for quite a while.

Shaftesbury Avenue, Piccadilly Circus. He doesn't hang around, and I cling on to the seat as we dart in and out of the traffic.

"Want to see Buckingham Palace?" he asks, checking his watch. "We've got time. Mrs Chamberlain won't be finished until six."

Six? I swallow. Mum or Dad will have found my letter by now.

"OK." I try to sound enthusiastic.

We've slowed down to a crawl. The traffic's heavier than ever. I feel a bit sick so I open my window and the heat rushes in.

"Has my grandmother said anything about me coming?"

Charlie doesn't answer straight away. "Nope. Just said for us to have everything ready. She's been busy setting up your schedule."

"My schedule? What sort of schedule?"

"Dunno. I just drive."

Charlie doesn't strike me as a person who "just drives".

We circle Trafalgar Square. I want a better look at the top of Nelson's Column and I stick my face so far out of the window that a passing taxi nearly knocks my head off.

"Watch yourself," Charlie says, pulling me back into my seat.

We head through an archway and on to a wide open road.

"This is the bit you see on the telly," says Charlie. "The Mall – all the way up to the golden angel and the palace."

I like the feeling of openness after the buildings

and heavy traffic. I sit back in my seat and feel the cool breeze on my face. This is the right decision – I know it is.

"There you go," says Charlie. "Buck House in all its glory."

It's pretty impressive. Huge.

"Not exactly cosy, is it? Imagine having soldiers outside your house all the time."

Charlie laughs. "You'd be a hard one to please."

We leave the palace behind and keep going and going.

"Hyde Park," says Charlie as we catch glimpses of a green area on the right. "Great place. I run round there most mornings, before work. It's lovely at this time of year. You could join me if you want."

"Are you having a laugh? Thanks but no thanks. Running's not exactly my thing."

"Well, you never know. You might get into it." He's almost laughing. I can't see what's so funny.

He checks his watch. "We'd better get a move on. Don't want you starting off on the wrong foot with Mrs Chamberlain. That wouldn't be clever."

"Why? What do you mean?"

"Oh, she can get pretty angry when she wants."

I bite my lip. I'm not at all sure that explaining to

her I've run away will be too clever either. Charlie must notice the worried expression on my face.

"Don't worry, we'll be there in good time," he says.

What am I going to say to her? I try out a few things in my head. Charlie turns on the radio but keeps the volume down.

"Do you like music – apart from classical stuff?" he asks.

"Just because I play the violin, it doesn't mean I only like classical music. Why do people always think that?"

"Sorry I asked."

"Don't be. It just narks me off that people think I'm a complete weirdo because I play the violin. And I don't just play classical music either, since we're on the subject. Rock, pop, heavy metal. You'd be amazed what you can do on a violin. Have you heard Judy Kang on tour with Lady Gaga?"

"Who's Judy Kang?"

"A virtuoso violinist. Brilliant."

"Oh." Charlie is silent for a moment. He seems unconvinced. "Foo Fighters. Bet you can't do that on your violin?"

"How much do you bet?"

"Why? Can you?"

"Maybe."

"Good thing I'm not a betting man." He's smiling again now.

I try to keep talking, to keep my mind off things, but the worry's gnawing away at my stomach. Soon, too soon, we turn into a smart street with big houses and start slowing down. No peeling paint, smashed glass or dog shit here. Charlie parks.

"Here we are," he says.

Number 68. I remember the number from Grandmother's letter. Now it towers up beside me, smooth and white. I can't see the roof without putting my face right against the car window. I count four storeys. As I look up, my stomach sinks further and further down. The nerves have kicked in hard and everything's jangling around inside. Is this my new home? Is this where Mum was brought up? I'm not sure I want to go in. This doesn't look very cosy either.

Charlie comes round and opens my door.

"Getting out?" he asks.

I stand on the pavement. Five steps lead up to the front door, which has pillars on either side. The door is painted navy blue with a massive polished doorknob in the middle.

He gives me a gentle push.

I force myself to move. The pale stone steps are so clean that it doesn't feel right to tread on them.

"Is this all hers?"

"What?"

"Does this whole house belong to my grandmother?"

"Yep," says Charlie as he lifts my suitcase from the back.

I follow him up the steps, tucking my hair behind my ears.

He presses the bell.

"Don't worry," he whispers, "if you play by the rules, you'll get along fine. Mrs Chamberlain's set in her ways but you'll soon get used to it."

Will I? I've never been known for playing by the rules.

Chapter 4

I take my usual deep breath to prepare myself. A woman opens the door. It's not my grandmother.

"Jessica, this is Sarah Partridge, Mrs Chamberlain's housekeeper," Charlie says.

"It's Jess," I say. "No one calls me Jessica."

Sarah grips my hand firmly as she shakes it. She is small and slim and dressed smartly in a blue skirt and white shirt. She looks about the same age as Mum – a bit younger, perhaps. She gives me a huge smile.

"Nice to meet you, Jess. Welcome to London." Her voice is friendly and kind. She stands to one side to let me in.

I take a few steps and stop. The hall is as big as the whole downstairs of my house, the floor a shiny pale marble that's slippery under my feet. In the centre is a round table with a huge vase of lilies.

Charlie nudges me forward.

"There's nothing Sarah doesn't know," he says. "If you've got any questions, you can go to her. That's what I do."

The air is cool inside the house. Sarah's heels click across the floor and I follow her, staring around me as I go.

"I'll tell Mrs Chamberlain you're back," says Sarah to Charlie. "She'll be wanting you to take Mr Ritchie home at some stage. They've just finished a lengthy phone call."

"OK. I'll pop Jess's things up in her room," says Charlie, "then I'll be ready."

"Don't worry," I say, "I can take my own things up."

"It's fine. Charlie will take them. I'll take you to see Mrs Chamberlain."

I scuff along behind Sarah to a door at the end of the hall. She gives quick knock and walks in. I tuck myself against the wall outside.

"Sorry to disturb you, Mrs Chamberlain. Charles is back, so just let me know when Mr Ritchie is ready. I've got Jessica here."

"Well, I don't want to see her now. She's caused me enough trouble already."

It's like a punch on the jaw. I've only just walked through the door and she doesn't want to see me already. Trouble? It must have been Mum on the phone. I wanted to tell Gran first. I wanted to explain.

I hear a man's voice. "Calm down, Tara. We've sorted it out with Susan for the time being. I'd like to meet the girl."

So I was right, it was Mum. What have they sorted out? And who is the man? I shrink away from the door and wait, heart pounding.

"Oh all right. Well, I suppose you might as well bring her in."

Doesn't Grandmother realize I can hear every word she's saying?

Sarah puts her hand on my shoulder and I prepare myself for the storm. I hope my cheeks aren't burning too pink. I count to three, hold my head high and walk in.

"Hi," I say, putting on a cheerful voice.

Grandmother stares at me and you'd think I'd just climbed out of the sewer.

"Good evening, Jessica." She makes it sound like an accusation. "I'd like you to meet Mr Ritchie. He is an old friend of mine."

"Very old," says the old man from his chair. He waves his walking stick at me in a cheery way. "I hope you'll forgive me for not getting up, but my pins aren't as steady as they used to be." He pats his legs with his hand.

His bushy white moustache dances as he speaks. I can't keep my eyes off it. His hair is bushy and white too. Not a hint of baldness. He leans forward and rests his chin on the curved handle of his walking stick.

"How was your journey?" he says. "It must have felt like something of an adventure." His eyes twinkle.

"George!" says Grandmother. She looks furious.

"I love the train, don't you?" he continues. "Such a pleasant way to travel. Much nicer than an aeroplane or car, don't you think?"

"I wouldn't know. I've never been in a plane."

"Never mind. Plenty of time for that."

Grandmother folds her arms. "Jessica, you have some explaining to do."

"I know," I say, and I launch into a long, garbled explanation. As I prattle on, I find myself talking to each of them in turn, hoping that one of them will understand. I keep going and going, like a tap that won't turn off. "And anyway, I did leave them a note – so they knew I was safe and everything."

In the empty silence that follows, they both watch me. Standing here, in the middle of this large room, it's like being back on a stage, isolated under a spotlight once again, and I don't like it.

"You said it was *my* decision," I add, looking straight at Grandmother.

"Yes, but that is no excuse for running away. You should have talked to your parents."

"You don't understand!" I shout. "I tried, but if Dad decides *no*, then it's no. What choice did I have?"

"Please don't raise your voice like that," says Grandmother, touching her fingers to her ear.

"Well, you're here now," says Mr Ritchie, "so that's all that matters."

"And your mother has agreed to let you stay," says Grandmother, "but you have caused a great deal of bother."

"And Dad?" I ask.

"I am sure David will come round," she says.

And I'm pretty sure he won't – but I don't say that.

Mr Ritchie clears his throat loudly. "I hear you play very well," he says. His change of subject isn't exactly subtle.

"Who told you that?"

"Hmm . . . I don't know. Memory's not what it was. You have that look about you, though."

"George, will you stop talking complete gibberish?" says Grandmother.

"And you enjoy playing the violin?" he chatters on as if Grandmother doesn't exist.

"I've run away from home for it, haven't I? That should tell you something."

"Indeed it does." Mr Ritchie smiles and gives Grandmother a look. I almost get the feeling he's impressed I ran away.

"When you say you *love* it, what do you mean?" he asks. "How do you feel when you play?"

"George, will you *stop* asking ridiculous questions."

Mr Ritchie ignores her and looks at me. I'm not sure if I should answer or not. He nods encouragingly.

"Depends on the day. Different, I guess." I'm staring at the carpet, shuffling my feet. It's so hard to explain. "Sometimes it's like the world disappears and it's just the music. That's when it's best. But only sometimes. If it's working."

"If what is working?"

"I don't know." I've said more than I meant

53

to. I don't want to sound like a nutter. I'd say it if Grandmother wasn't here. I'd admit that there's some kind of magic that works inside me. But I can't. She'll laugh at me.

"Well, let me know when you find out," he says. "And what have you been working on recently?"

I look at my grandmother. "Wieniawski's *Légende*, mainly. For my scholarship. I suppose she's told you what happened." I nod towards her.

"She might have mentioned it."

"It was the worst day ever."

"So at your performance, the *something* wasn't working?" says Mr Ritchie.

"Nothing was working. I didn't play a note."

"Oh well; these things happen. I'm looking forward to hearing you perform." He says it with such enthusiasm that I smile directly at him and his eyes twinkle back.

"We're all looking forward to hearing Jessica perform." Grandmother's voice is hard and dismissive. "But no one will hear her until the time is right. And that will be my decision. I am not having any outside interference. Not even from you."

"Understood, sir," says Mr Ritchie, giving a salute.

Grandmother raises her eyes to the ceiling, then strides over to the door. "Charles," she calls.

After a couple of seconds, Charlie appears in the room.

"Mr Ritchie is ready to go home. *Now*."

"Am I?" says Mr Ritchie. "I suppose I am, if you say so. Would you mind giving me a hand?" Mr Ritchie is trying to stand up. Charlie hurries over to help.

Mr Ritchie takes a few uncertain steps before finding his balance.

"Goodbye, Tara," he says. He takes Grandmother's hand and lifts it towards his lips. He hardly touches it. Her face softens for a moment. It's like watching an old movie.

"And goodbye to you, Jessica," he says, turning to me.

"It's Jess."

He takes my hand and brushes his lips against it, just as he did with Grandmother. I giggle.

"Stop that silly noise," says Grandmother.

He gives my hand a little shake and whispers, "Keep your chin up."

I'd like to hug him. Instead I watch him leave with Charlie. The door closes and Grandmother fixes her gaze on me, her eyes sharp again.

"Right. First you must ring your mother to apologize."

"I can't. My phone's broken."

"Really. In that case we will go through to my office."

I follow her to a small room with a large desk and a carved chair. There are shelves and shelves stacked with magazines and books. My eyes run over the titles. She's definitely keen on music.

She points to the telephone and stands over me as I press in Mum's number.

It rings. Once. Twice.

"Hello. Susan Cooke speaking."

"Mum – it's Jess."

There's a silence at the other end of the phone.

"I'm sorry." I can't think of anything else to say.

"What do you think you're doing? Your dad and I are . . . well, how do you think we feel? How dare you run away?"

"I'm sorry," I say again, and hear a faint scuffle at the other end.

Then Dad's voice comes on and this torrent of words comes at me. I stare at a tiny oval photo on the desk. It's an attractive, dark-haired young woman with a baby.

"I warned you, Jess, didn't I? I'm coming straight down to pick you up whether you like it or not."

"No, Dad," I say. "Don't. I'm not coming home."

"You're my daughter and you will do as I say." I can hear Mum talking in the background.

Grandmother takes the phone from me. "We have already discussed this, David. Let's not go over it all again."

Dad's shouting so loud I can hear his words. "*I haven't discussed it with Jess. Put her back on the line right now.*"

Grandmother sighs and hands me back the phone.

"I'll not say this again, Jess." Dad's voice is so loud I have to hold the phone a little way from my ear. "If you don't come home now, there'll be no running back. Do I make myself clear?"

I nod.

"Jess?"

"Yes."

"Do I make myself clear?"

"Yes!" I shout back and hang up. There's no point in continuing this conversation.

Grandmother shakes her head. I can't tell if she's

angry with Dad or me or both. She interlinks her fingers and her knuckles stand out, hard and white and bony.

"I suggest you go to your room and unpack."

"Suits me." I don't want to talk any more. I want to be by myself.

"Dinner is at eight o'clock," she says. "Don't be late. And please put on a proper skirt."

I look down at my old black body-con.

"Something a little more decent," she adds as if I haven't understood her.

"Well so-rree, but I don't have another skirt."

"Oh. We will need to do something about that."

"Like what?" I ask.

"I will obviously need to provide you with some clothes; clothes suitable for London. You will have to go shopping. I can't have you wandering around in things like – those."

"But I don't have any money. I spent the last of my cash in getting to the station."

"That won't be a problem."

Not a problem for her, obviously, living here in this smart house. Even the furniture in her office looks expensive. My eyes wander back to the photo.

"Is that you and Mum?" I ask.

"Yes," she says without even looking. "Now I'll get Sarah to take you to your room."

She presses a little button on a phone on the wall and, as she hurries me out of the door, Sarah is already coming towards us.

"Oh, and Jessica, please take that ridiculous thing out of your nose. You are not a bull."

What is she talking about? I raise my finger to my nose ring and laugh. Is she for real? Grandmother walks back into her office and closes the door.

"Come on," says Sarah, "I'll take you up."

I stomp up the stairs behind Sarah. Remove my nose ring? Wear a longer skirt? My grandmother needs to get out a bit more.

"Here we are," says Sarah, pushing open a door. "I hope you'll like it."

My room is on the second floor. It's the biggest bedroom I've ever seen. At one end there's a bed twice the size of Mum and Dad's, a dressing table and a whole wall of built-in cupboards. At the other, there's a sitting area with a couch, a chair and a desk.

"Is this all mine?"

Sarah nods.

I run my fingers across the silky blue bed cover; look at the curtains hanging in heavy folds, held back with thick blue and gold ropes. I wish Beth could see me now. This makes her swanky apartment in Dubai look like a shed.

"And this is your bathroom." Sarah pushes open another door. I can't help gawping and I try to force my mouth shut. It's ten times the size of our bathroom at home and everything is oversized to match. Huge mirrors, huge shower, a bath like a swimming pool. The whole room gleams silver and white. No mould. No scum, no cracks in the tiles.

"And we have wifi," says Sarah. She's back in the bedroom. "So you can use your laptop anywhere in the house. Charlie will help you if you have any problems."

"One problem – I don't have a laptop."

"Gracious. I thought all teenagers had laptops these days."

"Mum's got one. I shared that when I was at home."

There's a knock at the door. Charlie's outside and he motions Sarah out to the corridor. When she comes back in she has a box in her hand.

"I gather you don't have a phone either," she says, holding out the box. "Mrs Chamberlain says to give you this one for the time being."

She hands me a brand-new mobile phone.

"You have to be kidding," I say. "My grandmother is giving me this?"

"Well, she's loaning it to you, yes."

"Wow. And there was me thinking we'd started off badly."

Sarah smiles. "Don't be too quick to judge your grandmother. It's going to be quite an adjustment for her to have a teenager in the house. You'll have to make some allowances."

"Yeah, well, it'll be an adjustment for me too and *she'll* have to make some allowances."

Sarah puts her arm around me. "Take it slowly, Jess. Let things settle. She's an elderly lady."

"That doesn't give her the right to boss me around and tell me what I should look like."

Sarah sighs. "Make sure you're ready by eight," she says and leaves me alone.

I open the cupboards and poke my nose into a few drawers. All empty. The contents of my suitcase hardly fill a shelf. I stack my music in a pile on the desk and I put my two photos on the bedside table. One's of Mum, Dad and me at my auntie's house. Our faces smile from the picture. I wonder if Dad'll ever speak to me again. I think of the photo in

Grandmother's study. Her and Mum together. Why did Mum never talk to me about her? Why haven't they seen each other for seventeen years? Perhaps Mum and Dad'll never want to see me again after what I've done.

I pick up the other photo, the one snapped for our local newspaper when I won a competition. I'm playing my violin and Stefan is bent over the piano in the background. I touch his face with my finger. I'd give anything to talk to him. I pick up my new phone, but what's the point? I don't even have his number – or not one that works. And now he won't have mine either.

I lie on the soft blue bed and bury my face in the pillow. I'm tired and I'm lonely. I will not cry though. I'm through with crying for the time being.

I go to the bathroom and my pale face stares back at me from the mirror, my eyes a smudge of black make-up. I look terrible. I start to remove my nose ring, then stop. If Grandmother thinks I look like a bull that's her problem. Anyway, I don't. This is what teenagers look like and she'll just have to get used to it. It's hardly breaking any rules – we were allowed piercings at school. I leave the ring where it is, then slip off the rest of my clothes before stepping into the shower cubicle.

I should've asked Sarah how to work the shower. Simple on and off is all I know – not all these knobs and levers. I play lucky dip. The first knob sends jets of freezing water from every side. I squeal and turn it off, then stand shivering as I concentrate harder on the controls. I turn up the temperature and then risk another lever. Water pounds down from a huge circular spray straight above my head. It's like standing under a waterfall. I don't move, just close my eyes and let the hot water stream over my body and gurgle down the plughole. I imagine all the misery washing down the drain with the water. Things will work out all right. I'm going to look on the bright side. Just like Dad always tells me to. This could be my best chance yet.

Chapter 5

It's past eight by the time I hurry down the stairs. Only five minutes late – not too bad. I've added a bit more eye make-up than usual and tried to tidy my hair but the results aren't great. Oh well; it's best she gets to know me as I am.

"You're pushing it," says Charlie as he looks at his watch and points me into the dining room.

Grandmother is waiting at the far end, standing behind her chair with her hands resting on its back. Between me and her is a long table with silver candlesticks and a glass bowl filled with roses. Dark portraits stare down on me from the walls. I pull at my skirt.

"You're late," she says.

"Sorry. I was having a shower."

"It rather looks like you forgot to wash your

face. You are not to be late again. Ever. Do you understand? It is rude and disrespectful."

Her anger takes me by surprise and the tone of her voice winds me up. OK, so I was a bit late and that might have been stupid but I've only just arrived and she can't expect me to get everything right straight away. It's hardly fair to get so worked up about five minutes. As we face each other, she stares hard at my nose and raises one eyebrow. But she doesn't tell me off.

"Dinner is ready. We had better sit down."

There are two places set at one end of the table. Grandmother at the head, me at the side. Just her and me, no Sarah or Charlie.

"I thought we'd have dinner together tonight so that we can get to know each other a little better," she says. "Normally I don't eat in the evenings."

Sarah comes in carrying two plates and I smell the fish before I see it. If it's not fish-and-chips fish, I don't eat it. The sight of the pale pink flesh on the plate turns my stomach. Sarah offers me potatoes, then spinach. I take five potatoes but refuse the spinach, and I start to eat.

"Hasn't your mother taught you any manners?" says Grandmother.

I stop with my fork halfway to my mouth. I've got no idea what she's talking about.

"First," she says, "you wait for me to begin before you pick up your knife and fork. That is common courtesy."

I stay frozen for a moment, staring at her, not quite believing what I'm hearing.

She leans towards me. "You wait for me to begin eating before you begin," she says slowly and carefully, as if I can't speak English.

I push the bit of potato off my fork and thump the cutlery back down on the polished table. I don't mean to thump it that hard and I know I shouldn't but I can't help it. I wait. She waits. Then she picks up her knife and fork and begins eating.

What was that about? I stab my potato again and put it in my mouth before she can stop me. She's still staring at me and I wonder what else I've done wrong.

"We hold our fork like this and our knife like this," she says, indicating her own.

"Well *we* don't," I say. It's not strictly true. Mum does, but not Dad or me.

I may as well give up now if I can't even get eating right.

"While you are in my house, Jessica, you will do as I say."

I nod. I know I've agreed to follow her rules but I didn't expect these kinds of rules. I squeeze my toes tight, then try to alter my knife and fork. How does anyone eat like this?

I push my fish round the plate, then put the tiniest bit on the end of my fork and press it between my lips. I gag and take a gulp of water to wash it down. I eat three potatoes, then prod around at my fish again.

"Don't play with your food. If you don't like it, don't eat it. I won't force you to eat. You could do with losing a little of that puppy fat."

That's the final straw. I stab a large potato on the end of my fork and stuff it in my mouth, whole. My eyes start to water. My mouth is too full. Puppy fat? That is not acceptable. Hasn't she heard about teenagers and anorexia?

Grandmother's eyes widen and I widen mine back, then quickly look away. I must not lose my temper, but why is she treating me like a two-year-old? I am not fat. I am not two.

"Is your bedroom quite comfortable?"

"Yesth," I say, my mouth still full of potato.

"And did Sarah give you the phone?"

I swallow with a loud gulp. "Yes." Then to prove I have got manners, I add, "Thank you."

"It's important you keep in touch with your mother. We don't want her worrying unnecessarily. I would ask you to use your phone wisely. I can check your bill, should I choose to do so."

My knife clatters against my plate. "It's none of your business who I call."

"Maybe. But I don't want you getting into trouble."

"You can't snoop on what I'm doing. I've got to have some privacy." I realize, too late, that I am pointing my fork at her.

"Don't wave your fork. I am not going to listen to your calls. And while we are on the subject of your phone, it is never to be turned on during mealtimes or if we have guests."

"Fine." I pull the phone out of my pocket and hold it so she can see me turn it off, then put it back.

"I do not appreciate your attitude, Jessica. If we are going to get on, then you are going to have to make more of an effort."

"I'd say that works both ways." It's out of my mouth before I can stop it. I'm used to answering back. I'll do my best while I'm here, but she's not going to walk all over me, and I think *her* attitude is pretty unreasonable right now.

We lock eyes until I give in and lean back in my chair. *Suck it up*, I tell myself. *It's only the first day*.

Sarah clears the plates and brings us raspberries and cream. I pour on the sugar and when I see Grandmother watching, I add an extra teaspoon, very daintily, for good measure.

I wolf them down. Grandmother eats like a snail and I am forced to watch every mouthful. It's torture. The silence stretches and stretches.

I stare around at the portraits. "Are those pictures of my relatives?" I ask.

"Yes."

"They're not very good-looking, are they?"

"There, at least, we have found something we can agree on. That is your great-great-great-grandfather." She points at a bloke with long curly hair wearing a blue and gold coat. "The one at the end there is your great-great-grandfather and the one behind you is my father, your great-grandfather."

It's a funny thing being related to all these people. Up to now it's just been Dad, Mum and me. Now I've got all these others, even though they're dead – and ugly.

"Where's my grandfather?"

Grandmother's eyes close for a second too long and she puts down her spoon. She dabs at her mouth with her napkin. She pushes her chair back and stands up. "We'll have coffee in the drawing room. Come with me." Her raspberries are left unfinished.

I'm surprised by how she reacted to my question. It intrigues me. She sweeps out of the door and into the living room – *drawing room*, as she calls it – and I'm sucked along behind.

"We have a lot to discuss," she says.

"Mum hasn't told me much about my grandfather," I say. "Apparently he died before she was born. That must've been hard for you."

Grandmother's face is etched with pain. She gives a brief nod and then busies herself picking up a folder and various sheets of paper. Perhaps I'd better shut up.

"Sit down, Jessica." Grandmother sits on the couch and points at the seat beside her. I do as I'm told. She's businesslike now and full of energy. When she opens the folder I see a complicated-looking timetable.

"This is your schedule. As you can see, your

lessons with Dr McNair and Professor Jenniston are arranged in two, two-hour blocks each day."

"Four hours a day?"

"Do you have a problem with that?"

"Yes. No. I don't know. I only had one hour a week at home. The rest was up to me."

"One hour a week? In that case you have done well to get to your current standard."

I take that as praise. "I do as much as I can. I normally get up at five thirty in the morning and practise for two hours and then try and fit in another couple of hours in the evening – depending on my homework."

"Gracious! You must have woken the whole street, not to mention your mother and father."

I laugh. "The neighbours threatened to kill Dad if I didn't shut up so Mum organized for me to practise at the library where she works. It was OK. Books make a good audience."

"I see. Well, I hope we can improve on that. Celia McNair will be your violin teacher. She's recently retired from the RCM – Royal College of Music – but she's one of the best."

"I know what the RCM is; I'm not stupid."

Grandmother gives a little sniff. "I'm pleased

to hear it. Margaret Jenniston will be covering the theoretical aspects of your studies and your music A-level. She is also a performance psychologist."

"Which is. . .?"

"She looks at ways to achieve the optimum performance even in high-pressure situations. She will help you to manage performance anxiety and nerves."

"Like stage fright, you mean."

"And other things."

"Stage fright is my own issue. I don't need someone else telling me what to do about it."

"You're wrong. Professor Jenniston is an expert. You are extremely fortunate and you should be grateful."

She's right. I should be grateful. I am grateful. I'm just not used to being told how to behave, how to think, how to dress. I'm used to running my own life and now someone I hardly know is running it all for me. I look at the blue blocks labelled PRACTICE: one between six and seven in the morning and another between six and eight in the evening. Three hours. Plus the four hours of tuition. My arms are hurting already. I'm not sure if I'm excited or terrified. Both, maybe. This is what I've always wanted – what I've dreamt of – and I need to make the most of it. Right now, it's all a bit overwhelming.

"Finally we have your physical fitness to consider," Grandmother says. "I have employed a personal trainer, three times a week, to work on your core strength and endurance."

"I'm not here to run the bloody marathon," I laugh. I assume she's joking.

"Jessica, I will not tolerate swearing. Playing an instrument is very demanding on the body. If you are to avoid injury, you will need to make sure your body is in perfect condition. Breathing, posture, stamina. They are all key to your success."

She is not joking. "But I'm not an exercise person!"

"From now on you will become an exercise person. Exercise is good for the mind as well as the body."

"It's not good for my mind or body, I promise."

"I think I will be the judge of that."

I swallow. "What will I be made to do?"

"That will be up to Rosie – your trainer. Your music programme will not begin until Tuesday morning. However, your fitness programme begins tomorrow. The rest of the day will be spent sorting out your appearance."

"My what?"

"Your clothes, your hair. We can't have you looking like some down-and-out."

I look down at myself. I'm not that bad, am I? I'm torn between resentment at her criticism and the nice idea of getting some new clothes.

"Thanks," I say, "but I'm sure I'll be fine." I can't have her wasting her money.

"You may be fine for suburban Manchester, but not for your life here. If you want to be successful, you have to look successful. Appearance counts for a lot."

I don't like the way she talks about my home. But I think of the terrible dresses from the charity shop that Mum forces me into for performances. I think of that green dress for my audition. That was the worst of all. Having new clothes would be cool. Except. . .

"What kind of clothes?" If Grandmother is going to come with me to *sort out my appearance*, then she'll probably force me into skirts below the knee and sensible shoes. Grandmother clothes. I know what I like. I wouldn't be seen dead in a flowery dress.

"Well," says Grandmother as she looks me up and down carefully, "I rather think you need clothes for all occasions. For that reason I have enlisted the help of Selina Marsh for the day. She is the daughter of a friend of mine and she works in the retail fashion industry. I think she calls herself a personal shopper. She will pick you up tomorrow morning and will help you find the things you need. I believe she is very good."

"Someone is going to pick me up to take me shopping? What about the money?"

"We don't discuss money. I said in my letter that I would fund your living expenses. Clothes are a living expense."

"And will she listen to what I like? Do I have to buy what she chooses?" My heart is racing now. I can't believe this.

"She will give you advice. Whether you choose to take it or not is up to you."

Wow! An all-expenses-paid shopping trip. I feel like laughing out loud.

Grandmother closes the yellow folder and hands it to me. "Do you have any questions?" she asks.

I look at the schedules. "I don't get much free time – to go out and stuff."

"Go out? But who will you go out with? Do you have friends in London?"

I shrug. I don't know a single person in London.

"As I thought. There is little point in us discussing going out until you have someone to go out with."

"But how will I make friends if I'm not allowed to go out?"

"I didn't say you were not allowed to go out. Should you want to go out, you may come and ask and I will make the appropriate decision. I'm sure you understand that while you are in my care, I must fulfil my responsibilities to keep you safe and well. I don't believe in young people being allowed to roam the streets without purpose."

"But I roam the streets without purpose at home. It's what people my age do."

"This is not home. This is London. And, as you say, you won't have a lot of free time. I'll be monitoring your progress and I am expecting to see one hundred per cent commitment and hard work."

"I always work hard. You don't have to worry about that."

Grandmother is on her feet now so I stand up too. We're almost exactly the same height.

"I hope I have made everything perfectly clear?" she says.

"I think so."

"Do you have any questions?"

I have hundreds of questions, but I don't think this is a good time to ask them, so I keep my mouth shut. She gives a quick nod, as if we have reached agreement.

"I'm going to bed now," she says. "I suggest you do the same."

It doesn't sound like a suggestion, more an order. "Goodnight, then," I say. I'm not sure what's expected of me. I step forward and kiss her on her cheek.

Grandmother stands like a board, as if I'd just slapped her. She seems confused. She hesitates, touches her cheek, then walks straight past me and out of the door. I'm feeling stupid and angry. Everything I do seems to be wrong. I make sure she's not looking and then I stick my tongue out and give her the finger. It makes me feel better — but not much. I watch her go up the stairs. She walks slowly and doesn't look back once. She's one weird woman.

I give it a few minutes before I head to my room. I don't want to bump into her again this evening — or ever. Left alone in the living room I have a snoop around, picking up dainty bits of china and putting them down again. I'm used to clutter: scribbled notes and discarded homework, cat hair and Coke cans and old family snaps. Everything here is clinically neat and tidy. I have no idea where Sarah and Charlie have gone. The carpeted silence makes me uncomfortable.

I tiptoe back to my bedroom and throw open the windows wide so I can hear the noise of the cars and the yowls of two cats fighting on the street. There's not much going on. I think of the twins from next door back home, kicking their football in the street, driving me nuts. Imagine if they did it here. I can't help laughing. They could do some real damage in this street.

Eventually, I close the window and shut the curtains.

I need to talk to someone but I can hardly ring Mum and Dad and theirs is the only number I know by heart – apart from Stefan's.

I check my watch. Ten sixteen.

I check Stefan's number in my head and dial. He won't realize it's me with this new number. Perhaps he'll answer. The phone rings and rings. Please answer.

Nothing. I flop down on the bed.

Six months stretches ahead like eternity.

Chapter 6

Heart racing, gasping for breath, spiralling out of some nightmare, I snap open my eyes. It's pitch-black and I sit up and grope around for a light switch. It takes me a few seconds to figure out my surroundings. I sit for a while with the light on, telling myself it will all be all right. I must fall asleep at some point because next thing I know, Sarah's shaking me on the shoulder.

"Time to get up, Jess. I've brought you these to wear." She puts a neat pile of clothes at the bottom of my bed. "I couldn't find much in your wardrobe that looked suitable for running, so I asked Rosie to pick up a few things for you."

I groan. "I'm not running and who's Rosie?"

"Rosie is your fitness trainer."

"Oh." Now I think about it, I do remember Grandmother mentioning someone called Rosie.

"Come on, it's a lovely morning. Here's some orange juice and a banana for you."

She switches off the light and opens the curtains. The hazy light streams in.

"I don't care if it's a lovely morning," I say, hiding my head under the duvet. "I hardly slept."

"Jess, *up*. You don't want to get into trouble, do you?"

To be honest, this morning, I don't much care. Grandmother's not really going to send me home if I don't go running. I stay buried under my duvet.

Sarah pulls it off the bed completely. "Come on, Jess. This is not an option."

"Whatever." I hang one leg off the bed, then the other, and I force myself to stand. My head is foggy.

"Twenty minutes," Sarah says firmly as she goes out and shuts my door.

I swallow some orange juice. It's fresh and the bitterness makes me shiver.

The clothes are hideous. These are things athletes wear, not musicians. Lycra. Yuck. The shorts have a kind of gusset in them. Do I wear knickers or not? I decide yes. The shorts are tight and they make my thighs blob out at the bottom. I quickly pull them off and put on my jeans.

I pray the trainers won't fit. I can't run without trainers. But they do fit – they fit perfectly.

I sneak downstairs and follow the sound of laughter to what turns out to be the kitchen. When I peep round the door, Sarah's talking to some stick-thin girl who's doing impossible stretches with one leg up on the back of the chair. The girl sees me and puts her foot back on the floor.

"Hi," she says, "you must be Jess. My name's Rosie; I'm your trainer."

"Hello," I say, looking as sulky as possible.

"Don't worry, we'll start slowly," she says. "You've not done much running before, have you?"

"I ran in a race once, at primary school. I gave up after that."

Rosie's got one of those irritating fake laughs. "Well, like I said, don't worry."

"I'm not," I say.

"And get those jeans off or you'll roast. Where are the shorts?"

"They're revolting."

"OK. Have it your own way." Rosie shakes her head as we walk out to the street. I check around to see who's watching as she tries to make me do stretching exercises on the pavement. I make a half-hearted attempt to touch my toes. Rosie shrugs and sets off at a jog.

The first few minutes are all right. Then my throat starts to tighten and before long I'm wheezing. I stop and hang forward, my arms swinging, gasping for breath. I didn't know it was possible to feel like this.

"Bet you wish you had those shorts on now?"

"I wouldn't be seen dead in those shorts." We walk for a way, then jog again. It's all right for Rosie. She spends her life doing this. I'd like to see her playing the violin. Finally, we stop in a green area with a few trees. I'm hotter than hot and sweat's pouring down my face, stinging my eyes and making a salty taste in my mouth. Rosie looks as though she's stepped out of a fridge.

"You'll soon get into it," she says. "You're doing well."

I am not doing well. I will not *get into it*. I lean heavily against the tree and gulp down water, wiping my mouth with the back of my hand. Now she gets me lying on the ground, doing stretches and twists and goodness knows what. It's nuts.

"Just a gentle jog home, downhill all the way."

"You go, I'll follow on behind."

I hobble my way back, Rosie running on the spot every now and then to let me catch up. I could kill her. My legs are like concrete; my nose is running. We get back and she rings the doorbell while I collapse on the steps like a blown-up strawberry.

"Thanks for your delightful company," she says. "I'll look forward to next time."

I swear at her under my breath.

"Having fun?" says Charlie when he opens the front door.

"No."

He holds out his hand to pull me up. Every muscle in my body hurts.

"I think you should go and take a long bath and have some breakfast," he says, "before I take you and Selina shopping."

I groan again. "Shopping is the last thing I feel like."

"I thought girls liked shopping."

"I just want to sleep for the rest of the day."

"It may not be so bad," he says. "Wait till you meet Selina."

Two hours later and I'm on the King's Road with Selina Walsh. She is not what I expected. She's young, she's sassy and she's fun. Much better than

Rosie. She wants to know what I like to wear, what I like to do, who my role models are. I don't give her much to get excited about. She says a cross between Lily Allen and Yehudi Menuhin might be hard to achieve.

"OK, we'll go with Lily then," I say.

We discuss skin tones, eye colour and hair colour, and she tells me what colours will suit me. I already know what colour suits me. Black.

"Black is not a colour and it's a bit dull for summer, isn't it?" she says. Well, she'd better know she's not getting me into emerald green or, worse still, pink.

Selina knows every shop and half the assistants. I check out each shop window before going in to make sure it's my kind of shop. I bet Grandmother's given Selina her orders but I'm not being turned into some prissy princess. Selina scans the display rails quickly and efficiently, picking things off, holding them up. She cocks her head at each one, then returns it to the rail or hands it to a waiting assistant. I hardly have time to think. She makes me try on things that I would never have looked at, but she's clever. A high-waisted black cotton skirt with a wide leather belt; neatly tailored blue trousers, narrow at the ankles with short silver zips; a grey silk dress with hooks all down the front. I love the feel of the silk and the little details of hooks and buttons. Then she hands me a green skirt. "Forget it," I say, and she puts it back on the rail. Casual, tidy, smart – she never does one thing at a time. It has to be the whole outfit. This with that, that with this.

Some things work and she cheers. Sometimes she just says "Horrible" and off we go again. After my run this morning, my whole body screams every time I stretch up or lean down to change. I curse Rosie under my breath. But Selina's enthusiasm is infectious and she makes me laugh. By the end I'm not sure what we've bought. But I know I've got good stuff and lots of it. This isn't so bad after all.

She consults her list. I've already got more clothes than I've had in my lifetime. Then we're galloping down the street again and she's grabbing my arm, pulling me into yet another shop. The smell is overpowering.

"Leather?" I say.

"A leather jacket. What do you reckon? Would you wear it?"

"I'd never take it off." Having a leather jacket would be the best thing ever.

She's sifting through the rails again. I catch a glimpse of a price tag and I nearly fall over.

"They're too expensive," I say.

"They last a lifetime," says Selina, and carries on.

"What will my grandmother say?"

"Do you care?" she asks, and then she smiles. "Relax. She's given me a budget and we're well within it."

"She must be rolling in it," I say, shaking my head. It strikes me as odd that someone who doesn't seem to like me at all, someone who I never even knew until last week, is spending a fortune on my clothes, on my phone, on me! It's confusing. We walk out of the shop with a fantastic leather jacket and nothing can wipe the smile off my face.

Selina checks her watch. "Let's grab some lunch before your hair appointment."

"Hair appointment? No one mentioned hair." Actually, now I come to think of it, I do remember Grandmother saying something about hair.

"Mrs Chamberlain says you need to have your hair tidied up."

"I don't want tidy hair."

"Don't worry. You can have tidy hair that isn't tidy."

"Can you?"

We sit out of the sun under the awning of an Italian restaurant and I order a lasagne and Coke. Selina picks at a salad and sips fizzy water while I scrape every last bit out of the dish. We watch the people walking past.

"See?" she says, looking at a woman in a tight grey skirt and yellow frilly shirt. "Her hips are wide and the shape of that skirt makes it worse. The yellow shirt is far too frothy for someone of her height and it looks terrible with her skin tone – washes her out completely. Not many people can wear yellow."

Selina continues her commentary on fashion mess-ups and I can't stop laughing. She should come and spend a day sitting on our front step in Manchester – that'd really give her something to talk about.

"Come on," says Selina, "or we'll be late."

The hair salon is only a couple of streets away. The heat of the midday sun bounces off the pavement and by the time we get there I'm a strawberry again.

Inside, the salon is sleek and cool, in spite of all the hairdryers. It has an atmosphere that's somewhere between catwalk and chemistry lab. I've never seen so many lotions and potions and weird-looking contraptions.

A lady drapes a black, shiny gown around my neck and guides me to a chair.

"I hope I haven't got nits," I say as I sit down.

Selina takes a step back. I grin. "I shouldn't. Mum checked the other day." Quite a while back, now I come to think about it. My head's not itching though.

"When did you last go to a hairdresser, Jess?" Selina asks.

"Never. Mum cuts my hair and sometimes I do it myself."

"Ah." What she means is *that explains a lot* but she's too polite to say it.

"Yeah, well, I like it like this."

A man glides over and introduces himself as Michael. It's hard to tell how old he is but he certainly isn't young. He's ruffling his fingers through my hair. Talking to my reflection in the mirror.

"So," he says. "You are Mrs Chamberlain's granddaughter?" He turns to Selina, who is flicking through a hair magazine. "Do we have a plan here?"

"Plan what you like," I say, "but you can keep the scissors in your pocket until I've agreed. I'm not having some posh hairdo, whatever you say."

He pushes my hair around. "You look so like your grandmother."

"I do not!"

"Your eyes. . ."

"And her character," adds Selina.

"Actually, I have my dad's character."

"And how is your mother?" says Michael.

"You know my mum?" I swivel my chair so I'm facing him.

"I've owned this salon for thirty-five years now, but don't tell anyone." He laughs and claps his hand theatrically over his mouth. "Susan used to bring Mrs Chamberlain in every week and, of course, I cut your mother's hair too. Not that she'd ever have more than a trim."

"When did you last see her?"

"Ooh – ages ago. Must be . . . seventeen, eighteen years?"

"That would figure. She works in a library now and in an old people's home. Except they might close the library."

"Oh I know, it's terrible, isn't it. Government cuts."

Not much evidence of government cuts in here, but I keep my lips buttoned. Michael's pulling bits of hair this way and that.

"Keep it edgy, contemporary and artistic," says Selina, "but keep in mind Mrs Chamberlain says she'll need to have it tidy for performances."

"Ah yes. The young violinist." He takes my hands, examines them. "Look at those hands. Such beautiful hands."

I do not have beautiful hands. My nails are bitten to pieces.

Michael stands back now, as if to observe my hair from afar. "Colour?" he asks.

"Black," I say.

"Just a few highlights to lift it," says Selina.

"If you turn me blonde I will shave every bit of hair off my head."

"Trust me, Jessica," says Michael. "I will not turn you blonde."

"It's *Jess*." I wish everyone would stop calling me Jessica.

It takes nearly three hours. I didn't know it was possible to spend this long having your hair done. The smell is overpowering and one hair magazine is a lot like another. This is beginning to feel like time-wasting. My violin is calling me. I haven't touched it since the morning after my concert and I'm getting withdrawal symptoms. Tomorrow's my first lesson and I certainly need a bit of practice before that.

I keep a check on what Michael's up to. I hate to think what I'm going to look like when all this foil and stuff comes off. I'm dragged to the basin. More lotions and potions. Back to the mirror again.

Now I watch Michael's every snip. He makes dainty, feathery little cuts. I wish he'd get on with it. All this attention is making me self-conscious. I don't like staring at myself and I hate everyone staring at me. Now he's blow-drying, scrunching my hair with his hands. He pulls the final few strands into place, puts a guard over my eyes and sprays.

"All done," he says as he whips away the guard. The face in the mirror is different. I look quite cool. Older. I can't help smiling.

"You see," says Selina, "untidy, tidy hair. Just like I said."

"Does it meet with your approval?" Michael holds a second mirror at different angles so I can see the back.

"Thanks, it's good."

"Good? After all these years of experience and

I only get a *good*? You are a hard taskmaster." He squeezes my shoulder. "I'll put in a bit more practice before I see you again."

I crank myself out of the chair. I'm stiff from sitting for too long – not to mention my run this morning and charging round shops half the day.

"Phew," I say as we get outside.

Selina laughs and looks at her watch and points up the road. "Charlie's waiting just up there. I have to rush. See you soon, I hope." She hands me all our shopping and waves as she trots off towards the underground. I wish she didn't have to go.

Charlie's parked on a yellow line. He beckons for me to hurry and opens the boot of the car for my bags. I collapse into the front seat of the car.

"You OK?" asks Charlie.

"Well, I've survived – just!"

"You're looking good on it."

I blush, which makes me feel stupid. "Yeah, well, after three hours with Michael, anyone would look great."

"I think I'll pass. Successful shopping trip?"

"We must've spent a fortune. I've never had this many clothes in my life. It's ridiculous."

"And you're complaining?"

I shrug. I'm thinking of Mum and Dad and everything we've never had. It was even worse after Dad lost his job. Every spare bit of cash went into my violin lessons and travelling to concerts and everything. I mean, Dad still goes to the pub and the footy every now and again – he likes to spend time with his mates – but what I've spent today, that would probably keep our family going for half the year.

Charlie's looking at me with an odd expression – he's probably trying to work out the strange dynamics of our family. He's not the only one.

"It doesn't seem right, that's all," I say. "Having so much."

"I'd make the most of it if I were you. Appreciate the fact that your grandmother is a generous lady."

"Is she?"

"Give her a chance, Jess."

"I suppose. But there's a difference between being generous with money and being a nice person."

"She's a very nice person."

"To you, maybe. Not to me. Not to Mum and Dad. I should've listened to Dad."

"You've only been here a couple of days. Things'll get better."

"I hope you're right. I'm not sure I'll ever be her kind of person."

Charlie laughs. "And you think I am?"

"You're not family."

"That's true. There's no accounting for families."

He's right. There isn't.

Chapter 7

Sarah insists on helping me put my new stuff away. She's tidied my room and made my bed and I feel bad for leaving everything in such a mess. No one cares at home. I never make my bed and my clothes live on the floor. Here it's different — everything has to be perfect. I don't know if I'm supposed to make my own bed or if that's Sarah's job. I feel awkward asking.

Bag by bag we unwrap tissue paper, shake out each item of clothing. Sarah keeps holding things up to me and smiling.

"Perfect," she says. "Absolutely gorgeous."

She refolds or hangs. I try to imagine Mum doing this with me. I can't. I try to think of any time Mum and I do things together. I try to fold things neatly like Sarah but it doesn't work so I end up sitting on the bed and watching her.

"Where do your family live?" I ask her.

"My mother is in London," says Sarah, "and I've got a brother in Australia."

"No husband or children?"

She stops folding for a moment. "No. I did have a husband, Anthony, but he died a long time ago, before we had the chance to have children." My new shirt hangs in her hands.

"I'm sorry," I mumble. I wish I hadn't started this conversation. I've put my foot in it as usual. I don't want to upset Sarah as well. "He must've been very young."

"Thirty-two. Cancer." She starts folding again. Goes backwards and forwards to the cupboard. "Actually, that's how I met your grandmother. It's why I'm here, really."

"How come?"

"In the last months of his life, Anthony went into a hospice. Mrs Chamberlain was a volunteer. She's been doing it for years. She was so caring – wonderful, really."

I cannot imagine Grandmother being a caring hospice volunteer – or a caring anything, come to that. I turn it over in my head.

"Grandmother's husband must've been very

young when he died." I'm thinking out loud. "He died before my mum was born. Maybe he had cancer too?"

Sarah looks surprised. "I wouldn't know. Mrs Chamberlain's never mentioned her husband to me. I have no idea how he died. I don't know anything about him at all."

"You're not the only one. I don't think she likes to talk about him. I asked Grandmother about him last night – *big* mistake."

"Well, I suppose I can sort of understand. These things are hard to talk about. Everyone deals with death in a different way."

"So how did you end up working here?"

"Mrs Chamberlain was very fond of Anthony. He was a trombonist in the London Symphony Orchestra and they'd spend hours together, talking about music. She'd bring in young musicians to play to him. It gave him enormous pleasure. I think it helped him a lot."

"That's cool." I feel kind of happy and sad at the same time.

"Anyway, when Anthony died, I lost touch with Mrs Chamberlain for a while. After a few months, I got a phone call out of the blue. She said she might have a job for me if I was interested. She was quite fragile then, quite unwell. She found it hard to cope with day-to-day life and she didn't like to leave the house. I needed to keep myself busy. So that's how I ended up here."

"How long ago was that?"

She thinks. "Seventeen years now – nearly eighteen. Goodness, how time flies."

"You must've met Mum, then?"

Sarah looks awkward. "No, I've never met your mother. I think she must have left London before I started."

"Does Grandmother ever talk about her?"

Sarah shakes her head.

"You mean she's never mentioned Mum, or Dad, or me? I mean, how did she explain me turning up out of the blue?"

"She simply said she had invited you to London to study the violin. It's not my place to ask questions. Mrs Chamberlain is a very private lady. She's not the kind of person to talk about her personal life."

"It's a bit odd, though, don't you think? Never once mentioning her family? Completely cutting us off?"

Sarah sits down, rubs her forehead. "I'm sorry. I didn't know. Things happen sometimes."

"No they don't. Not like that. Did you know my mum told me my grandmother was dead? She never talked about her either. Then suddenly Grandmother turns up at our front door. Why's she waited till now when she could've helped us before? You should see how we live at home." I pick up a pair of new shoes and fling them into the back of the cupboard.

"Don't be like that, Jess. The important thing is that you are here now and your grandmother is better than I've seen her for a long time."

"Well, I'm glad I didn't see her when she was at her worst! And I want to know *why* I'm here now. I'm grateful, don't get me wrong but – honestly." It's hard to explain how angry I feel; seeing everything Grandmother has, thinking of Mum and Dad.

"Maybe she just wants to make a new start. And with her love of music – well, you're very lucky she is able to help you."

"She could've done that at any time. Mum said she wrote to her loads of times to ask her for help."

Sarah sighs. "I can't answer your questions. You'll have to ask Mrs Chamberlain. But take one thing at a time. Give yourself a chance to settle in and get to know her first."

"That's what Charlie says too." I flop back on to my pillows. They're probably right, but I want some answers now.

"By the way, your mum called to make sure you were OK. I gave her your new number. She said to call whenever you want. I think she'd like to speak to you."

"Thanks," I say.

"Charlie and Mrs Chamberlain are out this evening so it's just us for supper. We'll have it in front of the TV if you like. I'll give you a call when it's ready." She closes the door quietly behind her.

I grab my phone and dial Mum's number. Dad answers.

"All right?" he says, grumpily.

"Please don't be angry with me."

"I've said what I've got to say. You've made your decision. I'm not going to hold a grudge."

"You'll be glad to hear I'm fine then." It's not completely true, of course, but I'm not giving Dad the satisfaction of saying *I told you so*. I tell him about the timetable Grandmother has set up for me. I tell him about Rosie and the shopping trip and the haircut, but I don't give him the details – not Dad's kind of thing. I just want to prove to him that I've made the right decision but his answers are monosyllabic.

"Dad, if you're going to be like this then you have to tell me: what happened between Mum and Grandmother? No one talks about it. It's like it's something terrible."

"Yeah, well, the way Tara treated your mum was nothing short of scandalous, in my opinion. Kept her shut up in that monstrous house. Your mum was like a servant. Running around day and night doing her ladyship's bidding."

"But Mum was grown up. She could've left, couldn't she?"

"It was more complicated than that."

"So tell me."

"I'm not the right person to ask. I was only the painter."

"The painter? I never knew you were a painter."

"Back then I was. I worked for a large company. We got the contract to do your grandmother's house – outside and in. Not that it really needed it. I was there for nearly four months. Mrs Chamberlain didn't like to mix with the workmen, which meant I saw quite a bit of your mum. She was the one who brought us tea and looked after us. She hardly went out. I felt sorry for her. She seemed lonely. I'd chat to her and then one thing led to another."

"Meaning. . .?"

"Let's just say that when Tara found out your mum was pregnant, she wasn't too thrilled. She gave your mum a choice. If Susan wanted to stay living at home, she had to promise never to see me again. If she decided to stay with me, then Grandmother would have nothing to do with either of us. Your mother chose me. And that was the last we heard of your grandmother – until your concert."

"Pregnant? Was that me? Was it all my fault, then?"

"How could it be your fault? You weren't even born. The only person at fault was your grandmother."

"But if Mum hadn't been pregnant. . .?"

"It would've made no difference. Your mum and I would've got married anyway and the result would have been the same."

"But what was wrong with you and Mum getting married?"

"People like me aren't good enough for the Mrs Chamberlains of this world."

"That's just stupid."

"You know that and I know that. I've never seen anyone as angry as Tara was. You'd have thought I was some kind of monster the way she went on."

Dad half laughs, but I can hear a hardness in his voice. I think of Grandmother's stony grey eyes and I shudder.

"You should've told me."

"You didn't give me a chance. You'd made your mind up and that was that."

"Perhaps she's changed since then," I say.

"And pigs might fly," Dad replies. "She'll never change. You should've listened to me, Jess, when I told you not to go. You should've listened."

I know I should – now – but I'm not going to admit that. It's time to end this conversation.

"Is Mum there? Can I speak to her?"

"She won't be back till late."

"Send her my love. Tell her I'll call tomorrow."

I put the phone down slowly and flip over on to my stomach. The pattern on the bedspread is like a complicated tune and I trace it with my finger – start humming the ups and downs and swirls of the patterns. Life is complicated but I'm here to play the violin. I don't need to get mixed up in all that other stuff. All I need is one more crack at that music scholarship and then I'm out of here. I can deal with Grandmother. It's only six months.

The thought of that scholarship makes energy surge through me and I roll off the bed. I need to practise before my lesson tomorrow morning if I'm going to impress this Dr McNair. I go to the cupboard to find my violin. I'm sure that's where I put it. I open all the doors, look under the bed, behind the curtains. I'm breathing hard, trying to think. I know it was in the cupboard. I look again. Where the hell is it? I shriek down the stairs to the kitchen.

"Where's my violin?"

Sarah looks up from the sink, startled. I stand there angry and accusing. It must be Sarah who's taken it, and I don't like people interfering with my things, especially not my violin. It's the most precious thing I own.

"I've put it in the music room," she says. "That's where you'll be doing your practice and having your lessons. It seemed the best place for it."

The blood is still pounding round my body. I know I'm overreacting. I do that when I'm stressed. I take a couple of deep breaths. "You could have told me. I didn't know there *was* a music room."

"Give me two seconds and I'll show you."

She drops the potato she was peeling into a saucepan and wipes her hands on a towel.

I feel my heartbeat calm as I wait, but I'm still angry. No one touches my violin. I follow her down the hall and round the corner to a door under the stairs. I hadn't noticed it before.

"This is the basement," she says, flicking on a couple of lights.

I always think of basements as dark, damp places, but this looks fresh and new. The stairs are steep and there's a mechanical stairlift attached to the wall on one side, the kind old people use.

"What's the lift for?"

"Some of your grandmother's elderly friends find it hard to get up and down the stairs, so she had this put in."

"Why does she take them down to the basement?" It sounds faintly dodgy. I have a sudden vision of her as some kind of mass murderer, bringing her victims down to the basement. It makes me giggle.

"Most of the people she knows are musicians. Sometimes they wanted to make use of the music room. Not any more, though. Apart from Mr Ritchie."

"I didn't know Mr Ritchie was a musician."

"Oh yes. A pianist."

Sarah opens a door at the bottom of the stairs on the right-hand side. "Here's the loo – saves you coming back upstairs."

We walk a bit further. "And this is the music room."

She pushes open a heavy door on the left and I walk into a large shadowy room. A dull grey light comes in through two high windows. They've got black bars on the outside, like a prison. They must be facing the street but I can barely hear the cars. The room feels heavily soundproofed.

Sarah presses a switch and everything leaps into focus. The lights are dazzling, set into the ceiling in two neat rows. Sarah adjusts the dimmer to make them a little softer. In one corner is a full-sized grand piano made of dark, almost black, wood. It gleams under its own spotlight. I lift the lid, give a little gasp. Stefan fills my head as my fingers touch the keys.

"It's beautiful, isn't it?" says Sarah. "It's a Blüthner."

I look at the signature marking on the underside of the lid. The wood feels warm under my fingers. "I have a friend who would love this," I say. "He used to be my accompanist. He's obsessed with this make of piano. It has a gentle playing tone, apparently."

I play a couple of notes. Stefan's right, the tone is gentle. I imagine him sitting at this piano caressing the notes with his fingers. I imagine us playing together again. For a moment I can hardly breathe. Then I shut the lid with a bang and the whole piano vibrates discordantly.

"It's lovely down here in the mornings," says Sarah. "The sun comes streaming in those two windows. I think you'll enjoy it."

"I'll have to enjoy it. I'll be in here about seven hours a day."

"And there is your violin," says Sarah, "safe and sound. Sorry about that."

My violin sits quietly in the corner. I'm happier now it's close to me.

"Thanks. I'm sorry I was grumpy; I'm a bit overprotective about my violin. It's on loan to me from a music charity. I had to fight so hard for it; I don't know what I'd do if I lost it."

"I can understand that."

"Why does Grandmother have so many friends who are musicians?" I'm delving into a cupboard stuffed full of music as I talk. I suddenly realize how little I know about my grandmother.

"I suppose through her work."

"She works?" That might explain the hours she spends in her office. "What does she do?"

"She's retired now. She used to be a music critic. She wrote for all the newspapers and magazines. My husband used to say that there was only one thing worse than giving a bad performance and that was giving a bad performance in front of Mrs Chamberlain. Apparently, she doesn't mince her words."

"I can imagine." I shut the cupboard door and swear under my breath. A music critic for a grandmother – that's all I need. I don't even want to think about it. I suppose it explains all the music books and magazines on her shelves – her interest in me. Why didn't she tell me? And how am I ever going to play in front of her now? Perhaps that's why she didn't tell me.

My stress levels bubble up again.

"Seen enough?" asks Sarah.

"I think I'd better stay down here and go through some stuff before tea if that's OK. I need to remind myself how to play before I meet Dr McNair tomorrow."

Sarah leaves. I sit on the floor and unzip my violin case. I hold my violin gently, pluck the strings softly. The acoustics in the room are incredible. I try to picture Stefan at the piano and I stand up and start to play. For the first time since my audition, I am back where I belong, my violin tucked under my cheek, my fingers on the strings. I feel the music inside me and all around me the tension of the last two days melts away.

Was it really only yesterday I left home? It feels like forever ago. Now I can only wonder what tomorrow will bring.

Chapter 8

Tomorrow brings Dr McNair. Dr McNair who never stops moving, whose thin, frizzy, ginger hair looks as though it's just come out of the toaster. The lines on her face match the crinkles in her hair and her eyes are fiercely blue. She conducts, she paces, she gesticulates, she demonstrates. I swear to God that woman is plugged into an electric socket. Her energy makes me nervous.

She wastes no time with introductions or small talk. It's straight into the music and it's insane.

"Again," she says. "Again, again, again." Everything goes in fours with Dr McNair. And she doesn't like my playing. Nothing's right.

"No, no, no, no." She spits the words quickly, like a machine gun. "Listen to me." She hums, demonstrating a tricky passage in the music. "You see, you're leaving that note a fraction too late and then you're forced to pull everything else back. You have to jump on it."

She pounces across the room, hands held like claws in front of her.

"Surprise your audience," she says in a dramatic voice, "then carry them forward." She sweeps her arms in a wave and flies in the direction of the door.

I swallow, try again.

"Stop!" The hand flies up. "Stop, stop, stop."

I've stopped, I've stopped. Does she think I'm deaf?

She hums some more, pacing, clicking her fingers. "This rhythm. Listen to it." *Click, click, click, click.*

I do it again.

"Now pounce!" she shouts at the top of her voice.

My pounce is more of a flop. Dr McNair rolls her eyes. "Work on it, Jessica. Work on it all night if you have to. I don't want to hear it again until you've mastered it."

At the end of my first session I'm sucked dry, frustrated and exhausted. My arms ache; I'm sweating.

"You've got a lot of work to do," says Dr McNair. "You'll need to fit in at least three hours a day."

I nod and blink furiously. She's pushed me to the limit already.

"If you want to be a violinist, Jessica, you need to give one hundred per cent. Anything less is hopeless."

I nod again. Pretend to rub my eyes.

"Are you listening to me?"

"Yes," I mumble.

"Now," she says, "who is your least favourite composer?"

I shrug. It's actually not a difficult question. I don't have to think too hard.

"Bartók."

"And what is wrong with Bartók?"

"He makes me want to scream." *A bit like you*, I'd like to add.

"Very good. We shall play Bartók until you learn to love him."

"Oh come on. You can't make me do that."

"Why not?"

"Because –" I stop myself before I swear "– because I'll go mad."

She smiles. "I'll look forward to it."

I screech with frustration and stamp my foot. It's

a stupid, childish thing to do and it doesn't make me feel any better.

"Doesn't look like I'll have long to wait," says Dr McNair as she sweeps her music into a briefcase and twirls out of the door. "See you tomorrow. I'm off to have a word with your grandmother." Her voice fades as she heads for the stairs.

The breath goes out of me and I collapse into a chair. I think of my gentle lessons with Mr Noble. So calm, so reassuring. Now I've got this fire-breathing lunatic. I half expect to see burn marks on the carpet. I massage my fingers; they're sore.

During lunch I haven't got much energy for conversation. It's just Charlie, Sarah and me. They decide I need chocolate. Charlie feeds me slabs like a small child.

"Have either of you met Professor Jenniston?" I ask. The word *professor* sounds scarier than *doctor* and I need to know what's coming. They both shake their heads.

"Great," I say.

When the doorbell rings, I peep out. Professor Jenniston is wearing a shapeless green T-shirt and a skirt that floats around her ankles as she walks. Dad would have plenty to say about Professor Jenniston.

I can hear him now. *Doesn't she realize that hippies went out in the seventies?* She's definitely younger than Dr McNair but her dark hair is flecked with grey and she's got it tied back in a thick plait that stretches all the way to her waist.

I walk out to the hall.

"Hi, Jessica," she says. "I'm Professor Jenniston. Most of my students call me PJ."

PJ? I hate teachers who act like they want to be your best friend. "Most of my teachers call me Jess," I say.

She shakes my hand, gives me a warm smile. Maybe she isn't so bad. I stop panicking about the afternoon . . . briefly.

"Mondays and Wednesdays we'll look at general musicianship," she says as we walk down to the basement. "The rest of your lessons will be theory, composition, et cetera. In general, you can expect about two hours of homework a night."

Two hours of homework a night? I'm going to need more hours in my day at this rate. I don't say anything. I usually find music homework easy so I'll probably get it done quicker than she thinks.

Once we're in the music room she arranges two chairs face to face.

"Right," she says, "we're going to begin with a questionnaire. Multiple choice. It's to find out more about the kind of musician you are."

"OK."

Professor Jenniston reads out questions and gives me four choices. It's pretty personal.

"How do you rate your overall confidence as a musician? Very high, high, average, low."

That's a hard question to start with. Up until my scholarship I would've said high. Now I'm not so sure.

"Average," I say.

"Do you suffer from performance nerves? Always, often, rarely, never."

I don't know the answer to that. I suppose I'll always be nervous now in case the stage fright comes back. She'll know about that, I bet. Grandmother will have told her. "Rarely," I decide. She gives me a knowing look.

It gets more complicated. My roles in musical groups, my ability to persevere, my ability to deal with frustration. Her eyes are steady, searching. I begin to feel more and more awkward. I try to answer truthfully but she must think I'm useless. By the time I've finished I hate myself.

Then she asks me about my family, my friends, my life at home. I can't believe anyone can be that interested in my home life. She asks me about drinks, about drugs. As if I've had the time or money for that. Then she asks me about my piercings. Why I've got so many. I've only got eight. I don't know why I've got that many. I just wanted them.

"Do you know if you were breastfed?"

"I'm sorry?"

Why does she need to know that? I don't know if I was breastfed. I can't imagine Mum ever doing anything like that. "No," I say, and she nods as though it's the most fascinating thing she's ever heard.

Questions, questions. What's all this got to do with playing the violin? Professor Jenniston twirls her plait around one hand and writes furiously with the other. Finally she smiles and puts down her pen.

"Well, we've got plenty to work on," she says. "We're going to build you into a really confident performer. That means understanding who you are as a person as well as a musician."

"If you say so."

"There must be no blocks to your musical development. Issues create blocks."

"But I don't have issues."

She gives me a sad, sympathetic look. I wrap my feet behind the legs of my chair and press hard on the palm of my hand with my thumb to stop myself from saying any more. I'll certainly have issues after six months with this woman.

"You see," she carries on, "often we seem like one person on the outside, but inside we're a very different person. That makes it difficult to perform effectively. If we are to give a true performance, then it must come from the person we really are."

I shrug. It's as if she can look right inside me. I don't like that.

"That's enough for now," she says, and she's up on a chair, sticking something to the ceiling. "Time for a bit of fun. I want you to lie on the floor and look up at that spot."

Doesn't sound like fun to me. I lie down.

She turns down the lights to dim and puts her iPod on the speaker system. Strange sounds fill the room. Whales or something.

We begin with a whole-body relaxation. I've done this before. Scrunching my toes, letting them go. Then my feet. All the way up to my nose and eyes and forehead.

Her voice gets softer and softer. "Now your body feels heavy and you are sinking down into the floor."

My body does not feel heavy. It feels uncomfortable and I'm not sinking anywhere.

"Relax, Jessica," she whispers. But I can't. Not shut in a room with Professor Jenniston.

"Close your eyes and picture yourself in a beautiful place . . . flowers and birds and a river that flows all the way to the sea. You are on a boat, floating towards that sea. Slowly, slowly, slowly, slowly."

I'm not on a boat. I am definitely still lying on the carpet in the music room. I giggle and she huffs grumpily.

"Sorry," I say, "but you've got to admit it sounds a bit stupid."

"On the contrary, it is not stupid at all. It will get easier in time. Now let's try again."

She takes me back through the relaxation once again. I try to sink down through the floor and to fill my mind with her pictures but all I want to do is laugh.

Eventually, she turns up the lights, very slowly,

and then holds out her hand to pull me up to the sitting position.

"If you are prepared to work on it, creative visualization can be very helpful when it comes to musical performance. It helps you to tell the story to your audience."

"I can't say I've ever played anything where I'm floating on a boat to the sea."

"That's just an example. You will create your own."

I somehow doubt it.

She sits opposite me on the floor, cross-legged. I can't stop looking at the long, dark hairs on her legs.

"I'm going to give you this book," she says. "I want you to write in it for two minutes a day. Anything that pops into your head. I will not look at it. It is private. But if things keep coming up – questions, or thoughts, or problems – then I want you to make a note of them in the back and discuss them with me."

I could probably fill the whole book in about two minutes with the amount of questions I've got at the moment.

She holds out an A4 notebook. It has a hard black cover with white writing on the front:

WHAT WOULD YOU
ATTEMPT TO DO
IF YOU KNEW YOU
COULD NOT FAIL?

"It's an interesting question, isn't it," she says and nudges the book towards my hand.

I don't want to take it. I don't want to write down all my thoughts. It feels heavy in my hands.

"It's been lovely meeting you, Jessica. You can make a start on your notebook in the morning and I would like you to begin thinking about the music you will be playing with Celia McNair. She tells me you'll be studying Bartók for the next few weeks."

"News travels fast."

It's after three thirty when Professor Jenniston leaves and I've got another two hours of practice to look forward to. Bloody Bartók. I need a strong cup of tea before even thinking about it.

Sarah's pulling something out of a bag. She holds it up. A pair of shorts. Baggy this time. She laughs when she sees my face.

"I thought you might prefer these," she says, "for your run tomorrow."

I roll my eyes.

"It's not that bad, is it?" she asks.

"Worse," I say.

I make tea, sip it slowly, and then I drag myself back down to the basement and get out the Bartók Violin Concerto. Number Two – the second movement – the worst. It's raw, angry music. I stare at the bars on the windows. Playing Bartók in a dungeon. Bloody perfect.

I should've guessed what Dr McNair was going to do. I should've chosen a nice, gentle composer. I didn't and now I'm stuck with this and it's so frickin difficult.

I lift my bow and start to play. I play phrases over and over and over.

What should I visualize for this piece of music? Tanks driving through barbed wire? I was looking forward to beginning my new violin lessons. Now I'm not sure I'm looking forward to anything at all.

Chapter 9

The heat doesn't let up all week. Not just my lessons but the weather too. Hot and sticky. The basement is like a sauna. Charlie's opened the two high windows but no air comes through because there's no air moving outside.

The heat doesn't affect Rosie's enthusiasm. She's there bright and early every morning for my fitness session. This morning, I actually managed to run a mile without stopping. A whole mile. Rosie says I'm almost ready for the Olympics . . . or not! And I'm grateful for my baggy shorts – plenty of air conditioning. Trouble is, I've got blisters on my toes to match the blisters on my fingers. All in all, I'm a mess.

I've barely seen Grandmother – just a glimpse every now and again. I can sense her, though, behind closed doors. She avoids me on purpose, I'm certain of that.

Mum's started calling every day. I talk to her more now than I did when I was at home. She wants to know if I'm OK. She keeps asking me if I'm happy.

Happy? I don't think happiness comes into it. It's a matter of survival. I tell her how I drag myself out of bed for morning exercise. I tell her I'm working hard on my violin with four hours of lessons a day. What I don't tell her is about the loneliness, the exhaustion, the frustration. I feed Mum enough info to stop her from worrying and hold in all the bad stuff.

"And how is my mother?" she asks.

"I hardly ever see her. I don't think she likes me much."

"She didn't like me much either, if that's any consolation. But I suppose I was a bit hopeless."

"She probably thinks I'm hopeless too."

"You're nothing like me. I wasn't clever, wasn't musical, wasn't even pretty. "

"Don't be silly, Mum." I don't like listening to her say those things. I realize I don't know much about Mum's childhood at all. I have to admit she's not that pretty; she hasn't inherited any of her mother's elegant, bony features. Genetics suck.

"I tried so hard when I was little," Mum's saying, "but I never seemed to be able to live up to her expectations, whatever they were. I couldn't do anything right. I think she just lost interest in me. She didn't seem to know what to say to me. I suppose that's why she sent me to boarding school. She wanted me out of the way."

"That's terrible. How old were you when you went away?"

"Eight."

"Eight? She sent you away to boarding school when you were eight?"

"Like I said, she didn't seem to like having me around very much."

"Well, I hope you had more fun at school."

Mum gives a dry laugh. "I hated it. I was bullied. I didn't know how to act around other kids. I knew they wouldn't like me before I even met them. I kept hoping it would get better but it never did. After failing all my O levels – twice – school didn't want me either. After that my mother had no idea what to do with me. She decided I should do a secretarial course and 'try to do something useful with my life'. But then she got sick and so I looked after her instead."

"What was wrong with her?"

"A severe form of depression, would be my guess. They weren't so good at diagnosing these things back then. She was constantly exhausted. She cried a lot. Sometimes she would stare for hours at one spot on the floor or wall. It was as if she had built a wall around herself so that no one could get in and she couldn't get out. She would never actually admit to me that anything was wrong. She would never speak to me about anything personal. It was as if she hated me being there yet couldn't survive without me."

I think about what Sarah said about Grandmother being unwell. "So how long did you look after her?"

"Twenty years."

"Did you say twenty? *Twenty?* She can't have been ill all that time."

"On and off. She became almost reclusive, yet she couldn't bear to be alone in the house. It was like she wanted me there but didn't want to see me. The only time she really went out was to do her charity work at the hospice. She was always a little better when she came back. But it didn't last for long."

"Why didn't you leave? There's no way I would've stuck around that long."

"I thought of it. I dreamt about it. But where could

I go? I had no money, no friends, no qualifications. Anyway, I couldn't leave her. She needed me."

"Used you, more like."

"You don't understand the situation."

"No, I don't, you're right. Why did you never tell me?"

"It's not a part of my life I like to talk about. I left it all behind a long time ago."

"But you didn't, did you? You wrote to her."

Mum gives a huge sigh and I wonder if I am pushing her too far. I wonder if there's other stuff she's not telling me.

"Only because I was desperate to help you, Jess. That's all. My mother loves music. I thought she might. . ."

"So why now? Why did she wait so long? Surely you must know."

"I don't know. I really don't know. I've been over it and over it in my head. I have no idea why she's decided to help you now. I just hope it's for the right reasons."

A silence hangs between us. So many questions unanswered.

"D'you think she's still depressed?" I ask. "I mean, her behaviour's not exactly normal."

"I don't think people with depression are ever completely cured. But if she'd been very bad she never would've come, alone, to Manchester."

My phone beeps. It's a reminder I should be starting my practice.

"I have to go, Mum. I'm sorry. Grandmother'll kill me if she discovers I'm not doing my practice."

"You would tell me, wouldn't you? If she started treating you badly?"

"I didn't mean it literally! She'll tell me off, that's all."

Mum gives a short laugh and we say our goodbyes. I can't help shaking my head – so many things I never knew about Mum. I feel like it's the first time she and I have ever properly talked. I've never thought about it before: Mum's always been just Mum. We've never been that close. Now, suddenly, I'm discovering a different person.

My practice is terrible. There's too much whirring round my head. I wade my way through Bartók. I hate it. Back in my room, I settle down with Professor Jenniston's notebook. I thought it was stupid at first but now I'm getting the hang of it and the results are quite surprising. I write without thinking and without stopping – anything and everything that pops into my head. It's become like my best friend – my only friend. Most of what I write is rubbish, most of it's illegible, but it doesn't matter because no one will see and I don't have to worry about making a fool of myself. The same phrases and questions come round and round. How I hate Dr McNair. Where is Stefan? Is he really still mad at me? Why can't I get through to him even on my new phone? Has he blocked my number? I honestly can't believe he'd do that. I write down all the odd things my grandmother says and does. Why has she brought me here if she doesn't want me around? And how will I ever make any friends when I'm stuck in this house all the time? Then again, it's not so easy just to go out and make friends in a strange city. I guess if I have no distractions, I will work harder – put all my energy into playing and studying and running. Maybe that's why Grandmother wanted me in London.

I tell the notebook everything, straight up. Now, turning back the pages, I begin to see a pattern. I'm tired, I'm lonely and I want to go home. But I lock these feelings away in the desk drawer. I will not give up.

I work on the Bartók in every spare moment.

Even in the shower, I play it through my head. I desperately want to impress Dr McNair and show her I can do it, but each lesson brings more thick grey pencil scratched over my music. As soon as I do anything wrong, she's like a cat with her claws out. In my opinion, she should be put down. I've only been working on it for a week but she complains that my progress is slow. What does she expect? And if I get it right, she yells at me for *not feeling it*. How am I supposed to *let go and be more spontaneous* when I'm terrified of getting it wrong?

Professor Jenniston asks me if any themes keep recurring in my notebook. I don't want to discuss my notebook with her. It's mine. I can hardly tell her about Stefan, and anything I say about Grandmother is sure to get straight back.

I decide, perhaps, that it's safe to mention my problems with Dr McNair and the Bartók. Bad move! She's *delighted* I'm developing an awareness of the *blocks to my progress*. She starts asking me loads of questions.

"And you say your notebook gives you the freedom to write because you know no one will read it?"

"Yeah," I say.

"OK, so let's think about that with your music.

Do you fear playing things because you worry about what people will think when they listen to you?"

Well duh! Who doesn't worry what people will think? Why else would I practise my butt off before a performance?

"Sometimes."

Professor Jenniston smiles. "Do you think that was the problem at your scholarship performance?"

I don't want to think about my scholarship performance. That took fear and worry to a whole new level. "It was my last chance," I say. "And I was up against the best. The judges were looking for mistakes and I couldn't afford to fail. Yes, I was worried. I didn't want to let everyone down. It doesn't get any more pressured than that."

"Oh, I can assure you it does. Anyway, how do you feel about the prospect of your next performance?"

"I don't know. I haven't got a performance planned, so how am I supposed to say?" I don't add minor details like the fact that I haven't entered any competitions and I haven't even got an accompanist any more. My eyes drift to the empty piano stool. Right now I don't know if I ever want to perform again.

"OK, let's imagine you have a performance next week. How do you think you might feel?"

I shrug. "I would feel like everyone would be waiting to see if I stuff up again. I don't think anyone believes in me any more."

"Anyone? What about *you*?"

"I dunno. Maybe I haven't got what it takes. I'd never had stage fright before my scholarship. What happens if I get it again? What happens if I get it every time? I mean, if I had to play the Bartók now, I'd die. It's bad enough doing it in front of Dr McNair."

It's time to shut up. I can't believe I've said so much.

"Now I think we're getting somewhere. Bringing these things out in the open helps. I'm sure all musicians face these fears at one point or another. I can assure you that I believe in you and there is no reason why it should happen again."

I wish I could believe her.

"So these difficulties with Dr McNair and the Bartók – can you try and explain them to me?"

"I don't like Bartók. I can't understand it. I can't play it. And she just yells at me to *let go*."

"And if you *let go* as Dr McNair wishes you to

do, you're worried about – how did you describe it – making a fool of yourself?"

"Something like that."

"Do you see a link here, Jessica? Fear of failure. Fear of what other people think."

"I don't care what other people think," I mumble.

"That rather contradicts what you've just said. Do you ever feel this way with other music? As if you can't let go?"

"Not so much. There's more to hold on to in other music. Bartók frightens me. It messes with my head. I can't control it. It's so angry and wild."

"Forgive me for saying so, but you give the impression of being the kind of girl who would like angry and wild."

"How d'you mean?"

"The dark clothes, the make-up, the jewellery. Not angry? Not wild?"

"What've my clothes got to do with it?"

"I'm just saying that you look like someone who would play Bartók quite well. Now we have to find the key for getting it out of you. I'll have a chat to Dr McNair."

"You won't tell her what I said about her?"

"I wouldn't dream of it."

"I mean it. If you repeat any of this. . ."

"Trust me, Jessica. And in the meantime, I want you to study the composer. Find out about his family, his politics, his motivation. I think it will help."

She hands me a couple of books.

It doesn't help. Nothing helps. For the next three weeks I struggle on. I'm note-perfect now, or as note-perfect as anyone can be playing this stuff. Dr McNair and Professor Jenniston continue to try to coax the music out of me, to make me perform it as it deserves to be performed, but somehow it's stuck inside. And the pressure is building and building and I can't take much more. I'm not sleeping, I'm not eating, and sometimes I shake because there's nowhere else for all that pressure to go. I hate everyone. Something's going to give. It's not a question of *if* but of *when*. If I had a gun, I'd shoot someone – but who? Myself? Professor Jenniston? Or maybe Dr McNair or Mr Bartók if he was still around to shoot – which he's not, lucky for him. This isn't my dream of being a violinist. This is a black hole that's swallowing me up.

Chapter 10

Normal kids are relaxing on holiday in July. Not me. I've already been out running and now I'm back in the basement again with my crazy violin teacher. And it's only nine thirty. I've just performed the whole of the second movement with only a few mistakes. I'm pleased with myself. I hope it's enough and I hope Dr McNair will let me out early because if she doesn't. . .

"Do you want to be a violinist or not?" she says.

Is she all right in the head? After the hours I've put in over the last few weeks? I give her a death stare.

"You communicate nothing to me with your playing. I've heard eight-year-olds play better than you."

"But I hardly made a single mistake."

"I'm not talking about that and you know it. I need you to hypnotize me with this music, to hold me enthralled; not to bore me to death."

"I can't help it. I hate it." My jaw is clenched so hard that it aches. Blood thumps through my ears.

"Well, play it as though you hate it, then. I want to see hate, feel hate. From the beginning." She jabs at the music with her fingernail.

I begin again and I haven't even got to the bottom of the first page when Dr McNair grabs the music from the stand and throws it on to the floor. I shrink away from her, wonder what she's going to do next.

"Play it," she orders.

"I can't. Not with music on the floor."

"Play it without your music. You've practised enough. You shouldn't need the music – it should be in here." Dr McNair points at her chest.

I stand there. This is stupid.

"Play it!" screams Dr McNair.

"No!" I shout back.

She raises her hand and, for a moment, I think she's going to hit me. I'm not sticking around to find out. I've had enough. I don't have to put up with this. I duck away from her, run out of the door and lock myself in the toilet. My heart's banging in my chest and I'm breathing fast. I can hear her footsteps coming closer.

"Come out of there immediately. You're behaving like a child."

"I am a child."

The frustration and anger that's been bottled inside me for days spills over and runs in hot tears down my cheeks.

"If you don't come out right this second, I'll get Charles to come and break the door down."

"Fine."

"Come on, Jessica. Open the door." She's coaxing now.

"Go away and leave me alone." I'm squashed in the narrow space between the toilet and the wall. As far away from her as I can get.

She starts pounding again. "Open up right now or there'll be trouble. Your grandmother will have something to say about this."

"I don't care. She can say what she likes."

"You'll never be a violin player, Miss Cooke. You don't have the discipline. You don't have the talent. You don't have the commitment."

That's it. I fling open the door, hard, and it

smacks her in the face. Serves her right for standing so close. But she doesn't give any ground. She's not letting me escape. I put my face right up close to hers.

"How can you say that? How dare you say I haven't got the discipline? Get out of my way!" I push past her, shoving her as violently as I can. "How dare you tell me I don't have the commitment? You have no idea how hard I work."

I storm back into the music room, pick up my violin, grab my music and begin to play. The anger flows out of me in great waves. I don't care how it sounds; I don't care if the notes aren't right. I fly into the last section in a white-hot rage, the heat flowing from my fingers into my bow. I kick over the music stand, send it crashing to the floor, carry on with the music pounding in my head. I'm ripping at the strings with my bow, tearing up the notes until something snaps.

The silence is sudden and my breathing loud. I stop, look down at my violin. The E string dangles free in the air, broken, the ends ragged.

"Much better," says Dr McNair. "Much, much, much better. I will see you on Monday. And don't forget to replace that string."

And she leaves.

She's wrong. She won't see me on Monday. I'm done with this. If I spend one more minute in this house I'm going to go insane. I leap to my feet and chase up the stairs two at a time.

Sarah and Dr McNair are chatting in the hall. They stop as they hear me coming, glance in my direction. I know they're talking about me.

Sarah opens the door for Dr McNair to leave and I grab my chance. I dart through under Sarah's arm, jump down the steps and run. I run and I don't stop. I don't stop until my legs turn to jelly and my heart is bursting out of my ribs. Then I slow down. I'm at the edge of the park, sun on my face, space all around me.

I collapse on to a bench near a muddy pond and feel my heartbeat return to normal. A family of ducks glide across the water. As they swim, little ripples float out and out until they're absorbed back into the flatness and become invisible.

A couple walk past, arm in arm. They kiss, and suddenly I feel so lonely, so unloved, that it hurts, physically hurts in my chest and I crunch forward. I want to be back in Manchester, brushing my teeth in our mouldy basin at home and mouthing off at the twins next door. I want Mum and Dad. I reach for my phone, then realize I've left it on the piano and swear out loud. The ducks don't notice.

Why did I come to London? Stupid question. There was no alternative. I came so I could carry on playing the violin and that's exactly what I'm doing. I thought it was what I wanted. But now? Now I'm not so sure.

And where's my so-called grandmother when I need her? What is she, some kind of dictator? She brings me to London, controls every aspect of my life, yet we may as well be living on different planets. I need more than lessons, money, clothes. I need support and encouragement. She's my grandmother, she's supposed to love me. I can't do this by myself. It's not just about the music. Surely she can see that?

Even in this sweltering heat, I shiver.

But I'm too proud to go home. I can't ring Dad and beg him for the train fare. He's already made it quite clear that there's no going back and I can't admit failure that easily. I can't tell him that he was right all along, that I'm trapped by my grandmother in London and now I understand, only too well, how Mum must've felt.

"There you are," says a breathless voice. "I've run all over the damn park looking for you."

Charlie plonks himself down on the other end of the bench. He's still wearing his suit trousers but he's got trainers on.

"Good look," I say, and angle my body away from him.

"What are you doing, Jess?"

"Talking to the ducks. And you?"

He sighs. "What d'you do you think I'm doing? Your running's improved, by the way. I'll be sure to let Rosie know." He laughs. I don't.

"Can't you leave me alone?"

"What, after running all this way to find you?"

"You needn't have bothered."

"I thought you might like some company on the way home."

"Home? If you're talking about Grandmother's house, it is *not* my home. Home is with Mum and Dad."

"Do you want to tell me what's wrong?"

I shake my head. Charlie shrugs. But thoughts pile up in my head and somehow they start spilling out of my mouth. Once I've started, I can't stop.

"I can't keep going like this. My schedule is

140

ridiculous. Work, work, work. I have no time to myself and even if I did, I don't have any friends. I'm young. I'm supposed to be having fun. Instead I'm tired, homesick, fed up. I just want to eat fish and chips and go to the movies. Do something normal for a change." I grip the bench, rock backwards and forwards.

"Is that all? Doesn't sound too serious."

"No. Since you ask, it is not all."

I tell him about Dr McNair and he laughs when I get to the bit about locking myself in the toilet.

"But it's not just that. It's Grandmother. I thought she understood. I thought she cared about what happened to me."

"She does. That's why she asked you to come to London."

"Do you normally invite someone to your house and then ignore them? Why does she avoid me all the time?"

"She's a very private woman. Anyway, would you want to spend a lot of time with her?"

"I don't know. I thought she'd be different. I had this kind of romantic idea about discovering my long-lost grandmother. I'd pictured us chatting together and going to concerts. Now I realize that was all crap. She didn't want anything to do with her own daughter, so why would it be any different with me? Dad's right. She's not a nice person."

"He's wrong. You're wrong."

"I'm not talking about money."

"Nor am I. I can prove it to you."

"How?"

The ducks flap around on the pond. Some kid is lobbing stones at them. What have they done to deserve that?

Charlie waits for the commotion to die down. When he starts speaking, his voice is quiet. "My dad was an alcoholic. Mum always beaten up. I couldn't read. I was excluded from school. Drugs, robbery — you name it, I've done it. Never violence, though. I've never done violence. Or not that I remember."

I stare at him.

"I ended up on the streets, sleeping rough. Until Mrs Chamberlain rescued me."

"She rescued you? Are you making this up?"

He shakes his head. "Come with me. I'll show you." He grabs me by the hand, pulls me up from the bench. We're walking fast, him almost dragging me along. He doesn't say anything. Eventually he stops.

"This is where I met your grandmother."

We're standing in the covered porch of a smart building. Rows of buzzers with names. It looks like apartments.

"It wasn't like this a few years ago," Charlie says. "It was scabby, run-down. God knows why in this area. I used this porch for shelter. It was winter. Coldest winter for years. I was about to turn twenty. I couldn't go back home, not this time."

He lets go of my hand and his fingers touch the scar near his eye. I wince. He stares at the entrance of the building and his face sags, every bit of happiness sucked away from it. He suddenly seems older than twenty-three. I put my hand on his arm and he gives me an unconvincing smile.

"Mrs Chamberlain spotted me by chance. I like to call it fate. She stopped and asked me if I was all right. She must've felt sorry for me because she came back later the same day and brought me a blanket and food. She talked to me. It's lonely on the streets. It's frightening too but most of all it's lonely. She started coming by regularly. I told her everything about my life. She'd sit on the step beside me, listening. I didn't have anyone else to talk to. She never judged me. Then I got sick – coughing, and pain in my chest."

He has both hands on his ribs, as if he can still feel it.

"She called an ambulance. It was pneumonia. My immune system was trashed." He scuffs at the pavement with the toe of his shoe and keeps his head down. "She visited me in hospital and, when I was ready to leave, she asked me if I'd like a job. She knew I was too sick to work but she took me back to her house anyway. She and Sarah looked after me. They taught me to read, taught me to drive, gave me back some self-esteem. There's not many people who'd do that for you." He gives a small shrug and looks up for the first time. "So now you know."

I puff out my cheeks. I can't think of anything to say. My problems are pathetic compared to what Charlie's been through.

"You probably wish you'd never met me now," he says.

"Why?"

"It's not a great life story, is it?"

"It could be worse. At least it's got a happy ending."

"It'll be the same for you as long as you don't give up."

"Maybe."

I want to believe Charlie but I can't. There's something different about his story and my story. Sarah's story too. It's as if the grandmother they know and the grandmother I'm living with are two different people. She'll sit on a step and chat to a homeless guy but she hates being with her own granddaughter. She'll organize music recitals for a dying man but not speak to her daughter for seventeen years. What's that about? Why are Mum and me so bad?

"Jess?" Charlie puts his thumb in the middle of my forehead. "You're frowning." He circles his thumb as if trying to wipe away the lines. "It doesn't suit you."

"Sorry." I attempt to smile.

"Do me a favour," Charlie says. "Keep what I've just told you to yourself?"

"I haven't got anyone to tell."

He puts his arm round me and gives me a friendly squeeze. "Come on, we'd better get back. It'll be OK, you'll see." We start walking. "Want to hear a terrible joke?"

I nod.

"What do you call a sheep with no legs. . .?"

Sarah's been waiting for us, that's obvious. She opens the front door before we get to the top of the steps. I see the look that passes between her and Charlie and I wonder what happened in the house after I did my runner.

"Are you all right?" she asks.

"I guess." But as she closes the door I feel trapped again, and some of the anger comes racing back.

"I'm afraid Mrs Chamberlain wants to see you straight away. In her office."

"She wants to *see* me? That's a turn-up for the books. Does that mean she might actually talk to me for a change?"

"She's not in a very good mood, Jess. I suggest you try to be polite."

I roll my eyes. It's all right for Sarah. She's always nice to Sarah.

Sarah walks me to the office door and pushes me in gently. Grandmother has her back to me and she keeps on writing as if she doesn't know I'm there. I stand with my back to the door and wait. I notice the photo of her with Mum has gone.

"So, young lady, have you got anything to say for yourself?" She still doesn't turn around.

I shrug.

"I'm sorry," she says, "what was that?"

"I didn't say anything."

She swivels her chair to face me. "This kind of behaviour is not acceptable. First you lock yourself in the lavatory and then you run away. You've got some explaining to do."

"I don't have to explain myself to anyone."

"I do not pay Dr McNair for wasting her time trying to coax you out of the lavatory."

"She's horrible. You should hear the things she says."

"That is no excuse. She is not here to be nice to you; she is here to teach you the violin."

"What if I don't like her way of teaching?"

"That is irrelevant. And you missed your afternoon session with Professor Jenniston."

"So?"

"She comes from the other side of London, Jessica. A wasted journey. Because of your wilful behaviour."

I shrug again.

"Is that all you can do? Shrug your shoulders?"

"What am I supposed to do? Turn back the clock?"

"We'd all like to do that."

She holds out paper and envelopes and stares at me over the top of her glasses. "I would like you to write letters of apology to Dr McNair and Professor Jenniston."

"I am not apologizing to Dr McNair. It was her fault."

"You will apologize or I will send you home."

"Fine."

"Fine? Fine you will apologize or fine you'll go home?"

"I'll go home."

"You don't mean that. I suggest you think before you open your mouth."

"I do mean it."

Grandmother is quiet. I look out of the window so I don't have to meet those grey eyes. I imagine myself on the train home, imagine Dad picking me up and banging on about how I should have listened to him. I think of what Charlie told me, of facing a future without playing the violin. My throat gets tight and it's harder to breathe. Nothing's clear any more.

Grandmother taps the end of her pen on her lips.

"Dr McNair tells me you have progressed with the Bartók – after a bit of encouragement."

"Encouragement? Is that what she calls it? Bear-baiting, more like."

"Ah, she used that old trick, did she?" Grandmother laughs.

"I don't see what's so funny."

She shakes her head. "Bartók is hard to play. It has to come from here." She taps her heart with her fingertips. "All your playing must come from here. If you don't feel it inside, you'll never convince your audience. I think that is all Dr McNair was trying to do, to get you to play it from your heart."

"I can assure you I felt it here," I say, jabbing my chest in the same place.

"So her tactics worked, then. You see?" Grandmother's eyebrows are raised. "Now you need to learn to use your emotions to good effect and not let them get the better of you. You know you can do it and it would seem a terrible shame to give up and go home just as you reach such a turning point."

I feel trapped. Maybe I've got her completely

wrong. Perhaps she is interested, after all. When I say nothing she simply smiles a cool smile and says, "Oh well. It's your decision."

I need to buy some time. I need to think.

"Charlie told me," I say.

"Told you what?"

"That you rescued him from the streets. That you brought him back here and looked after him and gave him a job."

"And?" she says.

"I think that was kind. But. . ."

"But what?"

"But I want to know how you could rescue someone you don't even know, yet never speak to your own daughter. I want to know why you cut us out of your life."

Grandmother turns back to her desk. "I am not prepared to discuss my daughter."

"She's my mum," I say. "I have the right to ask."

"You have no right at all."

"I'm your granddaughter, in case you've forgotten."

"Forgotten? Hardly!"

"It seems like you have. You never want to see me. It's as if I don't exist."

"I'm seeing you now, aren't I?" Her eyes drop. She fingers some papers on her desk. "Maybe you are right, Jessica. Perhaps you should leave. Maybe I can't help you."

I plonk myself down on the chair by her desk.

"What if I've decided I will apologize?" I pick up a pen and some paper off her desk. Under the paper there's a letter. The address looks foreign. But it's not the address that catches my eye.

Re: your late husband's estate: Jelinec family trust.

I don't have time to read more. Grandmother swipes the papers off her desk and shovels them into a drawer. She seems rattled.

"What was that?" I ask.

"Nothing of any concern to you." Her stony calm has returned. She's like a machine. "I have left you alone for too long," she says, smoothing her skirt. "I realize it must be hard being here in London. Away from your friends. I'm afraid I don't know any young people. Maybe it's time I heard you play. If you're staying, that is."

Her quick turnaround catches me out. This is what I've been waiting for. I want her to listen to me play. I want her to hear I can do it. But already a cold knot of pressure twists in my stomach. She's a music

151

critic and in my head I'm back on that scholarship stage and it terrifies me.

"When?" I ask.

"I will organize a small recital for you tomorrow."

"Tomorrow?" I can't help laughing – she's crazy. "That's impossible."

"Nothing is impossible. Have you other plans for tomorrow?"

"I can't prepare that fast."

"Of course you can. It will be informal."

"And there was me thinking I was off to the Albert Hall."

She closes her eyes and takes a deep breath. "Sarcasm is the lowest form of wit. However, I will arrange for us to visit Mr Ritchie at Harris House. It's a retirement home in North London. You will give a short recital to the residents. It will be nice for us to go out together."

Go out together? To a retirement home? With me as the entertainment. It must be my lucky day!

"You do remember Mr Ritchie, don't you? You met him when you first arrived."

"Yeah," I say, "of course I do."

"The word is *yes*, Jessica."

"Well, pardon me for offending."

"*Excuse* me."

I could throttle her. The knot of pressure has turned to fury.

"Do you like making trouble?" she says with heavy emphasis on the word *like*.

"Do you?" I throw back at her. I turn to go out of the door.

"Where do you think you are going?"

"To practise before my recital tomorrow, if you'll *excuse* me."

"You will be ready to leave the house at two o'clock. Charles will drive us."

I walk out.

"You may go," she says to my back.

"I've gone already," I say.

And I've gone without writing any letters of apology. One up to me.

Chapter 11

You don't want to play badly in front of Tara Chamberlain.

The sun is still shining, the sky is still blue and I'm still miserable. Sarah's words, or the words of her dead husband, go round and round in my head. I had nightmares all night and it's not much better now I'm awake. I'm not sure how Charlie managed to coax me into the car. As we drive across London, I feel my guts clenching, all my muscles tensing. I do not want to play badly in front of my grandmother. I don't want to play badly in front of anyone. What happens if I freeze up again? I'm wearing one of the dresses I bought with Selina — dark grey and orange silk with a zip from top to bottom at the back. Now the zip digs into my back and the material sticks to my skin in the heat. I try to peel it away. I feel sick.

It's not easy to do Professor Jenniston's relaxation exercises in the back of the car. I try but I keep catching a glimpse of Grandmother's face in the rear-view mirror, lips pinched as if she's sucking on a lemon. I'm not ready for this.

The retirement home is nothing like the place Mum works. It's like a smart private house. Very smart, in fact.

"Come on," says Charlie, "you'll enjoy it here."

He holds out his hand and half drags me out of the car. I'll be giving my recital in the conservatory and I follow Grandmother along the carpeted corridor. Mr Ritchie is there to welcome us, waving his walking stick. He's in the middle of a game of Scrabble.

"I've been waiting for you to arrive," he says. "I need your opinion. Daphne is trying to convince us that *wistings* is a word. It gives her thirty-three points. The rest of us haven't heard of it."

"I suggest you look it up in the dictionary then," says Grandmother.

"The dictionary has mysteriously disappeared," says Daphne, smiling.

"In that case it is definitely not a word," says Grandmother, and for the first time I hear genuine amusement in her laugh.

"Now then, Jessica," says Mr Ritchie, turning to me, "let's get you set up. I hope you're looking forward to entertaining us. I've told them all about you."

What has he told them about me? He doesn't know anything to tell. I try to look enthusiastic.

"Don't worry, we won't eat you," he says.

"There's nothing of her to eat," says a lady in a floral dress, getting out of her chair and coming towards me. "I'm Helena," she says and shakes my hand. Then she whispers in my ear, "Some people call me Hell – can't imagine why!"

I like her already.

"We're so glad you've come to play for us. It's very kind of you," she says.

"I didn't have much option," I mumble.

"I'm sure you'll be wonderful. But you needn't worry; everything's a treat when you get to our age. Our performers usually set up over here." She guides me towards the piano.

"Do you have many musicians, then?" I ask.

"Oh yes, most weeks."

My confidence plummets. They'll compare me to all the others. They'll decide I'm no good.

"I expect George will want to join you on the piano. He usually does."

"As in Mr Ritchie? Does he still play?"

"Oh yes. At every opportunity. Though he's not quite as good as he used to be." She whispers the last few words and glances over at Mr Ritchie with a smile.

"What are you two talking about?" he hollers, putting on a pretend-fierce face. "I hope you're not telling secrets behind my back, Hell." He's laughing away, and Helena makes shooing motions with her hand.

"Tara tells me you're sixteen," she says. "That's the same age as my granddaughter. She plays the clarinet." Helena turns her mouth down at the corners. "Not very well, I'm afraid – I think she's a bit lazy with her practising."

"It's not for everyone." I think of my crazy schedule.

"Very true." Helena is putting together a music stand. She does it in no time. I get out my violin.

"May I?" she says. She examines it closely. Plucks the strings. Hands it back, nodding.

"You play?" I ask.

"Oh, just a little these days." She opens the piano. "I'll give you an A."

I start to adjust my tuning. My new string is

misbehaving and it takes me longer than normal. The sound is harsh. There's so much glass in a conservatory and the sound bounces off it too easily.

The room is filling with people now – not quite the small audience I was expecting. It appears that some of the residents have invited friends and family along.

"We'll give everyone a few more minutes to settle," says Helena.

I wonder if I've got time to go to the toilet.

"What are you going to play?" she asks.

"I've been working on Bartók. I assume that's what Grandmother's expecting me to play."

Helena narrows her eyes, glances at Grandmother. "I don't think we want to hear that gloomy old stuff. It's rather intense. Have you got anything else? It's *your* recital, after all. You can choose. Shall we have a look?" She flicks through the music in my case. "Oh look," she says, "you could begin with a couple of Kreutzer études. They'll get your fingers warmed up and they'll bring back plenty of fond memories." She puts them on my music stand. "Oh, and this is nice. Do you enjoy Vivaldi? I think we'd all enjoy this – nothing like a bit of Vivaldi to cheer one up."

She lines up my music for me. It's all quite simple stuff and I begin to breathe a little more easily. But then I look at Grandmother and my confidence drains away.

"Are you ready, do you think?" Helena asks. "I'll introduce you."

Am I ready? My heart is beating fast and once again I'm back on that wretched stage in Manchester. My palms are sweating. I watch Helena hold up her hand and gradually the room falls silent. I close my eyes.

"Good afternoon. Today we are very lucky to have Jessica Cooke to play for us." Helena's voice sounds faint and fuzzy. I try to breathe like Professor Jenniston has taught me. "Jessica is studying with our great friend Celia McNair. Let's give her a warm welcome."

How do they know Dr McNair? I open my eyes and the room swims into focus. There's gentle applause. I try to pull myself together. I need to say something.

"Hello," I begin. I'm blushing, mumbling, awkward. "Um – as I haven't had much of a chance to warm up, I'm going to begin with a couple of studies to get my fingers moving." I wiggle my left-hand fingers in the air and then feel like I'm talking to a bunch of kids. I'd better just get on with it.

I loosen my shoulders a little. The music is on the stand but I don't need it. I play these studies every day and even the worst stage fright in the world couldn't wipe them from my memory. I look at Helena and she smiles. I'd never've thought of starting with these if she hadn't suggested it.

I lift my violin, lift my bow. I'm holding my breath and I force myself to exhale.

And I begin to play.

Quickly, I sense a change in the room. The air becomes lighter; backs straighten, heads bob, shoes tap on the carpet. I catch the eye of one person, then another, and it's like a tiny electric current between us. They become my friends.

As my bow skips over the strings, Helena's following my every move, and I know by the way she dips her shoulder, tilts her hand, that she's anticipating where the music goes next. In her head, she's playing with me, and it feels like we're playing together.

They clap and I give a little bow. I keep my eyes away from Grandmother but I can feel her gaze on me. Like an eagle.

I play some Vivaldi, Bruch, Mozart. With each new piece, I'm weaving a web with my music, drawing each person closer to me. It's a personal, powerful, physical connection that I've never felt before. The clapping becomes more and more energetic and a warm sensation spreads from my chest all the way to my fingers and toes.

When I come to a stop, they call for more. I can't help smiling.

Mr Ritchie is struggling out of his chair. I see Charlie step forward to help.

"Would you do me the honour?" he says as he approaches the piano.

Helena winks at me. I have no idea what I'm letting myself in for.

Mr Ritchie adjusts the piano stool and begins running his fingers up and down the keys. He can move them fast for an old person – fast for a young person come to that.

"I presume you know *Méditation* from *Thaïs*?" he asks.

"I do," I say, "but I'm afraid I haven't brought the music. I'm so sorry."

"Well, I don't need it if you don't," he says.

That really knocks me over. He must be

about ninety. And he can play the *Méditation* from memory?

"Are you sure?" I ask. It's standard repertoire for me. I've been playing it since I was about ten, but accompanists don't usually play from memory.

"Sure I'm sure. Anyway, what's the worst that can happen? Let's give it a go."

He gets all serious, rubbing his hands together. I stand back a little and wait for him to begin the introduction. This could be awkward.

He plays the first few notes.

I know straight away he's no ordinary piano player. He presses into the notes softly and gently, with immaculate timing, perfect tempo. I listen, stunned. So stunned I almost forget to come in. He stops straight away and holds up his hand.

"False start," he says, grinning. "Sorry, everyone, I think we'll give that another go."

They laugh. I blush. Mr Ritchie looks at me and I can tell there's to be no mucking about.

"Are you ready this time?" he asks. His eyes are twinkling.

"Yes, sir!" I say and give a sharp nod. There's something about him that brings out a good side of me.

I tuck my violin under my chin. For this piece, I need the close contact of the instrument to allow me to feel every note. It's a meditation. It's played inside. He begins again and this time I'm ready. His playing is magnetic. It binds me to him so our instruments become one. The music spirals down inside me, filling every inch of my body, stretching and pulling, and everything else disappears.

We finish and there is a heartbeat of silence before the clapping begins. It's hardly deafening applause, but it's real. I keep my eyes closed. When I open them, Mr Ritchie holds out his hand to me and smiles.

"The *something* is working today?" he asks quietly.

I nod.

He squeezes my hand, raises it to his lips. I know better than to giggle this time and I check to make sure Grandmother has noticed. She's clapping, politely, but her face is unreadable.

"Encore," comes the call, but Mr Ritchie holds up his hand again.

"I think that is quite enough excitement for one day," he says.

I'm disappointed. I'd like to carry on.

"Always better to leave on a high," whispers Mr Ritchie. "Anyway, it's teatime."

I place my violin back in its case. Someone has opened double doors into a small garden and I wander out to get some fresh air. I'm happier than I've been in months.

"Mind if I join you?" asks Charlie.

"It's not my garden," I say.

"That was very good." He nods his head towards the conservatory.

"But not really your kind of music. I know."

He laughs. "No, I mean it. It was good. You've caused quite stir in there. That's impressive, given your audience."

"They were hardly what I'd call threatening."

"Really? Even though most of them are past members of the London Symphony Orchestra?"

"Shut up, Charlie."

"Go and ask them if you don't believe me."

"Don't wind me up."

"I'm not. Well, I may be exaggerating a bit. They come from all over the place, but they're all musicians. Apparently, once Helena and Mr Ritchie moved in, other musicians started coming. Harris House has got quite a reputation."

"Are Helena and Mr Ritchie married?" I ask.

"No. Definitely not. Mr Ritchie's wife died some years ago, I think."

"So you're telling me they're all musicians – like real musicians?"

"Helena was a violinist, but you must have guessed that. Far as I remember, Daphne played the clarinet. She hasn't got the puff any more, poor thing. Old Gareth at the back there, he was percussion. You should see him with his knife and fork! Mr Ritchie you know about. I'm not sure about the rest. I've got a feeling Alfred played the trombone in a jazz band." Charlie points out a man wearing a bright bow tie. "Still looks the part." We laugh.

"You're not joking, are you?"

Charlie shakes his head.

"I'm glad I didn't know all that before I played. I'd have freaked out." I hardly know what to think now.

Helena's waving for us to come in and join them. I'm nervous now. What did they really think of my playing?

"Come on," says Charlie. "We'd better go in and have tea. It's a sin not to drink tea when you're here. Like the dress, by the way." He puts his hand against my back and presses me inside. His touch is reassuring.

The talk in the conservatory is all music. Helena congratulates me and praises my playing. Now I know she's professional herself, it means a lot. Others congratulate me and they are all so kind that I find it hard to stop smiling. I almost allow myself to believe their enthusiasm.

Daphne asks me about Dr McNair. I get the feeling she and Dr McNair don't see eye to eye either. Mr Ritchie and Grandmother are sitting away from the main group, talking quietly. I try to hear what they're saying but with all the other chatter it's hard. Mr Ritchie looks happy enough but Grandmother's got her back to me. Stiff and straight.

We drink tea, eat biscuits. I ask Helena about her career as a violinist and she tells me *it was all very easy in those days*. I don't believe a word of it. The goodbyes, when they come, are friendly, and I leave feeling about five times taller than when I arrived. I jump into the back of the car and wave as we pull out of the driveway.

The journey home is quicker. I wait and wait for Grandmother to say something – anything. I start to worry that she was disappointed in my performance. I tell myself I don't care what she thinks – but I do, more than anything. She's a critic.

Finally, Grandmother clears her throat and I hold my breath.

"Thank you, Jessica," she says, "you did well this afternoon. They enjoyed your recital."

They. The word sits heavily. I know *they* did. What about *her*?

"You didn't tell me they were professional musicians."

"Would it have made a difference?"

"It would when I started playing with Mr Ritchie. He took me properly by surprise."

"He played well today, though he's beginning to lose his touch."

"I don't think so."

"How would you know? You've never played with him before."

"No. But he's amazing."

I try to push away thoughts of Stefan. It's hard when the comparison is so obvious. Mr Ritchie is the first accompanist I've played with since working with Stefan and he's made me realize that even Stefan has a long way to go. Not that it's going to make a lot of difference to me now. I sigh. I'd give anything to see Stefan; everything. I wish I could just forget him.

I catch Charlie's eye in the rear-view mirror and see him smile. That cheers me up.

"It was gratifying to see that you were able to perform without too many nerves," continues Grandmother, "so I can only assume that Professor Jenniston's methods must be working."

"Yes, they are," I say enthusiastically.

"Of course," says Grandmother in a too-pleasant voice, "your audience was small and your repertoire undemanding. However, it's a start, I suppose."

"I'd like to see you play some of that stuff, and I don't see what difference the size of the audience makes. Anyway, they say it can be harder to communicate simpler pieces to an audience."

Charlie is slowing down to park. I can see his shoulders moving. If he's laughing I'll kill him.

"Oh. Is that what *they* say? We shall have to wait and see. I think we should reserve judgement until you try to perform something a little less simple."

"Like?"

"I haven't decided yet. I shall put my mind to it."

"Oh – and it might be handy to have more

than twenty-four hours' warning before I have to perform next time."

I'm out of the car, door slammed shut, almost before it's stopped. I wish I hadn't said that. I hate to think what she's going to come up with now. It's hard to imagine anything worse than the Bartók. But if anyone can find something, she will.

Chapter 12

Two extra squirts of bubble bath and I'm lying amongst mountains of foam. I make tall sculptures with the bubbles, then blow them over or smack them down as I think of Grandmother. When I go back downstairs, Charlie's alone in the kitchen reading the paper. Sarah's in bed with a migraine, he tells me, so he's in charge.

"Were you laughing at me in the car?" I ask.

"No, not really. I didn't know what to do, to be honest. It took me by surprise hearing Mrs Chamberlain going at you like that. I wasn't expecting it. You didn't deserve it, not today."

"At least now you know I'm not making it up. I told you she's foul to me."

"Don't rise to it. It makes it worse."

"What d'you expect me to do? Be a doormat? I bet you'd rise to it if she was your grandmother.

"She's old-fashioned. Maybe it's just her way."

"Her way with me, you mean. Not with anyone else."

"If you're talking about Sarah and me, then remember we only work for her."

"Yeah, and I'm only her granddaughter."

"Exactly. It's different."

"I thought charity was supposed to begin at home."

"I wouldn't know, would I? But she's got a lot invested in you, with your music and being responsible for you while you're away from your parents."

"You're just making excuses for her. Whose side are you on?"

"I'm not on anyone's side. I'm simply saying that things aren't always what they seem on the surface."

"Now you're sounding like Professor Jenniston."

"I'm no psychologist. But you're related to your grandmother by blood and so she's going to be far more emotionally involved with you. It's got nothing to do with liking or disliking you. Blood makes a difference, that's all."

"Emotionally involved? Grandmother? She's got the emotional capacity of a turnip."

"A turnip?" Charlie smiles. "Where did you drag that up from?"

"Under the ground?" I can't help laughing.

"That's a *terrible* joke!"

"Worse than a sheep with no legs being called a cloud? You're a fine one to talk."

Charlie starts laughing and it's infectious. I don't even know what we're laughing about but as soon as one of us stops, the other one starts. It's hopeless. I wipe the tears from my eyes.

"Honestly, though, she does me in," I say. "Can't she see how bored I am? Work, work, work. I've hardly met a single person under the age of seventy since I've been here."

"You've met me."

"That doesn't count."

"Thanks. And Sarah? And Rosie?"

"Don't remind me. We're doing five miles tomorrow. At this rate I *will* be running the marathon next year."

"At least it gets you out and reminds you there's world out there."

"Don't be stupid. I've got so much sweat in

my eyes, I can't even see where I'm going. It's like running in a fog." I lay my head down on my arms on the table. "I want to *do* something," I wail.

"So *do* something, then," says Charlie.

"Like what?" I sit up and cup my chin in my hands. "I have no friends. I can't exactly walk up to someone on the street and say 'Be my friend', can I? And even if I did meet a few people my own age, I've got no money. So far things aren't shaping up that well."

"Fair point, but at least it's not for ever. Tell you what, as Sarah's sick, I'll get pizzas tonight. Will that cheer you up?"

"Nothing will cheer me up."

"Fine. Stay miserable, then. I'll get pizzas anyway." He laughs as he gets up and walks out of the door.

I suppose pizza is better than nothing. I go to my room and dial Mum's number and give her the rundown on the day. Tell her about her stupid mother.

"I'm sorry to hear about my mother," she says, "but I'm glad George Ritchie played for you. How is he? I hope he's looking after you."

"Did you know him well?"

"He was my guardian angel when I was growing up. He often visited, and always brought me sweets and presents. It drove Mother mad. She said he spoilt me. He still sends me a birthday card every year, even now. If I hadn't known George would be there to keep half an eye on you, I definitely wouldn't have let you stay in London."

I think back to the day I arrived. I was in such a state I didn't take much in, but I remember how kind he was. I can't imagine why he'd want to be such good friends with my grandmother.

"He's a brilliant pianist," I say.

"He certainly is, or was."

Mum starts wittering on about Mr Ritchie but I'm only half listening. It's strange imagining Mum being a child growing up in this house. When she was little did she run around, play hide and seek, go to the park and feed the ducks? And when she was sixteen, like me? What was she like then? Still at boarding school, I suppose. Did she have any friends? What did she do in her spare time?

"Did you ever learn an instrument when you were growing up?" I don't know why I've never asked before.

"No." There's a pause. "Though when I was at

school I was desperate to play the violin. Mother didn't want me to. In fact, she got quite angry about it. She said I could take up ballet instead. I hated her for that."

"You'd have thought she'd have encouraged you, with her being a music critic and everything."

Mum gives a dry laugh. "That was the problem, I think. She always wanted me to be perfect at everything. Given her job, I suppose having a bad musician for a daughter would have been the final straw. I was always letting her down, or so she told me, so I expect the violin would have been the same. As it turned out, I was useless at ballet too."

"But you might've been a good violinist."

"I doubt it."

"What about Grandmother? Didn't she play an instrument? All her friends seem to be musicians."

"No. She just criticized."

"That figures. I wonder where I got my music genes from, then."

"Not from me. Anyway, not everyone believes talent is born. It's the old nature–nurture argument."

I've got no idea what Mum is talking about.

"You couldn't describe what Grandmother does as nurture. More like torture."

"Ah," she says. Then she's silent for so long I think she's hung up.

"Helloooooo?" I say.

"She's not being very unkind to you, is she? You would tell us if you're unhappy or. . ."

"She's odd. You and Dad warned me. I have to learn to live with it because I'd be dumb to give up a chance like this. It's the hardest thing I've ever done, but if it gives me another shot at a scholarship, then it's worth it."

"Yes, I suppose."

"Has Dad stopped being mad at me yet?"

"He's a stubborn old mule sometimes."

"He's worse than Grandmother — you can tell him I said that."

"I won't because it's not true."

"Mum . . . you know your father?"

"No, I don't."

"I didn't mean actually know him. But you must know something about him. Do you know if he had some kind of estate overseas, like in Europe?"

"What on earth made you ask that? I've got no

idea. My father could've been the tsar of Russia for all I know. Why?"

"Just wondered – I saw a letter, that's all. On Grandmother's desk. It had a foreign-looking address. Something about Grandmother's late husband's estate."

"That just means after he's dead. Ancient history."

"Didn't look that ancient."

"Well, what did it say?"

"No idea. Grandmother swept it away before I had the chance to read it."

"She's probably clearing out her filing cabinets or rewriting her will or something. Leaving all her money to the musicians' benevolent fund, no doubt." Mum doesn't have an expressive voice but there's a note of bitterness in it now.

"She must have shedloads of money," I say, staring around my room. "God, imagine if she left it to us. We'd be rolling in it. We could move house and Dad could get a new car."

"Don't waste your breath. It'll never happen."

"I guess not. Shame, though. Maybe if I get really good at the violin. . ."

"Nothing is ever good enough for her."

"Thanks for the encouragement."

"It's just the way she is. Anyway, I must go. Some of us have to work."

"You think I'm not working?"

"I'm talking about the kind of work that earns money. Work that pays the bills. You've probably forgotten about all that kind of thing living down there." Mum's tone of voice is irritating.

"You didn't have to run away with Dad. It was your choice."

"You're right. It was my choice. And it was the right choice. I'll call you tomorrow."

I say goodbye and throw the phone on the bed. What am I thinking? I shouldn't have said that about Dad. I wander over to the window and hang my head out. Nothing's happening – surprise, surprise. A middle-aged man in a smart suit walks past the house. Very proper. I put two fingers in my mouth and give a loud wolf whistle. That wakes him up. I duck down before he has the chance to see me. When I poke my head back up, he's still checking over his shoulder. Maybe he's been doing something he shouldn't. Visiting his girlfriend behind his wife's back. Now he's worried he's been spotted. Serves him right. God, I really must be bored.

I open Professor Jenniston's notebook and begin to scribble down thoughts. My conversation with Mum helps make some sense of the day.

Perfection? If that's what Gran wants, then I may as well leave now. Must practise more, play better. NO pressure. How far can she expect me to go in six months? Where will all her money go when she dies? I could be rich – imagine! Must stop biting my nails. Is talent born or made I wonder? Have I got any talent? Guess I'll find out one day – maybe.Wish me luck. I'm going to need it if I'm ever going to impress the great Mrs C. Stefan, you could learn a thing or two from Mr Ritchie. Perhaps you're not so brilliant after all.

I go back and cross that last bit out. It pisses me off that I can't get Stefan out of my head. If only I didn't think about music all the time. If only I had a life – then I might be able to forget Stefan ever existed. I rub the palms of my hands up and down my face, then pick up my pencil again.

I think I've become the most boring person in the world . . . thank goodness for Charlie. ♫

There's a knock and Charlie puts his head round the door. Talk of the devil! I slam my notebook shut and blush.

"Hello, Miss Mopey. I've just got to go and get

Sarah painkillers so I'll pick up pizzas on the way back. I'll be home in around forty."

"Is Grandmother in this evening?" I ask. "Will she be joining us for pizza?" I imitate her voice and giggle.

"She's in but she's not eating. She's hard at work, as usual. But for future information, she likes spicy pepperoni."

"You're joking, aren't you?" Charlie gives me an ambiguous smile. "What does she do all the time? She's always 'working'."

"Don't ask me."

Once Charlie's gone, I lock my notebook away and try to catch up on a bit of theory homework. But my stomach is rumbling at the thought of pizza and I can't concentrate. I leave my window open so I can hear when he gets back. As soon as the front door opens, I'm on my feet and down to the kitchen.

∫ ∖

I've never seen Charlie out of his suit or running gear before, but this evening he's wearing faded jeans and a T-shirt. I must be staring because he notices and kind of checks himself over.

"What?" he asks.

"No uniform tonight?"

"Off duty. I'm going out. Some mates of mine are doing a gig in Kentish Town."

We rip off quarters of pizza. Charlie offers me a Coke.

"What kind of gig?" The pizza tastes fantastic.

"Some Irish friends of mine. Ciaran's got a band. Pipeline. They play all sorts. Rock, mainly – with Irish influence."

"Are they any good?"

"They're great. They're beginning to make quite a name for themselves, especially in Ireland."

"Sounds fun." My attempt at saying it innocently doesn't work.

Charlie meets my eyes. "I can't take you," he says.

"You said earlier that I needed to get out more."

We sit in silence for a few seconds.

"It'd be more than my life's worth. If Mrs Chamberlain found out I'd taken you to a pub, I'd lose my job for sure." He rubs his eyes.

"Why? What's wrong with you taking me out? You're an adult. Anyway, she wouldn't have to find out, would she."

"You know her; she's got eyes in the back of her head."

"She'd never notice. Not in a million. Come on, I dare you."

"What about Sarah?"

"She's hardly going to be around tonight. Not with a migraine. Honestly, Grandmother couldn't give a monkey's where I am as long as I'm nowhere near her. She's not going to come looking for me. They'll both be tucked up in bed."

Charlie drums his fingers on the table. Says nothing. I can see he's wavering.

"OK. If I take you. *If*. You have to be sensible. No alcohol. No getting me into trouble."

"Of course I'll be sensible." I wonder what Charlie defines as sensible.

"And you'll need warm clothes. We're going on the bike."

"Uh-uh. I'm not biking anywhere." Charlie's fanatical fitness does my head in.

"Not a bicycle, you idiot. My motorbike. It's out the back."

"I didn't know you had a motorbike." I've never been on a motorbike. I try and act cool.

"Don't make me regret this, Jess."

"I won't."

We have to wait for Grandmother to go upstairs. Charlie teaches me poker hands and I get the hang of it pretty quick. Around nine thirty we hear her shoes on the marble floor. Charlie goes to check she's got everything she needs.

Once she's well out of the way, I whip up to my room, grab my jacket and boots, do my make-up and I'm set to go. I creep back down again, trying not to make a sound.

I notice Charlie giving me the once-over. I wonder if I've got the wrong clothes on for the bike.

"Ready?" he asks. He does a final check to make sure the house is quiet. "This way." He's flicking off light switches, grabbing keys.

He goes through the door at the back of the kitchen. It's a storage area.

"Come on," he whispers. "You'll have to go out first. I've got to set the alarms. This place is like Fort Knox."

"Tell me about it!" I say. "Who does Grandmother think is coming to get her?!"

He reaches up to a shelf, pulls down a big black helmet. Hands it to me.

"Put it on."

I fumble. Pretend to know what I'm doing. He helps. He's a bit rough. I reckon he's nervous. There's another door at the end of the storeroom. It leads to an alley down the side of the house with a solid gate out on to the road.

"I never knew this was here," I whisper, but the words are lost in my helmet.

He disappears back in the house, then re-emerges. I can see the huge shape of the bike under a plastic tarpaulin. When he pulls it off I gasp. Black and silver metal glint under the street light. *Kawasaki*. I whisper the name in my head and it sounds exciting. Dangerous.

Charlie's unlocking the gate, wheeling the bike out to the road. I follow. Grandmother's windows are at the back but I notice Charlie glancing up anxiously. He says something but I don't catch it.

He's pulled on his own helmet and he's on the bike. He jerks his thumb to the back and I climb on behind him, my legs straddling the soft leather of the seat. It's a good thing I've lost so much weight. I'd struggle to get on if my jeans were as tight as they used to be.

The bike thrums into action and the sound vibrates right through me. My adrenaline skyrockets.

He gives me the thumbs up and there's a surge of energy as the bike powers forward. I grab his waist, cling on tight.

We tip in and out of the traffic. Charlie's not patient and we race along, the wind pushing my jacket sleeves tight back against my arms. I lean the side of my helmet on Charlie's back and watch the street lights and buildings fly past in continuous streams of orange and grey. All sound mushes into a kind of deadened roar inside my helmet. By the time we pull up I'm breathless and laughing.

I climb off and shake the stiffness out of my legs. It's great to get the helmet off. Charlie locks both helmets on to the bike while I put my head forward and run my fingers through my hair.

"Pub's on the corner up there," Charlie says, and he puts his hand on my shoulder, guiding me towards the door. "What d'you think of the bike?"

"Brilliant."

"I only bought it last year. Costs me a fortune to insure. I don't get to take it out that much." He's grinning.

The music gets louder as we get closer.

"The Fiddler's Elbow? Great name for a pub. Is that why you brought me here?"

"I hadn't even thought of it. Could be a good omen."

Groups stand smoking on the street and the volume goes up a few notches as we push our way in. It's packed. I turn sideways to get through the crowd. People are sitting, standing, dancing. Charlie seems to know a few people here. They pat his shoulder as he goes past, raise their glasses, holler across the room. The room is full of life and energy and I let it soak into me. It's like being human again.

I stand close behind Charlie, pressed against him, as he gets some drinks. Some of my Coke spills as he passes it to me and I suck it off the back of my hand. He tries to introduce me to his friends but with all the noise it's kind of awkward. He starts talking to a pretty girl and I feel a bit of a spare part so I ease my way towards the band and find a spot near some empty seats. The table's got stuff all over it so I don't sit down but lean against the wall and listen. The band is playing a kind of rock ballad – nothing I recognize. The harmonies are good. The lead guitarist catches my eye, holds it for a moment and gives a quick smile. I blink it in. He doesn't look at me again.

It's not long until they finish the set and I stand

up a bit straighter, trying to spot Charlie over the other side. The guitarist is coming towards me now, followed by the others. I realize I must be standing by the band's table and I feel like a groupie.

"You all right there, girlie?" says the guitarist. "Enjoying the music?"

It's a breathy Irish accent. Friendly and gentle.

"Yeah. It's great."

"You're looking a bit lonely. Are you here by yourself?"

"No. I've come with a friend. Charlie. I think you know him."

"Charlie? So, what's he doing leaving you on your own?"

"I'm not exactly *with* Charlie. He just brought me along."

"Hey, Mr B, get . . . what's your name?"

"Jess."

"Get Jess a drink. She's a friend of Charlie's. And tell Charlie to get over here."

He pats the chair next to his. He looks older close-up. Late twenties, I'm guessing.

"I'm Ciaran. This is Seamus, otherwise known as Stubbie. That's Harry, and Mr B's over there. So now you know us all. How d'you know Charlie?"

"He works for my grandmother. I'm staying with her for six months. Studying the violin. I'm trying to get to music college." I feel childish.

"Wow, a real musician. We must seem like a bunch of amateurs."

I laugh. "I couldn't do what you do."

"Course you could. Come round some day and give it a try."

"If only."

Mr B puts down a tray of glasses full of golden liquid. They all take one. Ciaran hands one to me. I sniff it, wrinkle my nose.

"Cheers," says Ciaran and shoots his back. "Come on, drink up."

I take a sip. It burns my throat.

"Not like that." says Ciaran. "Knock it back."

I can hardly refuse; I'd look silly. So I tip back my head, throw it down. The heat fills my body. It's strong.

"What is it," I gasp.

"Irish whiskey."

They're reaching for a second. They wait for me.

"Come on, Jessie," they say.

I drink. Laugh.

I've just downed my third when Charlie arrives.

He swipes the glass from my hand. "What are you doing?" He stares around the band. "She's only sixteen."

I don't know why he's so worked up. I haven't done that much wrong.

"Whoa. Hang on," says Ciaran, "we didn't know how old she was."

I'm ready to sink through the floor. My cheeks are burning but maybe that's the whiskey too. I can feel it in my head and I have to try to stop myself from giggling.

"Oh for heaven's sake," Charlie says. "Get her some water." He makes me drink two full glasses. But the whiskey's warm in my body and I'm having fun. I don't care if Charlie's shouting at me. He can shout all he wants.

"You're a bunch of idiots," he says. They try to look serious for a moment but they can't keep it up. Once they start laughing, there's no stopping them, and I can't help joining in. Finally Charlie's face relaxes and he shakes his head. But as soon as the boys are back on stage, Charlie grips my elbow.

"I told you not to drink."

"Hey, loosen up, I'm only having a bit of fun. What's wrong with that?"

"Only that you shouldn't even be here, your grandmother doesn't know and if anything happens to you it'll be me who's in trouble. A lot of trouble."

"But nothing will happen, will it?" I shout it over the sound of the music.

"Lay off the whiskey, OK?"

I shrug one shoulder and let my body absorb the beat of the music. People start to dance and I pull at Charlie's shirt. He's sitting there like a dummy, staring into his Coke.

"C'mon," I say to him, "let's dance."

"No, thanks."

"Don't you like dancing?"

He doesn't say anything.

"Fine, I'll find someone else to dance with. Someone a bit more fun than you." I get to my feet.

He grabs me by the arm and pulls me back down.

"Get off me," I say, shaking him off. "Anyway, you can't tell me what to do. You're not my dad."

"Sorry," he says gruffly. "I didn't hurt you, did I?"

I glare at him, then feel bad and look at my feet instead.

Charlie puts his finger under my chin and tries to lift it. I resist at first. "I'm sorry," he says again. This time I let him raise my head. He holds my eyes and I don't blink. It feels like a game where neither of us will be the first to break the stare. Finally, he drops his elbow to the table and wipes his hand slowly across his eyes. "I shouldn't have brought you here. It was a mistake," he says.

"No it wasn't. Don't be boring. It's the best night I've had for months. If we get into trouble, so what?"

The music is getting louder and I'm not sure Charlie can hear me. I cross my arms and look around at everyone else having a good time. Charlie's knee is against mine and he's drumming on it with his fingers.

Suddenly he takes my hand and pulls me to my feet. "Oh come on then," he says, "I suppose one dance won't do any harm."

I smile as he drags me into the crowd. I'm a terrible dancer but I don't care. There's such a squish I can get away with not doing much. Charlie seems to clear his own space. He can dance, no doubt about that. In fact, he's really good. The band winds down to a slower song and people drift back to their tables. I move to do the same but Charlie puts his hand on my waist.

"I like this song," he says.

"I don't know it." I'm not sure what to do.

He nods over towards the band. "It's one of their new ones," he says as he pulls me towards him.

This is awkward. I'm even more rubbish at slow dancing. I'm glad I've had a bit to drink. The whiskey swims gently through my head. Charlie slips his arm further round my waist and I let my head rest on his shoulder. I close my eyes and try to imagine I'm dancing with Stefan – not that I've ever danced with Stefan.

The song finishes and another one starts. Slow again. I drape my arms round Charlie's neck. He pulls away slightly and I look at him. The look in his eyes confuses me and I drop my head back to his shoulder. I feel his hand touch the back of my head, a finger gently stroking my neck, and it sends little ripples down my spine. Then suddenly he pushes me away. It's not even the end of the song.

"I think we should go," he says. "Some fresh air will do us both good."

He makes me feel like I've done something wrong. "I thought you said you liked this music."

I'd never guessed Charlie could be so moody. He steers me outside and walks me up and down the pavement a few times, mumbling something about not wanting me to fall off the bike. The journey home goes in a flash and, by the time we're back at the house, the fuzziness in my head has mostly cleared and the pub seems a distant memory. I still manage to trip over the step to the back door and I snort with laughter. Charlie clamps his hand over my mouth.

"Be quiet," he hisses, "you'll wake the whole neighbourhood. Wait here while I do the alarm."

After a load of beeps, he pulls me into the house and escorts me to my bedroom, his finger raised to his lips in case I forget to keep my mouth shut. He pushes me through my bedroom door, then closes it. We are both in my room. He has his hand on the door handle but he doesn't move. My radiator is making a strange sound. I see him glance at it.

"Thanks for tonight," I say.

His hand falls from the door handle and he takes a step towards me. My heart beats faster. Then he folds his arms. Stands there.

"I'd better get to bed," I say. "Five miles with Rosie in the morning."

"Of course," he says, and he's got his back to me already. "Night."

He opens the door silently, does a quick check and leaves.

For a few seconds I'm like a statue. I'm not sure if I wanted Charlie to go. I'm not sure if Charlie wanted to go. Probably my imagination. I haul off my boots, wander into the bathroom and take a hard look at myself in the mirror. Not good. I'm not sure I like whiskey. I shouldn't have broken my promise to Charlie tonight. I can't blame him for getting angry. And then I made him feel bad and he had to be nice to me. He probably thinks I'm a complete idiot. And I am.

I'll apologize in the morning.

Chapter 13

It's the first thing I do. Seven thirty a.m. Apologize. But Charlie's so uptight it's crazy. He barely says a word to me. I'm quite relieved when Rosie arrives even though I have a blinding headache from that bloody whiskey. We're nearly four miles into our run when it starts to rain.

"It may be wet," says Rosie, "but that's no excuse to run like a duck."

"What d'you mean?"

"Think about your feet and your elbows. You need to make yourself more aerodynamic."

"I'll never be anything dynamic when it comes to running so I wouldn't waste time getting excited," I puff.

"OK, well, at least you might look a bit cooler

if you tuck in your arms and make your feet a little straighter."

As we get near the house, I do make an effort — in case Charlie is watching. He's not. Sarah opens the door to let me in. Charlie's out all day. I can understand that — it's his day off.

∫ ∫

As the days go by, it's clear he's avoiding me on purpose. Every time I walk into the kitchen, he walks out. I don't know what I've done. Perhaps I made a bit of a fool of myself the other night but I've got over it and so should he. It's not like anyone's found out.

On the Friday, I get a text from Ciaran, apologizing. Charlie must've given him my number. Apparently the boys feel guilty and they want to make it up to Charlie and me. He's invited us over to his place. He says to bring my violin. That makes me smile but I can't see it happening. At least it gives me an excuse to have it out with Charlie. I manage to trap him in the kitchen — stand with my back to the door so he can't escape.

"So have you heard from Ciaran too?" I ask.

"Yup."

"He wants us to go over there."

"Yup."

"It'd be fun," I say.

"Go, then."

"What, without you?"

"D'you want me to come with you?"

"Of course I do. Anyway, how else would I get there?"

"Oh, sorry, I'd forgotten. I'm just the driver."

"Cut it out. I didn't mean that."

"Sorry."

"What's up with you, anyway? You've barely spoken to me since last Saturday."

"Keep your voice down!"

"Why? I'm not saying anything incriminating. I've said I'm sorry – I know I shouldn't have been drinking, but. . ."

"Shut up," Charlie hisses. "D'you want to get us both into trouble? Anyway, it's not that."

"Well, what is it, then?"

He stares at me for a few moments. "Nothing. Look, if you really want to go, I've got an idea how we can do it."

"You have?"

197

"The thing is," he says, "I've been discussing a few things with Mrs Chamberlain. I told her that it seems a shame you're living here in London but not getting the chance to see any of the tourist attractions. I suggested I could drive you around on the odd Saturday afternoon to do a bit of sightseeing."

"Cunning! What did she say? I presume she didn't agree."

It's the first time I've seen him smile in days. "As a matter of fact, she did. She thought it was a very good idea. She thinks it will do you good to explore London. She recognizes that you're working hard and, as she said to me, 'that can be a little damaging without any balance.' So, all in all, we had a pretty good conversation. All we have to do is tell her where we're going."

I fling my arms round Charlie's neck. "You're a genius. I owe you one."

Charlie moves away and sits down.

"So –" he clears his throat "– on Saturday I thought we could go and visit Ciaran and the rest – though I think we might tell Mrs Chamberlain that we're off to London Zoo."

I stop then. "Charlie, we can't do that. We can't just lie to her."

"It didn't seem to worry you when we went to the pub."

"That was different. She didn't know anything about that. There's a difference between not telling and deliberately lying."

"I've told Ciaran we'll be there at two. If you don't want to come, don't come."

His mood has changed quickly. He walks out of the kitchen, slamming the door behind him. I thought you were supposed to grow out of being temperamental when you stopped being a teenager. Not Charlie. Now I'm not sure what to do. The thing is, I do want to go. I really want to go. It's a clever plan, but I can't stop the prickle of worry in my head. I suppose just the once can't do any harm. It's not as if we're doing anything illegal, and it's not often you get the chance to play the violin with a real rock band.

That evening, I bust out some of my rock covers and allow myself to forget that I'm supposed to be mastering the finer points of Brahms and Bartók. It's then that I realize I've almost forgotten what it feels like to enjoy playing. Suddenly I'm breathing again – having fun. I need Grandmother's financial support and I can't deny that I'm getting some good tuition, however much I may hate it, but there's more to playing than practice. I won't let Grandmother stop me from loving what I do. So yes, I will go to Ciaran's tomorrow. I'll tell Charlie in the morning. Now I'm excited.

On Saturday morning, I feel light-footed as I run with Rosie.

"You're chirpy this morning," she says when we reach our turnaround point.

"Yep – today is a good-mood day," I say.

"Why's that?"

I shrug. "Just is."

Rosie smiles. "Well, it's good to see you looking happy."

Dr McNair nearly manages to spoil everything by winding me up over six particular bars of music. She makes me play them about a hundred times. If I didn't have something to look forward to, I would've chucked my toys out of the pram by now. Instead, I just do as she says and eventually she grudgingly agrees that we've got it sorted. I lose concentration towards the end of the lesson and she lets me go five minutes early.

"So, Charlie tells me you're off to the zoo," Sarah says as we sit down to lunch.

I feel my face go puce and almost choke on a piece of sweetcorn.

"Yes," I mumble.

"You'll have a lovely time," says Sarah, patting my hand. "If I wasn't so busy, I'd come too. It'll do you good to have some time out from all your hard work."

I nod and smile and feel terrible. I can't even look at Charlie. It's not just Grandmother we're lying to, it's Sarah too. Worse still, I have to divert Sarah's attention by pretending I've lost an earring while Charlie sneaks my violin into the car. I can hardly claim I'm off to serenade the penguins.

Sarah waves us goodbye, and as soon as we're out of sight, I lean forward with my head in my hands.

"God, that was a bit tricky," I say.

Charlie laughs, winds down the windows and cranks up the music. I lean back in my seat and close my eyes.

"I can't tell you what it feels like to be out of that house," I say with a huge sigh. I massage my knuckles and try to undo some of the knots of tension in my fingers. "Time to have some fun at last!"

Ciaran's place is way out beyond Ealing Broadway – about half an hour, apparently. I don't care. I've got the breeze on my face and nothing is going to stop me from feeling happy. Charlie starts singing along to the radio and I join in. His voice isn't bad. I can't sing to save my life and that makes Charlie laugh. I hit him on the leg and sing louder.

London changes as we get away from the centre. It's more relaxed out here. Still plenty of traffic but the houses look friendlier. We turn right at some lights, then left into a road, and Charlie's parking up and getting out.

Ciaran's front door is like a suitcase: red and covered in stickers from all over the world.

"Has he actually been to all these places?" I ask Charlie.

He nods. "They go all over the place. They only work in London for as long as it takes to raise money for the next airfare and then they're off again. They play their way around the bars of wherever they are and come home when they've had enough."

"Lucky."

Charlie knocks loudly. There's no answer, so we take off round the side of the house to what looks like a garage or outbuilding of some sort. The muffled sound of music comes from inside. It must be well soundproofed.

"Hey," says Ciaran as we push open the door, "you've escaped." He's sitting up on a high stool, guitar in his hand, a few empty beer bottles at his feet.

"If anyone asks, we're at the zoo," says Charlie.

In fact, we're in an old, converted garage. Music kit everywhere – keyboard, guitars, drums, amplifiers, microphones, electric leads like spaghetti all over the floor. Better still are the graffiti-style pictures on the walls. Life-sized, black and white. Crazy stuff. I wish my rehearsal room was more like this.

"Cool," I say as I blink it all in. "Who's the artist?"

"Mr B. We've been wondering recently if he's related to Banksy."

"Perhaps I am Banksy," says Mr B. He and Seamus are jamming quietly in the background, mucking around with chords, changing the key. I listen in, enjoying the way the music evolves from just a few notes through to entire phrases. They seem to feed off each other's playing, but not in any planned way. Out of a jumble of chords, a melody starts to emerge, and they're away. The whole Irish thing comes through, yet the music's got a real edge. It's quirky. I like it. Every now and again, it all crunches into a horrible mess and they laugh and start again.

Listening to them rehearse compared to the way I have to rehearse makes me wonder if we come from different musical planets. I can't see them playing the same phrase of music a hundred times until they get it right.

"So, Jessie," says Ciaran, "are you ready to give us a demo of how it should be done?"

A surge of panic raccs through me and I shake my head. "Not likely," I say.

I thought I was up for this, but now I'm not so sure. I don't want to make a fool of myself in front of this lot. I'm happy to relax and let someone else do the work for a change. I can't see my violin, wonderful as it is, fitting in amongst all these leads and amplifiers and sound mixers.

"Come on," says Charlie, "you told me you could play rock. That's why we're here."

They're all looking at me and I dig in. I'm cross with Charlie for putting me on the spot.

"No, I'm fine," I say.

"You told me you could do Guns N' Roses," says Charlie. "I thought we had a bet."

"We did not," I say accusingly, but I've heard the challenge in Charlie's voice and now I've got no option. If he doesn't believe me then I'll have to prove it. Angrily I open up my violin case. I try to appear laid-back as I put the rosin on my bow, but playing in front of this lot is different to mucking around by myself in the music room.

"Are you sure about this?" I ask.

They all nod. I swear inside my head.

"OK – well, here goes, then. 'Welcome to the Jungle'."

Their eyes are on me. Something between amusement and condescension. I hate that look. OK – fine – I *will* show them.

But it doesn't start well. I'm shaky as I begin and don't hit the first few stops cleanly. Annoyed, I focus harder. The rhythm pumps through me and I start to ramp up the intensity. Before long, I'm smacking it out and I forget there's anyone else in the room. When I stop, all the boys are sitting with their eyes wide.

"What?" I say aggressively.

"Nothing," says Ciaran, shaking his head.

"Told you she was good," says Charlie. He's lounging on a beanbag in the corner looking smug.

"Yes. You always were the master of understatement." Ciaran hasn't taken his eyes off me even when he's talking to Charlie. He rolls a cigarette, puts it between his teeth. "Miss Jessie — you're wasted on the classics! You should stick with Guns N' Roses. D'you want to have a go playing it with some backing?"

The boys are all reaching for their instruments.

"I've never tried it other than solo. How's it going to work?"

"No idea," says Ciaran. "We'll takc it as it comes. I suggest you listen to us playing and then work out how you can improvise."

He makes it sound easy. They begin and I listen to the rhythm and try to pick a few lines. Each time I start, I lose my thread and stop again. It is not easy. In fact, it's impossible. I'm having to focus on about fifty things at once.

"Stop worrying so much," says Ciaran. "Don't fret about getting it right. Experiment. We don't care. Do what you want but keep going. If you stop, you'll lose it."

I nod, but now I'm feeling the pressure and there's no escape.

They start again. I wait a few bars, try to go in with the basic melody, and cock it up straight away.

"Keep going," shouts Ciaran, "don't worry. Enjoy yourself. It doesn't matter about mistakes."

I can't ignore mistakes. That's not the way I do things. If I make a mistake, I force myself to play it over and over until it's perfect. How can I enjoy myself if I keep getting it wrong? It goes against everything I've ever learnt. So I lose it again and give up.

They stop and I shrug. "Sorry." I almost throw my violin back in its case.

"What are you doing, you daft girlie? There's nothing to be sorry about. Relax. This is supposed to be fun." Ciaran comes over and starts massaging my shoulders. I can feel them scrunching under his fingers. "You're overthinking it. You didn't do that playing solo. Once you relax, it'll start to flow more naturally." He gives my shoulder a final squeeze. "RE-LAX," he says and hands me my violin.

I exhale loudly and try to let everything go. I know this music and I should be able to do it. OK, I have to let myself go. I have to stop worrying about what they'll think. This time I go for it straight away and I don't stop. Ciaran doesn't do the vocals so I let my violin take over the melody. It's not great, but it's not bad either.

"That's it," shouts Ciaran. "Now have some fun — improvise a little — whatever you feel like."

So I do. I rip out a few cadenzas and allow instinct to take over. The boys keep encouraging me and it's exciting. I throw in all sorts of stuff and it sounds amazing – well, most of the time. No one cares anyway; I'm not even sure anyone notices.

When we finish, I flop to the floor but I can't stop smiling. The boys are telling me I'm great, telling me I should give up Mozart and become a rock star.

"Thanks," I reply, fanning my face with my hands. "Grandmother might have something to say about that."

"How about a part-time rock star then? Surely she wouldn't mind if you did the odd gig."

I'm blushing so hard that the tips of my ears are hot. Seamus puts a cold beer bottle against each of my cheeks and everyone's laughing.

We sit around, the boys splayed out on beanbags. I'm squished up against Charlie's legs and I can't help being aware of the pressure of his knee against my back. It's kind of awkward, but he doesn't try to move so I guess he doesn't mind. We chat for a while, and then the boys test me on my knowledge of the zoo. Before we go, they play me their new song. It's quiet and gentle and I can hear a violin part in my head, clear as a river. When they finish, Ciaran looks at me and narrows his eyes.

"Have you got that, Jessie? Because we'll be expecting you to come up with something before next weekend."

"Next weekend?" I look at Charlie.

"Well, you'll be coming back, won't you?" Ciaran makes it sound as though his life depends on it.

"I don't know if we can," I say.

Charlie gives a little shrug and he stares at me with a kind of questioning grin.

"Couldn't you wing it with Madame Tussauds or something?" asks Mr B.

I look down and try to test my feelings on this. Charlie must catch my hesitation.

"It's not quite as simple as that," he says. I'm relieved. It's bought a bit of time, at least.

"It seems simple enough to me," says Ciaran. "This girl is a dream and we need her to play with the band."

I shouldn't be proud, but I can't help it. Somebody thinks I'm good. At last! I haven't felt like this in ages. None of Grandmother's sucked-in lips. None of Dr McNair's repetitive, miserable criticism. Both of them could do with a good session with Ciaran. It might loosen them up a bit. I smile at the thought.

"So, next week, then?" says Ciaran, taking my smile as acceptance.

Charlie makes a cut-throat sign at Ciaran, as if to say *that's enough*. "We'll talk about it," he says.

"Fine. But you should know we won't take no for an answer." Ciaran makes it sound jokey, but there's no doubt he means it — or part of it. I wish I could hold on to this feeling of success. Of being wanted.

Charlie's quiet on the way home. We stop at a red light and he taps his fingers on the steering wheel.

"Perhaps I should just be a rock musician," I say. "It's a lot more fun."

Charlie shakes his head. "Don't get too carried away. It's not all easy."

"It's easier than what I'm doing at the moment."

"So you enjoyed yourself, then?" he asks. "Playing with the band, I mean."

"Yeah, I did." I glance towards him and I can see he's watching me sideways.

The car behind us beeps its horn. The light's gone green. Charlie lurches forward and I laugh. He swears.

"I like the way they do things," I say. "I learnt

so much today. More than Dr McNair's taught me in weeks. I reckon having some time with Ciaran could really help me with some of my other stuff."

"It sounded more like you were teaching them a thing or two."

"I wish."

"You're dangerous with that instrument of yours. I honestly never realized what you could do with it."

I laugh.

"Listening to you today – it was like someone had flung open the cage door and let you out."

"Is that a compliment?"

"Definitely," he says, and he glances at me again.

Instinctively, I reach out my hand and put it on his arm. "Thanks, Charlie."

We drive the rest of the way home in silence. Something tells me this won't be the last time we make this journey.

Chapter 14

The heat of July collapses into massive thunderstorms and August is damp and grey. It gives everyone something to moan about.

By now, Charlie and I are supposed to have visited Madame Tussauds and Buckingham Palace, but after lying to Grandmother once, and then again the following week and the week after that, it doesn't seem so hard. Our visits to Ciaran's place have become the highlight of my week. Occasionally, Grandmother asks a few tricky questions about our sightseeing and I sweat my way through garbled answers, but she barely seems to listen.

I don't feel guilty, not really, because playing with the band has changed the way I think about my music – all my music. Charlie's right about that cage. Ciaran is teaching me not to worry about making mistakes, and that's given me the freedom to play. He challenges me to push myself to the limits and then further.

"It's all in the mind," he says when I don't get it right, "so leave the mind out of it."

He's right. I'm beginning to realize that what Ciaran and Dr McNair and Professor Jenniston are saying is the same thing, but in different ways. It's not that the technical aspects of playing aren't important. They are. I still practise for hours and hours. But that's only part of it. Now I'm working with my instincts instead of fighting against them. I use my imagination; I experiment and I take risks. I've even begun to use Professor Jenniston's visualization techniques. It's as though playing with Ciaran is making everything else fall into place. And I'm getting better – much, much better – and my teachers are smiling and patting themselves on the back, no doubt. If only they knew.

Some things don't change. Every Sunday, Grandmother takes me to Harris House. Helena and Mr Ritchie have decided to run "masterclasses" with me with all the residents watching. I'm not sure if Grandmother approves or not, but even she must notice how much better I'm getting. It'd be hard to ignore it with Helena and Mr Ritchie banging on about my incredible progress. As I play, they stop me less and less to give me hints and constructive criticism. Meanwhile, Grandmother sips at her tea and writes furiously in a notebook. She never says anything until the end.

"A critic's job comes after the event," says Mr Ritchie quietly. "She knows that."

Sometimes Grandmother says nothing. I take that as good news. Other times she lays into me, shredding my playing, and I have to sit there, humiliated, with everyone else listening.

"You played that like a complete beginner," she says one Sunday as she tears out a page of notes and hands them to me.

"But she is a beginner, Tara," says Helena. "She's only sixteen. She's at the beginning of what could be a marvellous career."

"Well, she'll never get her scholarship if she performs like that."

I tense, and the tears well up, but Mr Ritchie pats my hand and whispers, "Nod and smile. A critic will destroy you if you let them. Don't let them. You need to be tough in this game."

I try to do as he says.

"Learn to sift through the criticism," he murmurs. "Separate what is useful from what is simply unpleasant. Use what you need to use. Discard the rest."

I store his words away. I know I'll need them.

So day by day and week by week, my confidence grows. I now feel *part* of a world, not *set apart* from a world. I'm surrounded by people who are passionate about music. I don't always like them and it's not easy, but we all have the same aim: to make me better.

As for Grandmother, I'm not sure anyone knows what her aim is, and I find it very hard to like her. I try not to let it bother me. I know I'm on a roll and I'm not going to let her spoil anything. We now have dinner together once a week, and talking to her is getting easier, as long as I stay on safe subjects like concerts and musicians. She is so knowledgeable. I may hate the way she treats me but I can't help admiring her. And so the days pass – sometimes slowly, sometimes faster.

My exam results arrive. A for music, A for maths, B for physics and D for English. I'm not surprised about music or English but I'm really happy about maths and physics. Most importantly, my grades are good enough for me to apply to music college –

as long as I do well in my A2 music. When I tell Grandmother, she seems pleased, and congratulates me politely.

Saturday the twenty-ninth of August is my birthday. Seventeen. Now I can learn to drive. I wonder if Grandmother will let me. Charlie could teach me. I suggest this to him and he laughs.

"Not likely," he says, crossing his arms very firmly. "If your driving is anything like your violin playing, we'll be all over the place very, very fast. I'll let Mrs Chamberlain teach you."

"Imagine what fun that would be!" I roll my eyes.

I open a card and present from Mum and Dad. They've sent me some mascara and eyeliner. Mum's even managed to choose my favourite brand, which is pretty clever. It's strange not being with them, and I get a sudden pang of homesickness. I wanted them to come down and visit for my birthday but Dad said that I'd made my decision to go to London and I had to see out the six months before he'd set foot on the train. He can be stubborn like that. Still, it made me sad. Maybe they're enjoying life without me? I rub my fingers over the surface of the card, then slowly put it on the table next to my bed.

After breakfast, I get a summons to Grandmother's office.

"Well, Jessica," she says as I walk in, "many happy returns of the day."

"Thank you." I'm surprised she even knew it was my birthday, let alone took the time to wish me happy returns.

"I have a gift for you," she says. It sounds almost as if she's trying to remember words she has practised. "I hope you will like it." She hands me a small package.

I take it and turn it over in my hands – unsure if I should open it.

"My father gave it to me," she says, "when I was about your age. Now I would like you to have it."

I try to blink back the surprise. "It was a gift from your father?" I'm not sure how to react. This sudden family closeness makes me feel a little awkward. When I look at her, she meets my eyes and holds them for a moment.

"Are you going to open it?" she says with a small smile.

I unwrap the paper and inside is a scruffy, old-looking blue leather box with a gold pattern round the outside. I fumble trying to open it, then notice the tiny little button at the front. I press it and lift the lid. Inside is a slim gold brooch with a tiny diamond horseshoe.

"Wow! Is it, like, real diamonds?"

"No, it is not *like* real diamonds. It *is* real diamonds."

I'm almost speechless as I stare at the glittering stones. "Don't you want to keep it, though – if it was a gift from your father?"

"I never wear it, Jessica. They say the horseshoe is supposed to bring good luck, but it never worked for me." She gives a dry laugh. "I trust it will work better for you."

Her voice is suddenly so bitter that I almost snap the box shut. "What do you mean?"

"Oh, you know; all that superstitious twaddle. Anyway, I thought it was suitable for a girl your age."

I try to hold on to some enthusiasm, but the idea of an unlucky, lucky horseshoe freaks me out.

"Charles tells me you are going to the National Gallery today. That is a very nice place to visit for your birthday."

I think I manage to nod. The diamonds glint at me, alternating dark and bright under the light.

When I look up, Grandmother is almost glaring at me. Did I forget to thank her or something?

"Thank you," I say again, just in case. But it sounds unconvincing.

"Are you all right, Jessica?"

I try to think of something to say and mumble about it being the first time I've been away from home on my birthday.

"I have asked Sarah to bake you a cake for tea," she says.

I guess I'm supposed to be impressed by her thoughtfulness, but she manages to makes it sound more like a duty than a kindness. I let it go and thank her again. I've learnt when it's not worth wasting my breath.

"I suggest we have it when you get home," she continues. "I need you and Charles to be back by five, as I am going to a concert this evening. And, of course, you have your practice to do."

"I thought I'd have a day off as it's my birthday."

Grandmother sighs. "No, Jessica, you do not have a day off."

"But. . ."

"But nothing."

"Do you honestly think a day off is going to make

a difference? Anyway, I won't be having a day off. . ."
I stop myself before I let the cat out of the bag about
practising with the band. What am I thinking? Her
giving me this brooch must have got to me.

"Good girl," says Grandmother. "I know I can
trust you to put in the work." Her smile is cool. "And
as you are off to the National Gallery, I thought you
might like to borrow this book. It provides a useful
guide to some of the paintings."

I take the book, keen to get out before I land
myself in trouble. I leave, grasping the little blue
box in my hand, the corners digging into my palm.

∫ ℩

Charlie has his back to me when I walk into the
kitchen. He glances round, sees me and slams the
cupboard door shut.

"What are you up to?" I ask.

"Tidying."

He's lying. I frown at him and he grins.

"What've you got there?" he asks.

I show him the brooch. "Grandmother's dad
gave it to her, apparently."

"That's nice."

"Maybe."

He smiles and shakes his head as though he doesn't understand me. "You don't have to wear it," he says. "It's still a nice present. And the book?"

"Paintings. We're supposed to be visiting the National Gallery today. Remember?"

Charlie doesn't say anything.

"Charlie – perhaps we should visit the gallery today. Like actually visit it. It's not that I don't want to go to Ciaran's, but I think she might've started to suspect something. She looked at me strangely today when she mentioned the gallery."

Charlie looks down at his hands, rubs his palm with his thumb. "You're imagining it, Jess. You're just feeling guilty because she's given you a generous present. Anyway, there's no way we can change our plans now. Ciaran's expecting us."

"I know, but it's not going to make much difference to Ciaran if we're there or not. I'm not talking for ever. But maybe just this week we should do what we're supposed to be doing – to be on the safe side."

Charlie rubs his hands backwards and forwards through his hair. "But Ciaran'll be upset if we don't turn up. He wants to try out a new song with you."

"What's the big deal? He always wants to try out new songs. If they want a full-time violinist, they should hire one."

"They'd never find someone as good as you."

"Rubbish. Anyway, I'm sure this new song could wait until next weekend."

Charlie shakes his head. He seems unreasonably tense. "It can't," he says with some aggression. "They're going off on tour next week."

My stomach almost hits the floor. "You're kidding! Ciaran hasn't said anything. When did he tell you? Where are they going? How long for?"

"Keep your hair on. He only told me yesterday and he was going to tell you today. I told him you'd be upset. They're off to Ireland – until the money runs out, I guess. That's usually how it works."

The thought of not having Ciaran around makes me feel desperate. I've come to rely on his input. Playing with the band has become like a different side to my musical development and it's a side I don't need to lose. I flip the lid of the brooch box open and shut and stare out of the kitchen window. I don't believe in any of that superstitious stuff, but already I'm starting to wish that Grandmother hadn't given me this brooch. I make a decision.

"If this is the last week we can go to Ciaran's, then I agree, we have to go. I need to say goodbye to them all, apart from anything else. I could be back in Manchester by the time they come home." I blink hard as the thought brings hot tears into my eyes.

"Cheer up," says Charlie, giving my shoulder a squeeze. "It's your birthday. Come on, let's go and have some fun. We can catch up on all the sightseeing stuff over the next few weeks and then you won't feel so guilty. We'll need something to do on a Saturday afternoon."

I look at him and shake my head. "You're a bad influence, Charlie."

"So I've been told – many times. Now hurry up and get ready. We've got to be back by five."

"I know. She told me."

I jog upstairs and put the brooch in the bottom drawer of my desk. I shut the drawer, then open it again and put the box up on its side so the horseshoe is the right way up. I close the drawer carefully.

As I apply my eyeliner, I grump away to my reflection in the mirror. I can't believe Ciaran has decided to go on tour. Why now? I carry on whingeing all the way to Ealing – about all the things

Ciaran has taught me and how much I've improved as a result and what I'll do when he's not around.

Suddenly Charlie butts in. "Do we have to talk about music all the time?"

I shut up, surprised. "Well, sorry. I didn't mean to bore you." I inject a note of hurt into my voice.

"You don't bore me. I'd just like to talk about something else every now and then. There must be more to Jess than music. I don't know anything about your life in Manchester, your friends. Anything."

"You do *not* want to know about my life in Manchester. We live on a crappy housing estate, Mum works nights in an old people's home and part time in a library that's closing down. Dad was made redundant a couple of months ago. He says he'll never get another job at his age."

"That's not good. No brothers or sisters?"

"Nope. Mum was quite old when she had me and it's been bad enough trying to make ends meet with just the three of us. Though it should be easier now I'm not around and they don't have to pay for my music lessons and all the tripping around to rehearsals and everything."

"What about friends? I bet they're missing you."

"I doubt it. I didn't have a lot of time for friends,

really. While they were out getting pissed and pregnant, I was practising my violin. My best friend was Beth, but then her dad got a job as a security guard in Dubai and I haven't seen her since. I might see her this Christmas, though – they're coming back for a few weeks to visit family."

"Boyfriends?"

"What's it to you?"

"So I'll take that as a yes!"

I hit him on the arm. "I suppose – if you can count Ethan. He was a goth and deeply into music too. You know, remixing, that kind of stuff. A bit of a weirdo, actually."

"Nice!"

"Then there was Stefan." I stop. I don't know what to say about Stefan. I don't know why I've even mentioned him.

"Stefan?"

"He was my accompanist."

"Just your accompanist?" Charlie teases.

"*Yes*. Just my accompanist." I exaggerate the words. "We worked together for two years. He was cool – kind of. We couldn't have been more different if we tried. He was posh. Public school. Wealthy. You know the type. But he was the one person I could really be myself with; the one person who understood how much music means to me. I guess he's moved on now. He hasn't been in contact since I left Manchester."

"Oh well. You win some, you lose some."

I bite at the skin on the edge of my thumbnail. It starts to bleed. Thoughts of Stefan resurface and tumble round my head. I suppose I've stopped missing him quite so much now. Perhaps I've moved on too. We stop at some traffic lights and I refocus. They turn green and we drive straight ahead.

"Charlie, you've gone the wrong way. You should've turned right."

"No I shouldn't."

"You should – at the traffic lights."

Charlie grins. "Not today."

"What are you talking about?"

"Surprise."

"Surprise?"

"Close your eyes. I'll tell you when to open them."

I do as I'm told. My mood immediately improves. I knew Charlie was up to something. "What's happening? Tell me!"

"You'll see in a minute."

It's a bit more than a minute, but finally the car comes to a stop. "Keep them closed. No peeking. You'll have to trust me."

"Trust you? Chance'd be a fine thing!"

Charlie opens my door and leads me out of the car. My eyes are still tight shut and I'm giggling now. I can feel grass under my feet.

"This is ridiculous," I say as I stagger along beside him.

We stop. There's silence, but some sixth sense tells me there are people around.

"OK. One, two, three and *open*."

"Happy birthday!" everyone bursts out singing. I take it all in. Ciaran and the rest of the band, the picnic laid out on the rug, Stubbie strumming his guitar.

I'm so happy and my smile is so huge it's making my face hurt. No one's ever given me a surprise like this. I've never had a proper picnic before.

"I thought we should celebrate," says Charlie, and hands me a bottle of champagne.

I throw my arms round his neck and nearly knock him out with the bottle. I hug him and hug him and he hugs me back, nearly squeezing the breath out of me. "Thank you," I squeak into his ear.

The others are on their feet.

"Hey, it's our turn now," says Ciaran. "How come Charlie gets all the hugs?"

I put my hands on my cheeks to stop the muscles hurting. "Ow," I say, laughing, "stop making me smile."

They give me the bumps – eighteen of them. One for each year and one for luck. I can hardly stand when they put me down.

"I want you to know that this is the best birthday I've ever had," I tell them.

Charlie opens the bottle and hands me a plastic cup.

"You mean you're letting me drink?" I say.

"Just the one, or maybe two – as it's your birthday."

We clunk our plastic cups together and I take a large sip. The bubbles fizz in my head. We eat and talk and sing. Stubbie gently strums his guitar in the background. Then we play frisbee for a while before collapsing back on to the rug.

"So, Charlie tells me you're off on tour," I say to Ciaran.

He nods.

"Do you have to go?"

"Yes, we do. We want to go. This could be our big break and it'd be a sin to miss it. We have to take our chances while we can. You'll learn to do the same."

"I can't see my big break coming any time soon."

"You never know. Anyway, you haven't been working at it for as long as we have. You have to put up with at least ten years of misery first."

"I've nearly done that already."

"There you go, then. And you can't be miserable today because it's your birthday." Ciaran punches me on the arm gently. And again. And again, until I start to laugh.

"And in honour of today," says Mr B, "I have baked you this spectacular cake." He lifts the lid off a cardboard box. "You should know I made this all myself," he says proudly as he hands it to me.

Everyone laughs. He's tried to make it look like a violin but it's kind of wonky and the strings look like they're tied in knots.

"It's . . . amazing," I say and we all crack up, including Mr B. They huddle round the cake, trying to light the candles. Finally, they're all alight and everyone shouts, "Blow – quick."

One blow is all it takes and they clap.

"Who's the lucky man?" says Ciaran.

"What d'you mean?"

"Candles out in one puff. Means there's just one lucky man. So, who is he?"

"Shut up," I say, and I blush. Ciaran raises his eyebrows and gives Charlie a nudge and that makes me blush even more. Charlie's probably told him about Ethan already. Or, worse still, Stefan. I stuff some cake in my mouth to avoid having to say anything. It tastes heaps better than it looks and we devour most of it before the boys start apologizing and saying they have to leave.

"Too much to do," they say as they pack up.

Charlie and I help them carry stuff to their car.

"Don't let us stop the party," says Ciaran.

Charlie looks at his watch. "We won't. We don't have to go anywhere yet."

"Keep in touch," orders Ciaran, pointing his finger at me. "I want to know everything you're doing."

"Everything?" I say. "Trips to the toilet. That kind of thing."

"Well – not absolutely everything, perhaps. But everything you're doing with that violin of yours. I don't want to come back and find you've returned to all your bad habits."

"OK."

"And look after Charlie for us."

I roll my eyes and we wave goodbye. It's horrible watching the van disappear and I sit on the ground, pulling my knees up to my chest.

"When I used to feel sad, I'd lie on my back and try to find animal shapes in the clouds," says Charlie, and he flattens himself out on the rug. He tugs gently at the back of my shirt.

"Look, that one is just like an alligator," he says.

I laugh and look up. Then I stretch out beside him, staring up at the white clouds.

"How? It doesn't look like an alligator to me."

"Yes it does. Come here so you're looking at it from the same angle."

I shuffle towards him so our heads are together. "Look – there's the snout." He takes my hand and traces it in the air with his. "And the body . . . and the long tail."

"Oh yes." I can see it now. "And it's chasing that sort of . . . fat slug."

"Where?"

"There – look – just ahead of its nose."

We both laugh.

Charlie rolls over on to his side and props himself on one elbow. His face is very close to mine. I swallow hard, a mixture of panic and excitement.

"Enjoying your birthday?" His question is matter of fact. I keep my eyes firmly on the clouds. If I look at him . . . I don't know. Maybe I'm just imagining it.

"It's been brilliant."

I can feel his smile. He gently nudges my side.

"Really?"

I glance towards him. See the smile, my stomach swimming away as his fingers brush my cheek. A long moment passes and my brain is a blur and then his lips are on mine. It feels weird being kissed by Charlie. But nice at the same time. And I don't want him to stop, but then again, perhaps I do. He's pulling me closer to him and my arm slips easily over his waist as my leg slides between his. Then his fingers start fumbling with the buttons of my shirt and I push him away.

"We're in the middle of a park," I say.

He looks around. "There's no one watching." He pulls me towards him again.

"Charlie — no. We can't. Stop it."

He groans and flops on to his back. "God, Jess, you don't know what you're doing to me." He sounds agonized.

I smile inside. That strange sense of power is exciting. It's good feeling wanted. I roll on to my front and prop my chin on my hands so I can look at him. I'm not going to lie, he is good-looking. But I really hadn't thought about him like . . . this. I mean, he's twenty-three.

"So did you have this all planned?" I ask, pretending to sound angry. "Did you tell the others to go early?"

"I might have."

"I see."

He shifts his head slightly so his face is immediately below mine. "Do you see? Do you have any idea how I feel about you?"

The intensity in his eyes is almost scary, and I sit up. I need to put a bit of space between us. "Charlie — shouldn't we be getting back? Haven't you got to take Grandmother somewhere this evening?"

Charlie wraps his arms round my waist. "It can't be that time already." His voice is husky.

I tap his watch and he looks at it and leaps to his feet. "Shit, you're right. We have to go now." He pulls me up, folds the rug. I scoop up bits and pieces left on the ground and we pile into the car.

The journey home is awkward. Neither of us seems to be able to think of anything to say. I'm busy trying to unscramble my thoughts. One emotion piles on top of the next and the car feels claustrophobic.

"Are you OK with this?" asks Charlie.

"With what?"

"With us – you know. . .?"

I look out of the window. I'm not sure.

"Jess, please." He takes my hand and kisses it, then lets it drop to his lap as he returns his hand to the steering wheel.

He's so sweet. That's all I can think.

"Yeah, it's cool," I say.

I see his shoulders relax and I leave my hand resting in his lap. We start talking again – as if everything is normal. But it's not, and I really hope things don't get complicated. I don't need any more stresses in my life. I can't believe he really likes me that much.

"Your grandmother can't know anything about this," says Charlie as we come to a halt outside the house. "Nor Sarah."

"Like I'm going to tell them."

Charlie laughs. "We'll have to be careful."

I nod. I can already see this is not going to be easy.

Before he unlocks the front door he squeezes my hand. I give him a weak smile. Then we're back inside. It's four thirty.

I head straight down to the music room and get out my violin. I can still feel Charlie's body pressed against mine and see that intensity in his eyes. That's what's scaring me. I rip through a few pages of Bartók. I'm feeling out of control and the music helps. I begin to calm down and breathe. Having a bit of a fling with Charlie can't do any harm. I start playing through one of my new studies. It's a sad piece. Halfway through the door opens and Charlie walks in. He kicks it shut behind him. He hardly ever comes down here. This is my territory.

"I've come to apologize," he begins.

"What for?" I say before I even think.

"You know. Maybe I took things too fast."

"Yeah, perhaps. I was a bit surprised."

"But you must've guessed?"

I shrug. For some reason I'm embarrassed. Like I should've guessed.

Charlie comes towards me. He puts his hands either side of me on the wall. "Your grandmother is waiting upstairs for us to eat cake," he says, laughing.

"Oh no, not more cake."

Charlie brushes my lips with his fingers. "You have to tell me honestly, Jess. I need to know if it's OK. I mean . . . if you like me or not."

His body is tense again. His eyes locked on to mine.

"Of course I like you." I'm going on to say that I'm not sure if it is such a good idea right now, right here, but I don't get the chance.

He pins my hands against the wall and starts kissing me with such passion that I can't think of anything. I don't even hear the door opening.

"Charles! Jessica!" Charlie leaps away from me. There's nowhere to hide.

"What on earth is going on?" Grandmother's voice is strident, her face a storm.

"My office," she orders Charlie, and I see his eyes close briefly before he walks out of the door. "I'll deal with you later, young lady," she says. "Do not leave this room." She follows Charlie back up the stairs.

We're screwed. Why did Charlie have to come

down to the music room? Why did Grandmother have to walk in right that second? Why did today have to happen? I howl in frustration. Just when things seem to be looking up, everything crashes back down again. I sit on the piano stool, open the lid of the piano and pound the keys as hard as I can. Then I slam it shut, bury my face in my arms and don't move. I try not to imagine what is going on upstairs. I try not to think about what's going to happen to me. I close my eyes and feel the warmth of the wood from the piano against my cheek.

I don't hear Sarah coming in, but I look up when I feel the touch on my shoulder.

"Your grandmother wants to see you now."

I check my watch. It's nearly six. Over an hour since she found us. She obviously hasn't gone to her concert.

"Where's Charlie?"

"I don't know. What on earth has happened? Your grandmother is incandescent."

I don't know what that word means but it doesn't sound good. "I don't want to talk about it," I say.

Sarah shakes her head. She's looking pale. "Come on. Don't keep her waiting." She prods me up the stairs and leaves me outside Grandmother's office.

I knock and open the door. I want to get this over and done with.

"Come in and sit down," Grandmother says. Her voice is weary, her face strained. I walk in but I don't sit.

"Do you take me for a fool?" she asks.

"It's not what you think. Charlie was just apologizing."

"Oh, is that how you apologize nowadays? I have never felt the need to make such close physical contact with someone when apologizing." She spits out the words like an angry snake. "And what was he apologizing for, exactly?"

I don't have an answer.

"As I thought," she says, turning back to her desk. "But that is only part of the story, isn't it? I have my bank statements." She waves a piece of paper. "I can track all Charles's spending on the household account. I know you haven't visited the places you are supposed to have visited. It appears you and Charles have been going behind my back in more ways than one."

I hang my head.

"According to what you've told me, you have recently visited London Zoo, Madame Tussauds,

Buckingham Palace and the Royal Observatory. You have been lying."

The blood must be disappearing from my face as fast as the panic is rising.

"I. . . I. . ."

"Don't bother saying anything. I know what you have been doing. Charles has told me about your little visits to his friends in Ealing. What can you be thinking, playing your violin with some popular music group?"

"And I suppose you think it's a coincidence how much I've improved in recent weeks? Well, it isn't. It's all down to Ciaran."

"All down to Ciaran, indeed. I don't think your improvement is a coincidence at all. However, I think it is coincidental with your work with Dr McNair and Professor Jenniston – I find it very hard to believe that it can be attributed to some unknown who has never picked up a violin in his life."

"Well, you're wrong. I mean, of course my work with Dr McNair and Professor Jenniston is important. But I needed something else. Ciaran's taught me it doesn't matter about making mistakes. He's taught me to experiment and have fun. He's taught me to play from my heart and not my head. He's let me out of the cage."

Grandmother goes very pale and seems to struggle to gather herself together. "I wish you'd spoken to me, that's all."

"Right! Like that would've worked."

"Am I so unapproachable?"

"I'm not even going to answer that question."

"Surely you can understand that, whatever this Ciaran man has been doing, I can't just let you go off and play the violin with any old person. Your gift is very precious. You can't afford to throw it away. There's no telling what might have happened if this had been allowed to continue."

"I was only playing a few songs with the band – I can't see how that could do any harm. And Ciaran is not any old person, he is a friend of Charlie's."

"Charles's troubled background hardly makes him a reliable source of friends, Jessica."

"But I don't have any other source of friends, so what do you expect? Charlie's the nearest thing to a friend I've had since moving to London. I'm seventeen. I can't hang out with old people all the time and I can't work all the time. I need to have some fun. Charlie was only trying to help."

"What, by forcing himself on you? By taking advantage of your inexperience and seducing you?" Two red spots have appeared on her cheeks.

"He didn't seduce me or force himself on me. He only kissed me a couple of times. Where's the harm in that? It's not as if you caught us shagging in your bed." It rushes out of my mouth before I have a chance to control it.

Grandmother's face is tense with anger; a grey shell ready to crack apart. "Thank you for enlightening me on the younger generation," she says through tightly pursed lips. "I suppose you think me completely naive. But I know what men are like and you are an attractive young lady, in your own way. For this reason, I must ask you to give me your word, truthfully, that you have had no sexual relations of any sort with Charles."

"It wouldn't be illegal if I had. I am seventeen, you know."

"That was not my question."

"Not that I can see it's any business of yours but, as it happens, no, I haven't. Does that satisfy you?"

She nods slowly. Relaxes a little. "I blame myself," she says, turning to her desk and tidying some already tidy papers. "I should never have let you and Charles spend so much time alone together. Who knows what might have happened if I hadn't discovered this little relationship of yours?"

"I suppose I could've got pregnant and then run off like my mum."

"That is *enough*."

"But you're being—"

"I said *enough*."

I button my mouth.

"You have put me in a very difficult position, Jessica. I cannot decide what I should do. Charles has already left, but what to do with you?"

"You've given Charlie the sack? You can't do that. He hasn't done anything wrong."

"Apart from take advantage of my granddaughter and lie to me. However, if you must know, it was his choice to go. It is, I believe, a temporary arrangement. He says he needs some time for consideration."

"I don't believe you. Where will he go? He can't go back to his family. What if he ends up on the streets again? Goes back to drugs?"

My words hang in the air. Grandmother taps a pencil on her desk. "Do you really think I would let that happen?"

I shrug.

"You, however, *can* go back to your family. In fact, I should have sent you home weeks ago when you first ran off. You have been disrespectful, ungrateful and have taken little notice of our agreement. I expected better of you."

"But I've worked so hard! I've done everything you've asked. You're being completely unfair. I bet you weren't perfect when you were my age."

"If I had behaved like you when I was your age, my father would have given me a good spanking. I was allowed nowhere without a chaperone."

"So why can't you understand, then? I bet you hated it. I bet you longed for freedom and fun."

Grandmother is silent. She stares out of her window at the darkening sky. Maybe I've given her something to think about. Maybe I've pushed things too far? I hold my head, press my fingers into my scalp. I'm completely shredded. The fierce reality is that I do not want to go home. Not now I've got this far. More than anything, I want that place at music college, and I believe I can get it. Another few months of tuition – working on those scholarship pieces – and this really could be my big break. I'd be a fool not to fight for it. I can't let her send me home.

"I will talk to you again in the morning," she says as she gets up and opens the door for me to leave.

She can't leave me wondering all night. That's not fair.

"Please," I say. "Please give me one more chance."

"You should have thought of that before. One must always consider the consequences of one's actions, Jessica. You have put me in a very difficult position."

"I'm sorry."

"That is something, I suppose."

I look at her, silently begging her to give me an answer; to let me stay. My feet are refusing to move. There are so many things I want to say.

She raises one eyebrow and I take my chance.

"Can I ask you to do one thing before you make your decision?"

She moves her head very slightly, as if she's ready to listen.

"Talk to Professor Jenniston. She can explain. She told me, right at the start, if I want to learn to give a true performance, then it has to come from the person I really am. I've tried to do everything you've asked me. I've worn the clothes, changed my table manners, practised until my fingers are bleeding. But underneath all that, you've got to let me be *me*. I'll never be the person you want me to be. I'm sorry. I'll do anything, absolutely anything, if you let me stay, except I won't change who I am and you can't make me."

She's watching me closely. I'm proud of myself for saying what I feel. But I'm terrified that I've ruined any chance I might've had of changing her mind.

"You may go now!" she says firmly. "I will give you my decision in the morning."

I still don't move.

"Go!" she shouts, and the loudness shocks me into action. The word echoes round my head all the way to my room.

I sit on the floor in my room with my back against the wall. I try to call Charlie. No answer. I leave a message telling him to call me. Then I call Ciaran, and when he answers I blab the whole lot out.

"I've already heard," he says when I finally pause for breath.

"Oh. So is Charlie with you?"

"No. He's called, but he won't say where he is. I think he's pretty upset."

"It's all my fault."

"Don't be silly. If it's anyone's fault, it's mine. It was my idea to get you over to my place. In fact, it was my idea to clear off and leave you two alone together yesterday. Eejit that I am. Now the whole thing's a sorry mess."

"My grandmother has no idea about real life. She's a dinosaur."

"Charlie says he reckons she might let you stay now he's out of the way. He's a bloody good friend, Jessie – I hope you appreciate that."

"I do. I wish I could talk to him. And I wish he was right. But Grandmother's pretty pissed at both of us and I didn't exactly do a great job of apologizing. She'll send me home for sure. And then I don't know what I'm going to do." I choke out the last few words as I try to stop the tears. Already I can feel them hot on my cheeks, salty in my mouth.

"Calm down, Jessie. Tell me what she's said to you."

"She's sleeping on it. She'll tell me in the morning. But I think she's already made her decision. I may as well pack my bag now."

"She'd be dumb to send you home."

"I told her I was sorry. And I did mean it. But I

said a few other things too. It's me who's dumb. I should never have. . ."

"We all do stupid things – even your grandmother must understand that. You're way too talented to give up on. She'll work it out."

"Will she?" I try to find a glimmer of hope but I'm not optimistic.

"If not, you can always have a job with us."

"Thanks. When do you go? Save a place on the boat."

"We leave first thing tomorrow. The forecast is bad. You'd be sick all the way on the boat. You're better off in London, tell your gran. In the meantime, I'm sending you some good Irish luck."

"Don't bother. Luck doesn't work for me."

"Of course it does."

"If you talk to Charlie again, tell him to answer his phone. I need to speak to him."

"Get some sleep, Jessie. Tomorrow is another day."

The phone goes dead. I listen to the quiet. How can everything have gone so wrong?

I leap off the floor and get the brooch from the drawer of my desk. I open up the box and take another hard look at it. She said it didn't work for her, so why give it to me? Does she want me to have bad luck? If she hadn't given me this stupid present, perhaps none of this would've happened.

I snap the box shut and wrestle my window open. I hurl the brooch out on to the street and it lands on the pavement. I watch and wait for someone to pass. First a lady, then a nanny in a funny uniform with a child in each hand, then an older man. He scuffs it with the toe of his shoe. My heart misses a beat. He bends and picks it up. Opens it. Then he checks his watch, looks around and slips the brooch into his pocket.

"Enjoy," I say quietly and shut the window.

I wait to feel better, but it doesn't happen.

Chapter 15

That night, I drift in and out of a stomach-churning sleep. Hour after hour, I play out every scenario and try to prepare myself for the worst. I can manage my thoughts but I can't control my nightmares, so I end up trying to stay awake, sitting up with the light on. I think about writing Grandmother a letter. I think about asking Mum to ring her, but that might make things worse.

At six, I get up and start practising. Perhaps that will remind her how determined I am. I need her to know how much I want this.

Just after eight, she appears like a spectre in the music room. I drop my violin to my side. Her eyes are as red as mine.

"You can stop leaving messages for Charles," she says. "The phone went with the job. I have it now."

She waves it at me. "However, I am glad to hear from your messages that you are concerned for his welfare."

"You said he hadn't lost his job."

"And he will get his phone back if he returns."

So she's listened to all my messages to Charlie? It's a good thing I wasn't slagging her off.

I wait. Watch as she twists his phone round and round in her hands.

"You are a talented violinist, Jessica. And I do acknowledge that you have worked hard. I understand that it can't have been easy for you coming to live here with me, and perhaps I should have done more. However, I have invested a lot in you and you have thrown it back in my face. I find that very hurtful."

There's another long pause and I hold my breath and wait for the axe to drop.

"I am told things are different for seventeen-year-olds nowadays and I know you haven't had the most advantageous upbringing. Perhaps my expectations were too high."

I clamp my teeth together to stop myself from saying something. She's a fine one to talk. My upbringing might've been a lot different if she hadn't cut us off from everything. And Mum and Dad haven't done a bad job, all things considered.

She's pacing up and down in front of me. Finally she stops. "I do not want to be unreasonable. I have listened to everything you have said and I have decided to let you stay."

"You have?" The breath bursts out of me and I have to stop myself from hugging her. My body is physically shaking with relief.

"Things will have to change from now on. I hope you understand that."

I nod.

"You will never, ever deceive me again. Do you understand?"

I nod again.

"And you will have no further intimate contact with Charles. Neither personally nor by telephone."

"But. . ."

"I'm sorry. That is how it has to be."

"As long as you promise he can come back as soon as I've gone."

"That will be his decision. He can come back when he is ready. And I have asked Celia McNair to organize for you to play in a string quartet at the Royal College of Music with some first-year students. I can see it is important to spend time with people your own age. I hope this may help."

I can see she's thought about this, but I'm not sure first-year music students will have a lot of time for me. She's probably had to bribe them to accept me. I try to smile but I doubt it's too convincing.

"And perhaps another trip with Selina is required. For your winter wardrobe."

Now that does make me smile. "That would be good. Thanks."

"And, finally. . ." She pauses for a little too long. ". . .I am going to set you a challenge which will really show me the kind of person you are."

"What kind of challenge?"

There is a dangerous sparkle in her eyes. "You will be giving a solo performance at the RCM on the fifteenth of December. It will be a performance for invited guests and the general public."

I count on my fingers. "That's only just over three months away. A performance of what?" Something tells me this is heading somewhere bad.

"You will play Sibelius's Violin Concerto in D Minor."

"Sibelius? D Minor?" I have to force the words out.

So this is how she's going to punish me: slow, painful torture. Setting me up for failure.

"Are you familiar with it?" she asks.

"Yes, of course I am. Who isn't? But I can't perform it. It's massive. I'll never learn it in such a short time. It's too hard."

"Too hard says who?"

"Says everybody. It's. . ." I can't find the words.

"This is not up for debate, Jessica. I recollect you said you would do anything if I allowed you to stay. Well, I've allowed you to stay and I want you to prepare the Sibelius."

"Why? Why not Elgar or Brahms or even Bartók?"

"Do you *want* me to send you home? It is *Sibelius*. Take it or leave it."

She's got me completely trapped and I'm hardly in a position to negotiate. I stare at the grey morning light filtering through the bars on the windows. It fills the room with shadows. I've touched on the first and second movements of this concerto before. They're bad enough. But the third is just survival. I can't think of anything more difficult – not for me, at any rate.

"Perhaps you would rather pack your bags after all?"

"No," I say quietly. A fiery determination fills my body. If she wants a fight, she's going to get one.

I am not going to lose — even if it kills me. "I will start working on it straight away." My voice is so hard, I barely recognize it. I wish I felt as strong as I sound. "I will be ready to perform on December the fifteenth."

We stare at each other and neither of us blinks. She breaks first.

"In that case, your new schedule will begin as of today. I have informed Dr McNair of your repertoire for the concert. And your first quartet rehearsal will be this coming Saturday."

"And what about my sessions on Sunday at Harris House? Can I still have my classes with Mr Ritchie and Helena?" I'm going to need all the help I can get. I bet Helena's played the Sibelius. She can pass on some experience.

"In case you have forgotten, Jessica, I no longer have a driver. I can hardly ask Sarah to take us all the way to North London every Sunday. Her workload has doubled as it is. There will be no further visits to Harris House."

So this is how it will be. As a punishment, it couldn't get much worse. I wonder if Grandmother ever had any intention of sending me home or whether she had something like this planned from the start. She'll enjoy watching me suffer. She looks at her watch.

"Dr McNair will be here in a few minutes for your lesson. You had better continue with your practice."

I pick up my violin deliberately slowly. I'm not going to give her the pleasure of seeing me angry. I turn to my studies. Grandmother watches me.

"Oh, and good luck," she says with a thin smile.

Once she's gone I grip my violin so hard it almost breaks.

"OK, I can do this," I tell myself out loud. "I have to do this."

I hear Dr McNair coming down the stairs and I begin to play loudly and violently. When she walks in, she almost has to shout. She only says one word. "Sibelius." I stop playing. I can hear the anger in her voice and it sets me off. I rant and rave for about five minutes. She sits in a chair with her arms crossed.

"Have you quite finished?" she asks. "It's all very well for you to complain, but I have to teach you the wretched thing. Under four months to get the Sibelius to performance standard. I don't know what your grandmother can be thinking."

"I know exactly what she's thinking."

"I told her, when she first mentioned it, that I thought it was completely unreasonable. She said we should wait and see. I honestly thought she'd put it out of her head."

"What do you mean, when she first mentioned it? When did she first mention it?"

"Before you arrived in London."

"Before!" It explodes out of me. "I don't understand. Has she simply been waiting for the opportunity to throw it at me? Is there some hidden agenda here I don't know about?"

"Don't ask me. She's *your* grandmother." Dr McNair slams her briefcase down on the top of the piano. "We'll just have to do the best we can in the time we have." She violently flicks through sheets of music, then places something on the music stand.

I point the end of my bow at Dr McNair. "The best we can is *not* good enough. We've got to do better than that. I'm prepared to throw everything at this. We're going to prove to Grandmother that I can do it. We'll work twenty-four hours a day if we have to."

Dr McNair's chin rises a little, and then a

small smile twitches at her lips. "All right. Good, good, very good." She stands up, all businesslike. "We have a deal." She puts out her hand and we shake. "But I hope you know what you're taking on."

I nod.

"In that case, let's go straight into some chromatic scales, please."

So we begin.

She nurses me through that first week, but my progress is frighteningly slow. We set deadlines for the first, second and third movements and within those, I set myself daily deadlines. The structure is reassuring, as long as I don't get behind. But by Friday I'm already lagging and I'm so tired. Day after day there's no let-up.

Saturday comes and I'm due to start the string quartet at the RCM. It's the last thing I need. I dress deliberately dark. Black jeans, a silvery silk shirt, leather jacket and boots. I know what these little string groups are like and I'm not going to get pushed around. I check myself in the mirror, add a bit more eyeliner.

Sarah drives me and she makes sure to let me know how inconvenient all this is for her. I'm not going to let her make me feel that guilty. I offered to walk and it's not as though I asked to play in this string quartet. I don't have the time and I don't want to be here. Worse still, I'm nervous. Playing with students at the RCM is a big deal. I'm just a wannabe and, even now, I'm probably nowhere near good enough. I can't bear the thought of making a fool of myself.

Sarah finds a parking spot and edges her way in. I stare out of the window of the car. There are masses of people around, mostly very young.

"Must be the first weekend back for the Junior Department," says Sarah. "My husband used to help out sometimes at weekends." The memory seems to cheer her up a little. "Look at those little things. Some of them have only just learnt to walk."

She's right. There are tiny kids struggling along with huge instruments. I always dreamt of coming here to the Junior Department. We couldn't afford it, of course. Not with the travel and all. Now I'm here and I don't want to be. Typical.

A beautiful girl with long, straight, blonde hair walks past the car carrying a violin. She has a dark suntan and she strides into the building like she owns the place.

"She looks more like one of yours," says Sarah.

"I hope not. Not sure we'd have that much in common."

"You never know; you both play the violin." Sarah checks her watch. "Well, are you getting out of the car or not? You're going to be late."

I clamber out, take my violin from the back seat and slam the door.

"I'll be back to pick you up in two hours and I'll be in a hurry, so please make sure you're waiting."

"OK, OK." She's made her point.

I head towards the entrance and ask for Dr McNair at reception. They direct me along a corridor to a rehearsal room. The door is open and I see the blonde girl there with two others. Just my luck. Dr McNair isn't there yet. When I walk in, the room goes quiet. I curl my lip slightly as they look me up and down. They're a tight little group.

"I'm Jess," I say.

The blonde gets up and shakes my hand. "I'm Harriet," she says, "and this is Su-lin and Flora. Welcome to the group."

They give me a quick smile, then go back to chatting to each other. I may as well not be there. I busy myself getting out my violin. Harriet's voice is irritatingly loud.

". . . And oh my God, I couldn't believe it when he said he was going to be studying in London too *and* he's living down the road from me. It's all too perfect."

"Ridiculously perfect," says Flora.

"I know!" Harriet squeals.

Please may I never be like Harriet.

As second violin, I'm in the seat between Harriet and Flora, which makes it harder for them to ignore me.

"Harriet's been at a music summer camp," says Su-lin, making an effort to include me in the conversation. I suppose I should be grateful.

"Good for Harriet," I say without enthusiasm. There's an awkward silence.

"It was wonderful," she says, drawing out the word to make sure none of us is in any doubt. "Italy is the most beautiful country in the world."

"Well, I'm glad someone's had a good summer."

I see Harriet roll her eyes at the others and that bugs me even more.

"So where do you come from?" she asks.

"Manchester."

"Oh. Nice."

"Not really. Not my part of Manchester, anyway."

"It must take you ages to get here."

"Ten minutes. I'm living in London with my grandmother."

"Nice," says Harriet again.

If only she knew. They go back to chatting about boys again. I think about Charlie and feel miserable. I get out my duster and meticulously wipe over my violin. For the first time in my life I wish Dr McNair would arrive.

"So are you officially an *item*?" asks Flora, making little speech marks with her fingers.

"No. Well, nearly!" I watch Harriet cross her fingers. "Just wait until you meet him. He is the most gorgeous thing on two legs."

Harriet is straight from a bad film script. There are little sighs and giggles from Su-lin and Flora. If I had a bucket, I'd vomit. Poor bloke. I wonder if he knows what he's letting himself in for. The thought of it makes me grin, and I pretend to search for something in my violin case so they can't see my face.

There's a hush in the room. Harriet gives Flora a kick on the side of her foot. It's not very subtle – or not from where I am, with my head at floor level.

I glance up to see what's happening.

There's someone walking down the corridor.

A jolt goes through me because that someone is too familiar. But it can't be. He's walking towards us. Closer and closer.

Stefan? Shit. It *is* Stefan. My heart nearly jumps out of my chest. I'm off my seat long before he's reached the door and I fling my arms round his neck.

"Jess?" he says, coolly. "What are you doing here?"

I let go and take a step back. He looks around, anywhere but me. I hate myself for my lack of control and I'm gutted by his reaction. I wish the ground would swallow me up.

"It's a long story." I try to sound light-hearted, uninterested. "And you?'

"I'm studying here, of course."

"I thought you were going to study in Manchester."

"I changed my mind. I got a last-minute place – some kind of private endowment for accompanists."

"Oh. That was lucky."

There's a silence that needs to be filled and I wish he'd look at me instead of over my shoulder.

"So what are you doing here – like now – in this room?" I say.

"I came to drop something with a friend. She said she'd be here this morning." He makes it sound like it's all perfectly normal, but it is not normal for me and I refuse to carry on pretending.

"This is crazy. Where have you been all summer?"

"Italy. On a music camp. I only got back three days ago. It was incredible." He runs his fingers through his hair. He does that when he's worried.

"Italy . . . oh, I see." I turn to look at Harriet and my worst fears are confirmed. She seems uncertain what to do and is simply staring at me with a horrified expression on her face. "OK," I say, "I think I get the picture."

"What picture?" asks Stefan, shrugging slightly.

"I'm guessing she is the friend you've come to find." I jab my thumb in Harriet's direction.

"I didn't realize you knew Hattie." Stefan acknowledges her now, gives her a kind of half wave.

"Actually, I don't know her. I just met her a minute ago. She told me her name was Harriet."

"Hattie, Harriet. Same thing." Then he whispers, "She's a brilliant violinist."

That does not make me feel better and him whispering in my ear seems to have got Hattie on her feet too, heading towards us. She gives Stefan a too-long hug while I shrivel up inside.

"Hi, Stefan," she says, tucking her hair behind

her ears. "How's it going?" She's almost fluttering her eyelashes. It's pathetic.

"Great. I've brought you the memory stick with those photos."

Those photos? I wonder what that means, exactly.

"How do you two know each other?" she says, barely keeping the sneer from her voice.

"We used to work together," says Stefan. "I was Jess's accompanist."

"Oh, you're not *that* Jess, are you?"

I raise my eyebrows at Stefan. "*That* Jess?" I say.

"The one who got the terrible stage fright? Stefan told us all about you. How you messed up your performance. You poor thing. It must have been awful."

My chest and throat fill up. Tears threaten. I hold them back. I'd like to punch him.

"Thanks, Stefan," I say. "It's nice to have friends."

Stefan tries to grab my hand but I shake him off. I'm not hanging around to take any more of this. I set off down the corridor, back towards the exit. I'm stopped by Dr McNair striding towards me.

"Ah good, you're here," she says. "You're going the wrong way."

"Toilet," I say, brushing my eyes with the back of my sleeve.

"Well, hurry up. We're late as it is."

"You're late, I'm not."

I find my way to the ladies'. I put down the toilet seat and sit there letting silent tears fall. I thought Stefan was a friend. I trusted him. How could he tell stories like that about me – especially to people like Harriet? I hear someone come in and I know I have to pull myself together. I wait until I hear the next-door cubicle lock, and then I let myself out, turn on the tap and splash water over my face. I can't avoid going back. Apart from anything else, I've left my violin in the rehearsal room. I wipe my face with a paper towel, dab away mascara, check my reflection and head back down the corridor.

They're all waiting for me. Stefan's gone. Harriet's got a self-satisfied smile glued to her face. I can feel all three girls watching as I pick up my violin. Dr McNair does some brief introductions and explains what we'll be doing.

"Right," she says, "let's get going."

It's hopeless. I can't concentrate at all. I keep making silly mistakes and Harriet keeps tittering. I sigh loudly.

"You'll get the hang of it soon," she says, and I have to resist the urge to put the heel of my boot on the toe of her neat little shoe and press hard. I want to get to the end of this session and get out. Fortunately, Dr McNair has a meeting, so we finish ten minutes early. The girls give me stiff little hugs as they say goodbye – after all, we're a quartet now.

"See you next Saturday," they say, almost in unison. It makes me squirm.

I wait until they're out of sight, then pack up slowly. I'm hoping Stefan might reappear so I can tell him just what I think of him, but there's no sign of him, and I drag my way back to the front steps to wait for Sarah.

"Pssst."

I turn my head in the direction of the sound.

"Jess! Over here. It's me, Stefan. Has Harriet gone?"

"Yes," I say. I feel a small sense of victory that he's waited for me. But I'm not going to get my hopes up.

He appears from behind a pillar, sits down beside me.

"It's so good to see you," he says.

"You could have fooled me."

"I'm sorry – I was shocked, that's all. I had no idea you were in London."

I keep my eyes firmly glued to the ground. "I could kill you," I say. Then I look at him square on. "How could you talk about my stage fright to other people? How could you tell them about my audition? Stories like that can damage a career."

"Please, Jess, I'm sorry. It wasn't like that. I didn't just tell them. Not in a nasty way. You have to believe me."

"Do you have any idea what it feels like? Knowing they all know? It's the first time I've met them. It's already bad enough being forced to come here to play with them."

He shakes his head. Looks down. "Why didn't you answer any of my texts or calls? That wasn't exactly friendly either."

"Bollocks you tried to call. You didn't answer one of my texts. You just blanked me. It kept coming up *message sending failed*."

"Well, you probably didn't bother to change my number."

"What d'you mean? Why should I change your number?"

He takes an iPhone out of his pocket and waves

it at me. "New phone, new number," he says. "All thanks to you."

"You mean you actually changed your phone so I couldn't get hold of you?"

"Don't be stupid. I'm just saying it was your fault, or kind of, that my old one got wrecked."

"How come?" I can't imagine how I could possibly be responsible for breaking his phone.

"You remember the day of your scholarship?"

I roll my eyes.

"Someone saw you race off out of the emergency exit of the theatre. It was pouring with rain – do you remember? I searched for ages. I wanted to find you."

"Did you?" I can hardly remember what happened immediately after my audition. Maybe it was raining.

"I looked everywhere, running up and down the streets around the concert hall. I was worried about you." He's waving his hands around in a Stefan-like way – the Stefan I know – the Stefan I love. "I was so busy looking for you that I missed the edge of the pavement, tripped, and my phone fell in the stupid gutter. Running water – wrecked."

I can't help smiling at his dramatic presentation.

"Ha ha. Nice story."

"I'm not joking."

"You really expect me to believe you chased me round the streets of Manchester?" I've got his phone in my hand. Checking his contacts. I'll soon see if my name's still in here.

"What are you doing?" he asks, trying to grab his phone back.

"Wait." I pull it back and scroll through until I get to J. And I am there – with my old number. I hand him back his phone and wrap my arms around my knees. What is it with my life?

"What's the matter?" he asks.

I unwrap myself. Take my phone from my bag. Wave it at him. "New phone, new number. Threw it at the wall when I couldn't get through to you."

"Ah." He sighs loudly. "Shit."

I ball myself up again. I can't think of anything to say. Our phones may be an unlucky coincidence, but that still didn't give him any right to blab about me to his new girlfriend.

"So what are you doing in London?" he asks. "You look different. You even sound different."

"Do I? That's what living with my grandmother does to you."

"Grandmother?"

"Yep. Turns out I have a wealthy grandmother who's decided I'm a worthy cause. She arrived on my doorstep after the evening of the scholarship performances. She's pretty well connected in the music world, it seems. Anyway, I'm here until Christmas – private music tutors, all the bells and whistles. She pays for everything. I do as I'm told. If I survive my final three months with her, I'm hoping I'll get another shot at the scholarship."

"That's amazing. But how . . . why did you never mention her before?"

"I didn't know about her."

"You're joking."

"Nope. Some big family row before I was born. Mum told me she was dead."

"That's a bit excessive, isn't it? At least it's all worked out in the end."

"I wouldn't be so sure about that. Living with my grandmother has been an unusual experience, to say the least. Now she wants me to commit musical suicide."

"Sounds exciting."

"*Not*. She's organized a concert for me in December – here at the RCM. She's decided I will play the Sibelius violin concerto. Trouble is, she only told me on Tuesday."

Stefan laughs. "You're not being serious. You'll never do it in that time."

"I'm being deadly serious. And I have to do it in that time. She's doing it because. . ."

"Because what?"

What do I say? I don't want to tell him about Charlie. ". . .because that's the kind of thing she does."

Stefan is quiet for a while. He interlinks his fingers and twiddles his thumbs round and round.

"Who's going to accompany you?" he asks quietly.

"I don't know. The only accompanist I've worked with recently is a man called George Ritchie, and he's nearly ninety."

"George Ritchie? Now you're really being funny."

"Why, what's wrong with that?"

"Not *the* George Ritchie?"

"I don't know who *the* George Ritchie is. Should I?"

"Only one of the best-known post-war accompanists. He's a legend. I did a project on him once."

"There must be hundreds of George Ritchies."

"I doubt it. God, imagine if it was him! I'm going to have to check it out."

"Whatever."

Stefan laughs. "I've missed you, Jess."

"That's not the impression I get from Harriet."

"What's that supposed to mean?"

"Nothing."

Stefan gives a small shrug. "Look, I'm going out for a drink with the others this evening. D'you want to come?"

"Others?"

"Harriet and the rest."

"Oh."

"I know she'd be happy for you to come and join us."

"I'd rather have drinks with a python."

"Sorry?"

"Thanks but no thanks." I look at my watch. "I have to go."

Stefan grabs my arm. "When can I see you, then?"

"Dunno."

"Can I phone you?"

"If you want."

"Why are you being so difficult?"

"I'm not." I give him my number in a deadpan

voice and watch while he punches it into his phone. He'll probably forget about me as soon as he's in the pub with Harriet.

I see Sarah pull up in Grandmother's car. Stefan trails after me as I walk towards it.

"Don't go, Jess. Not yet."

"Sorry, but my lift is here."

"Tell them to come back later."

"I can't."

I climb into the car and open the window.

"I'll ring you," he says.

"Have fun with Harriet." I give him a sarcastic smile. We drive away and I wish I'd kept my mouth shut.

"Who was that?" asks Sarah.

"My old accompanist from Manchester."

"He's rather good-looking!"

"Looks aren't everything."

I gaze out of the window, not seeing. The overwhelming sense of wanting to be with him and anger at what he's done is a poisonous mixture and it makes me feel sick. I keep the window open and let the air blow on my face.

"Did you know he was going to be here?" Sarah asks.

"Uh-uh. I thought he was studying in Manchester."

"What a lovely surprise."

"Kind of."

"And how was your quartet?"

"Don't ask."

"Was the blonde girl there?"

"Harriet. Yes, worst luck. It seems she's been studying in Italy most of the summer – with Stefan." I hate the way my voice gives everything away and I scuff my foot hard against the floor of the car.

"Ah – Stefan being your accompanist," says Sarah. She's got it all worked out already.

"Oh well. At least I've got some good news for you."

"What?"

"Charlie's coming back."

"Already? How? When? I thought he wouldn't be back until Christmas."

"I talked to him today. He said Mrs Chamberlain had told him that she'd decided not to send you home." There's a pause. I wonder how much Grandmother has told her.

"And?"

"Knowing you were allowed to stay, he thought Mrs Chamberlain would need him after all. To do all the driving. Apparently she agreed to let him return, but not until next weekend. Apparently she wants to give him a *cooling-off period*?" Sarah is fishing for answers.

"It was my fault he got into trouble," I say. "He'll probably never speak to me again."

"Look, I don't know what happened, Jess. But it sounded like a joint effort to me and I don't think he's one to hold grudges. I'm sure he won't hold it against you and, between you and me, I think your grandmother is delighted. She's very fond of Charlie, and I really can't be expected to do all the driving as well as everything else."

I nod and wonder if this means I'll be able to go to Harris House after all.

Sarah puts her hand on my arm. "You will take care, won't you? Whatever happened – and I'm not asking you to tell me – don't you and Charlie go messing things up again."

"We're not that stupid," I say.

"Charlie isn't as young as you but he *is* still young. He doesn't take knocks easily."

"I know about his dad and everything, if that's what you mean."

"I didn't quite mean it like that, but if he's told

275

you, then you'll understand what I mean. And you'll understand that it's even more important. . ."

As Sarah continues to lecture me, I let my mind wander back to Stefan. I wonder if he'll call me.

"Sorry?" I say. I realize Sarah has asked me a question.

Sarah sighs loudly. "I'm asking you to be sensible, that's all."

Chapter 16

Sensible! How can I be sensible? Everything is happening so fast. Charlie is coming back and Stefan is here in London. I keep trying to push Stefan out of my thoughts but he's there, all the time, sitting in the front of my mind where I can't ignore him. Worse still, he's sitting there with Harriet. I can't concentrate on anything. I should be really excited about seeing Charlie, but now it's not so simple. On the other hand, at least I can show Stefan he's not the only one who's moved on.

That afternoon, I check my phone over and over for a message from Stefan.

Late on Saturday, I get a text. It's from an unknown number.

Can't wait to see you again.

I don't know if it's from Stefan or Charlie. I so desperately want it to be Stefan. I bite my knuckle. This is getting complicated.

A bit later I get a second text – different number.

I think it is *THE* George Ritchie. Did you say he was in a retirement home?

No guessing who that's from, which means the first message must've been from Charlie. I push my phone away from me across the table. Clearly all that Stefan cares about is George Ritchie. Great. I sigh, pull the phone back towards me.

Yes. Harris House.

A few seconds later my phone rings.

"Jess. Can you talk?"

I hope he can't hear how fast my heart is beating.

"Yup. I think I've been able to do that since I was quite small."

Stefan ignores my sarcasm. "I can't believe you've met George Ritchie. He's actually accompanied you?"

"Yup."

"And you didn't know about him being so famous?"

"Nope."

"Jess?" He sounds irritated now.

"OK, I'll admit it's obvious that he's a brilliant accompanist. I just didn't realize he was so well known. I'm a violinist, not an accompanist. I study violinists."

"Can you arrange for me to meet him?"

"No! Why?"

"He's my hero. He's the person who made me want to be an accompanist. He's the one who made me fall in love with Blüthner pianos. I've listened to hundreds of his recordings."

I'm smiling in spite of myself. It's so good to hear Stefan's voice again. I love it when he gets stupidly enthusiastic. I just wish he was enthusiastic about seeing me and not Mr Ritchie.

"And what if I told you Grandmother has a Blüthner in the music room where I practise?"

"*What?*" I hold my phone away from my ear as he yells. "Are you sure? In that case, I'm on my way over *now*."

"You can try, but you'll never get in. The way this place is guarded, you'd think we kept the crown jewels here. Strangers not allowed."

"I'm not a stranger."

"You are to my grandmother."

"When can I see you, then?" He sounds serious now.

"I don't know." I keep casual; try to sound as though it doesn't matter either way.

"I know you're angry with me and I don't blame you. I know I shouldn't have said anything to Hattie about. . ."

"No, you shouldn't. What's with you and her anyway? You seem very cosy."

"We are not cosy at all. Come on, give me a bit of credit, she's hardly my type."

"That's not what she thinks."

"And you care what she thinks?"

"Should I?"

"Depends what she's said."

"It's not important."

"It is to me."

"Stefan, it's fine. It's nothing to do with me anyway."

"I don't know what she's told you, but if it's anything about her and me, then it's rubbish. It was just a kind of holiday. . ."

"I'm really not interested."

"I have to see you," he says. "Please."

"Me or the piano?"

"Oh, for goodness' sake. What do I have to do?" He sounds desperate now. Or I think he does. It's hard to control my own excitement; hard to keep sounding as though I don't care.

"Let me think about it," I say.

"Jess!"

"I'll call you." I hang up and hug my phone to my chest. My face is hot and I'm smiling inside and outside. Maybe I could arrange for him to meet up with Mr Ritchie. I bet Harriet couldn't pull that out of the bag.

I run downstairs and find Sarah.

"Where's Grandmother?" I ask.

"In the drawing room. Why?"

"Is she busy?"

"I'll go and ask if you like," she says.

"No, it's OK. I'll go."

I walk to the door, knock gently and go in. Grandmother is sitting in her usual chair, ankles neatly crossed, reading the paper. She glances at me over the top of her glasses.

"Good evening," she says.

"Can I speak to you for a moment?" I'm learning how to play the game Grandmother's way.

281

"If this is about Charles coming back, then you must understand that I have set strict conditions and I will not tolerate any inappropriate behaviour. You are not to encourage him. Not under any circumstances. You will avoid being alone together."

"Yes," I say. For once I agree with her. I think about Charlie's text. This isn't going to be easy. Not at all. I almost wish he wasn't coming back — not yet.

"Actually, it wasn't about Charlie."

"Oh." She folds her newspaper. "How did your morning go at the RCM?"

"It was fine."

"Good."

"You never told me George Ritchie was famous — like really famous."

Grandmother looks confused for a moment. "It's hardly a state secret, Jessica." She gets up, walks over to the corner of the room and picks up a photo off the table. She hands it to me carefully. Black and white. A young man playing the piano. Obviously it must be Mr Ritchie, though I wouldn't have recognized him. He has a mass of thick dark hair.

"Did you know him back then?" I ask her.

"Yes. Yes, I did."

"Was he very good?"

"One of the best." She takes back the photo. Looks at it, then puts it down in her lap. "So who told you about him?"

"Someone I met today at the RCM."

"And why would this person be so interested in George Ritchie?"

I could be imagining it, but I feel as though Grandmother already knows what I am going to say.

"Because he also wants to be an accompanist," I say carefully.

"Ah. As I thought. Would this person be Stefan Montgomery, by any chance?"

"How did you know that? How could you know about Stefan?"

"I happen to know he has recently started studying at the RCM and, of course, I recognized his name from your concert in Manchester. I presumed you would be in contact with him sooner or later."

"How would you *happen* to know that? And for your information, you presumed wrong. I had no idea he was in London. It was a fluke that we met today."

She's watching me very closely. "His teachers at the RCM speak very highly of him," she says.

"Probably because he's very good."

She tips her head on one side, thoughtful. "Would you consider working with him again?"

My cheeks start to burn. "Maybe. Once I'm ready."

"Dr McNair tells me your progress with the concerto is rather slow."

"I've been working on it for less than a week; what does she expect?"

"She expects you to meet your deadlines."

I scrunch up my toes inside my shoes and try to keep my temper. "That's easy for her to say. I'm the one who has to put in the hours."

"And are you? Putting in the hours?"

"You know I am. It doesn't help having the quartet on a Saturday morning."

"Everything helps." Grandmother crosses her arms. "I thought you might like to invite your friends from the quartet to dinner one night."

"They're not my friends."

"Oh – well, maybe in a few weeks, then."

I have to recognize that she is trying – in her own way. I don't bother to tell her that I will never be friends with Hattie and her loyal followers. Just not my type.

"And I thought we could invite Mr Montgomery to audition as your accompanist for the concert. Finding you an accompanist is important. It has been concerning me. It is fortuitous that Mr Montgomery is in London." Her voice doesn't waver.

"Fortuitous or strangely coincidental?" I ask. I have a strong sense that Grandmother's got a hand in this somewhere and I don't like it.

"Indeed. It is a happy coincidence, I hope."

"Did you *know* that Stefan was going to be studying in London?"

Grandmother gazes rather vaguely towards the window. "How could I possibly know such a thing?"

I'm not sure. But she did know – I'm certain of that.

"Do you have a problem working with Mr Montgomery again?"

"His name is Stefan. He's not an old man. You should call him by his name. And yes, I might have a problem working with him again."

"Oh?"

How can I explain that I'd like to know where I stand with Stefan before going any further with this? I certainly don't want him to be forced into this by Grandmother. He's got plenty of choice now –

brilliant young musicians from the RCM. Why would he want to work with me? It's not as though our last effort was up to much. I try to choose my words carefully.

"What if Stefan doesn't want to work with me again after what happened last time? He's got his own reputation to think of. I think he's moved on."

"Last time was hardly his fault. I thought he came out of it rather well."

"I wouldn't know," I say with a sarcastic smile. "I seem to remember I didn't hang around to find out. But the point is, he'll never be able to trust me now, will he? Not after what happened."

"What is more important is whether or not *you* trust *him*."

I wonder if she means musically or in general.

"I wouldn't want to let him down again."

"And what makes you think you would let him down?"

"Well, since you ask, it could be something to do with the fact that the Sibelius concerto is about a hundred times harder than anything else we've ever played. Or it could be that you've only given me three months to prepare the whole thing. Or perhaps, when the time comes, I'll just get stage fright and have to face failure all over again. Are those enough reasons?"

"Jessica. We must put the past behind us. We all experience failure at one time or another. We have to let it go."

"*We?* Where does the *we* come into it? Don't try and pretend you know what it feels like."

She sighs. "Failure is just one step on the road to success. The sooner you recognize that, the better. If you don't, it will destroy you."

"If I stuff up this concert, it will destroy me."

"In that case you'd better not *stuff it up*." She imitates my voice.

"You should bloody try playing it."

She's got no answer to that. She just looks down at the photo in her lap and whispers, "Language, Jessica."

"Look," I say, "I know I did wrong with Charlie, but even Dr McNair thinks you're being ridiculous. She told me you talked about the Sibelius concerto even before I arrived. I don't know if you're using it as a punishment or what. I'm not sure why you brought me here in the first place, and God knows why you've let me stay, though I'm grateful that you have – don't get me wrong – and I'd really like to know how you know so much about Stefan being in

London." I'm gabbling because I haven't got a clue what it is I'm trying to say but my mouth won't stop. "You need to tell me what's going on here."

Grandmother has her hand up in the air. "Settle down, Jessica. Now, as I recall, when we first discussed the Sibelius, you promised not to let me down. Assuming you keep that promise, you will not let Stefan down either."

"Funnily enough, I don't remember any *discussion* about Sibelius. And yes, I did promise not to let you down, but that was before I started on this crackpot idea of yours. Now I know what it involves, I'm not so sure I can keep that promise."

"Oh, I think you can. As I said at the very start, I can help you – if you'll let me. Though lord knows you haven't made it easy for me thus far."

"And you think you've made it easy for me?"

"No, not always. But being a musician is not easy. I do not want to wrap you in cotton wool."

"You haven't answered my questions."

"I think you should focus your mind on your music and stop wasting time with silly questions."

"And I think it would help if you gave me some answers."

"Sometimes there are no easy answers."

"I didn't ask for *easy* answers."

"And sometimes it's simply better not to know." She stands up and takes the photo back to the corner table. "Now, what did you come to talk to me about?"

"Don't change the subject. I want to know what you're playing at."

"I don't *play* at things, Jessica, and I will change the subject if I want to."

Anger gets the better of me. I pick up a cushion and hurl it towards her. It misses. I should not have done that. I definitely shouldn't have done that. I wait for her to erupt.

"Pick it up, Jessica," she says calmly, "and then tell me what you came to talk to me about."

"What's the point?" I don't move to pick up the cushion and I watch as she steps over it and moves to sit down next to me.

"Well?" she says. "Come on, out with it."

My shoulders slump. "Stefan asked if I could arrange for him to meet Mr Ritchie. I thought you might help. Anyway, it's not important."

"Of course it's important. You should have said at the beginning. It is a very good idea. I'll invite George over to hear Stefan play. He will be the perfect judge of whether Stefan is the right person to accompany you."

"That wasn't exactly what I had in mind. If this has to be like a formal audition, I think we both need more time."

"Whatever do you mean? I'm sure Stefan is keen to meet George as soon as possible, if he's so interested in him."

"Yes. But I'm not ready to play the Sibelius with Stefan yet. Not even nearly."

The thought of it makes my throat tighten. I have to be good – very good – before Stefan hears me play again. Stress swims into my stomach and a sharp pain stabs at my guts. I try to breathe slowly but I can't seem to gain control. I badly need to do something about this. I wonder if I'm going to be sick. Is it possible that I will always associate playing with Stefan with stage fright? If so, there's no way I should work with him. But if not with him, with who?

Grandmother doesn't interrupt my thoughts. She waits. It's as if she can see inside me.

"Are you feeling unwell?" she asks.

I realize I'm pressing my hands against my stomach. "I'm fine."

Her eyebrows rise. There's not much gets past

the old baggage. "Well, I'm afraid I must get on. I'm sure you have work to do too."

Our conversation is over. She's already up and walking towards the door.

"Don't forget the cushion," she says as she walks out.

As soon as she's gone, I drop to my knees and pummel the cushion with my fists. She's extraordinary. She manipulates every conversation. She manipulates my whole life. She only listens to what she wants to hear and she only tells me what she wants me to know because *she* thinks it's better that way. She's incapable of seeing anything from anyone else's point of view. I've got no idea of what she'll plan for Stefan and me and she probably won't tell me until the last minute. She'll announce that *surprise* is something a musician needs to learn to deal with – like stress, and ridiculous practice schedules, and challenges which are way too hard. The more she tries to control me, the more out of control I feel. Everything churns around in my head and my stomach grumbles away and I fold myself in a ball around the cushion and try to make all the sums add up right.

But they don't. None of them.

Chapter 17

What is it *better not to know*? Those were Grandmother's words. Why are there no easy answers? I
chew the end of my pencil as I write in my notebook.
Then I get a bit stuck. I know I'm not supposed to
think too hard when I write, but there's something
going on with Grandmother. She says she's not
playing a game but I don't believe her, and if she is,
I don't want Stefan to be part of it. But what is she
doing and why? If she's somehow organized all this,
there must be a reason. There must be more to it
than wanting to help me get my scholarship.

I want to ring Ciaran, but I might blab out
something stupid about Stefan that would get back
to Charlie, and that's going to be a whole other issue.
So I have to work this out for myself. I put down my
pencil and lean back in my chair. I'm unbelievably

tired and my stomach is still hurting. If I'm going to work with Stefan again, it's going to be on my own terms. I want to be ready. I need to impress him. I will not be made to feel like an idiot. Whatever happens, I'm not having him and Harriet laughing at me behind my back.

I wonder about ringing Rosie to cancel our run tomorrow but I'm sure I'll feel better by the morning. I know I should text back Charlie but I haven't got the energy and I don't know what to say. Finally, I decide to call Mum, and I moan down the phone at her for about half an hour. She blames my stomach pains on stress, as if this is going to come as news to me. I tell her about Stefan being in London. I don't make a big thing of it. She's pleased – says it'll be nice for me to have a friend my own age.

Dad comes on. He says if I've got stomach ache I need food. He asks me, jokingly I think, if Grandmother is feeding me. I tell him yes, but he's right in one way. I haven't been eating enough recently. I just don't seem to feel like food. I take his advice and head for the kitchen. I force down a quick supper, then go down to the music room. I need to stay on schedule. I practise late into the night, going over and over and over the first movement. I try to master the trills and the endless arpeggios. I try to keep Ciaran's advice in my head as I play. I try not to overthink it. I wonder what he's up to. Drunk in a pub in the middle of a bog in Ireland, no doubt.

♪ ♩

My stomach ache gets worse, but I refuse to let myself stop until I've got this first movement sorted, even though I'm feeling sick, really sick. If I'm like this now, what am I going to be like by the time I get to the concert? My stomach heaves and I run to the toilet, where I throw up supper. It makes me feel a bit better, so I go back to my violin. Within ten minutes I'm back hanging over the toilet again and again.

Eventually I crawl up to bed. The sickness doesn't let up all night, or the next day. I haven't got time to be ill but I'm too weak to fight it. Sarah keeps putting a cool flannel on my head and she's put a bowl by my bed. There's nothing left in my stomach but still I keep reaching for the bowl.

On Tuesday, Sarah calls the doctor, but he says it's probably a virus. I hope he's right. I can't believe stress could make me this bad.

I lie in bed and force myself to listen to Sibelius on my iPod. I've got to get it into my head. Initially my feverish mind pushes the music away, but then I start to hear it properly. Without the pressure of having to play it, I discover things I haven't heard before. Slowly, it begins to make more sense.

As the nausea improves, I ask Sarah to bring me my music score so I can follow along as I listen. I shadow-bow some of the phrases and passages. Suddenly I'm desperate to get back to my violin. I get out of bed too fast and blackness swims behind my eyes. I flop back down again and sleep.

On Tuesday evening, I manage to keep down some toast. I've got so many hours of practice to make up but I can barely stand. I pray Grandmother hasn't been in touch with Stefan. I check my phone. Just a message from Mum asking me how I am and one from Rosie telling me to get better quickly. The following morning I'm out of bed. I look paler than ever but I've got a new energy. I strip off my sheets, have a long, hot shower and throw on some clothes. My jeans are loose round my waist and my collarbone is visible above the neckline of my dark T-shirt. Stefan's right. I do look different.

But I haven't heard a word from him. I want to text him but I'm not sure what to say.

When I finally make it down the stairs, Sarah's in the kitchen.

"Hello, stranger," she says. "Feeling better?"

"Yes. Much."

"I'm afraid Dr McNair has succumbed to your bug, so she won't be in today. And Professor Jenniston's decided she doesn't want to come either – in case you're still contagious."

"Oh great, that's just what I need," I say sarcastically. There was a time when I would've loved to miss a lesson. Not now.

I take a cup of tea and a banana down to the music room. For the first time in a few weeks, my fingers are tingling with anticipation. Sometimes I wonder if they have a mind of their own.

It's cold in the basement and I put on a heater, stand with my bum against it as I do my warm-ups. Then I open up the concerto to the first page. My eyes trace across the notes and I hear it my head, every note just where it should be. A little knot of energy gathers below my ribs, hot like the sun, and it's a feeling I recognize. I don't pretend to understand it, but as I wait, the energy tracks from under my ribs and through my shoulders, arms and hands. Only then do I start to play and the music is no longer fighting me, it's flowing through me in a continuous molten stream. I keep going to the end, enjoying every note.

I finish with a flourish. I should get sick more often.

I sit down when I've finished, shaking and exhausted. It wasn't perfect – far from it – but I start to believe, just for a moment, that I might be able to pull off this crazy idea of Grandmother's. And I know I want Stefan to accompany me. The knot of energy burns hotter.

At lunchtime I sit with a sandwich in one hand and a pencil in the other, scribbling notes and dripping tomato all over my music. I jump when the phone rings. My heart goes double-time when I hear Stefan's voice.

"Hi, Jess. I'm sorry. I've been so sick."

"Oh, not you too. So have I, since Sunday."

"Half the students at college have gone down with it. Norovirus. They're thinking of closing the whole place for a few days. They've had enough of people throwing up into their trumpets."

"Yuck." We laugh.

"Can you meet me on Saturday?" he asks. "After your rehearsal – assuming the place is open, that is? I really need to talk to you."

"I need to talk to you too."

"We could go and get lunch. We might feel like food by then."

"I'll try to arrange to be picked up later than normal, but I'm not sure I'll be allowed to do lunch. I've been in a bit of trouble recently."

Stefan laughs. "Why am I not surprised? Well, do what you can. We're going to have to be careful around Harriet. She's driving me mad. You have to believe me, Jess. Nothing, I repeat *nothing*, happened between Harriet and me."

"And I repeat that I am *not interested*."

Stefan sighs. "I've got classes. Have to go. See you on Saturday."

"Get better."

"You too."

I tap my phone against my chin a few times. Surely he would've told me if Grandmother had contacted him. I want to talk to him face to face first. I need to know he wants this as much as I do. I don't want to talk over the phone so I'll have to risk the wait.

Our string quartet on Saturday is interesting and quite funny. Harriet makes endless mistakes and tries to blame me. Dr McNair snaps at her. Harriet leaves in a huff at the end and even Su-lin and Flora roll their eyes. They're OK.

I hang back as I put away my violin and make sure they're all safely out of the way before I text Stefan to give him the all clear. As soon as I see him, he comes sprinting towards me and picks me up off my feet, spinning me around.

"What's that for?" I ask, trying to keep hold of my violin.

"How did you do it?

"What?"

"You're amazing!"

"Thanks. But what?"

"Persuade your grandmother – to let me accompany you again. Or at least to try."

"Oh, so she's been in contact with you already?" I try to keep my voice even. "That's typical. What did she say?"

"She sounds nice – in her letter. You gave me the impression she was a dragon."

"You haven't met her yet."

He hands me the letter. I skim through it. She

wants to hear us playing together, blah, blah . . . could he come on Sunday afternoon at four, blah, blah. . . So no mention of George Ritchie. I wonder if she's forgotten our conversation. I doubt it. I'd better not say anything to Stefan.

"God, that woman is a nightmare," I say, having finished reading.

"Why? Aren't you pleased? Don't you want me to come tomorrow?"

"Yes, I do. It's only that I'd asked her to hold off until I was ready and she's completely ignored me as usual."

I start wandering in the direction of Hyde Park. I guess Sarah will meet me somewhere up here. Stefan tags along beside me. I need to find out what he really thinks about all this.

"What do you mean, until you were ready?"

I shrug. "I wanted to talk to you first. I didn't know if you'd want to play for me after last time. And I wanted to be good enough to prove to you that it was worth us having another go."

He plants himself in front of me so I have to stop. "How could you think like that?"

"I didn't think you'd fancy being humiliated by me all over again."

"Are you crazy? It's time you forgot all that. It happened once. Stop obsessing about it."

"I can't help it. Harriet ramming it down my throat didn't make things any better."

"Can we forget that too?" He takes a step in front of me so he's facing me and I have to stop walking. He puts his hands on my arms. "I want this more than anything. I know you're still angry with me, but we have to move on from that. I've missed working with you – more than you could ever know. I don't think I'll ever find another person who has the connection we have. The musical connection, I mean."

His words warm my whole body, but now he's stuttering an embarrassed apology and he lets go of me. I preferred it before.

"Please, Jess," he says, "you have to trust me."

"That's exactly what Grandmother says." I laugh to try and lighten the situation. "Have you met her before, by any chance?"

"No, I've never set eyes on her. I'm thinking three-headed monster." Stefan does his best monster pose – teeth bared, fingers clawed.

"Close!" I say and I can't help giggling. "Are you sure you didn't have any contact with her before coming to the RCM?"

"Why would I? First I heard of her was when I bumped into you."

"Hmm. She's got her fingers in all this somewhere." I chew my nail as I think. Stefan pulls my hand away from my mouth. "She's no pushover, Stefan. This isn't going to be an easy audition, and if you do start working with me, you'll be sucked under her control." I admit I'm laying it on a bit thick, but he needs to know what he's up against.

Stefan crosses his arms and sighs. "Are you trying to put me off? If you'd rather work with George Ritchie, then go ahead."

"I don't think Mr Ritchie would want to accompany me. The Sibelius would probably give him a heart attack."

"It's enough to give anyone a heart attack."

"Tell me about it! Have you had a chance to look at it?"

"Kind of. I don't have a lot of spare time at the moment. But don't worry, I'm sure we'll be fine."

"I wouldn't count on it."

Stefan turns and we start walking again – slowly.

"Is your grandmother really that bad? Honestly?"

"Worse sometimes! She wants nothing less than perfect and she wants it immediately."

"Great." He pushes his hair back with both his hands.

"She knows what she's talking about, though, I'll give her that."

"Perhaps we should find somewhere to run through some of it now."

"I can't. I'm sorry. Sarah'll be here in a minute to pick me up."

"Your life seems very regimented."

"You'll understand why when you meet my grandmother. Here, hold this, I'll see if I can spot Sarah. Parking's not easy at this time of day – and it's not her strong point either." I hand Stefan my violin and head up towards where Sarah normally waits.

A voice yells at me from behind. "Hey, Jess!" I spin round to see Charlie bounding towards me.

"Charlie?" I can't hide my surprise. "I . . . I didn't think you were back until tomorrow."

He gives me a massive hug. "I'm not supposed to be here but I couldn't wait. Sarah sent me to pick you up, but don't tell Mrs Chamberlain. Apparently we have to avoid being alone together." He laughs and gives me another hug. His voice is too loud, and I glance over at Stefan. What's he heard? He hasn't moved. He's watching, holding my violin.

"We'd better be careful she doesn't find out then," I whisper through gritted teeth. "We're not likely to get a second chance – third in my case." I distance myself from Charlie a little.

"I can't believe you're still here. I thought she'd send you home and I didn't want her to do that. That's why I went." Charlie's eyes are twinkling; he looks so unbelievably happy. "It feels like weeks since I last saw you."

"A lot can happen in a short time."

"Come on," he says, "get in the car. Then you can tell me all about it."

He takes my hand and starts pulling me in the direction he came from. I drag back.

"Hang on, Charlie. I have to get my violin." I pull myself away. "Stefan's got it."

"Who?"

"Stefan."

"What – the Stefan you told me about? From Manchester?" It's Charlie's turn to look surprised.

Stefan still hasn't moved. He looks frozen to the spot. Charlie follows me over and I realize I have to introduce them. "Charlie, this is Stefan, and Stefan, this is Charlie."

They do a kind of boy thing of eyeing each other

up before they shake hands. There's an awkward silence.

"We'd better get going," says Charlie. "Nice to meet you, Stefan." He doesn't hang around, heads back towards the car.

Stefan sticks his hands deep in his pockets. "I thought you said someone called Sarah was picking you up. That's why we couldn't have lunch. Funny-looking Sarah." Stefan's tone is flat, accusing.

"Sarah was picking me up. I wasn't expecting Charlie. He wasn't supposed to be back until tomorrow. I'll have to go now. Sorry."

"Fine. Whatever."

I suddenly realize that Stefan doesn't even know who Charlie is. I can only imagine what must be going through his mind. He hasn't a clue about Charlie or Ciaran or anything. Charlie's still within earshot and I need time to work out how I'm going to explain everything to Stefan.

"Look, don't worry, I'll explain tomorrow," I say.

"If you don't want me to come, I'd rather know."

"What are you talking about? Of course I want you to come." I'm walking backwards now, away from him.

Stefan looks at me as if trying to figure me out.

"Stefan, I'm sorry, I have to go."

Charlie's waiting, arms crossed. I'm making such a mess of this.

"Fine; go then," he says, and strides off in the opposite direction.

"Hey, Stefan," I shout. He turns round. "Don't be late tomorrow." I blow him a kiss.

He gives me the briefest of looks, then keeps walking. Fast.

"What was that about?" says Charlie.

Nightmare.

Chapter 18

I'm angry with Charlie. Angry with him for turning up when he did. Angry with him for breaking Grandmother's new rules. Things have changed.

"Do you want to stop for a walk in the park?" he asks.

"Are you mad? It's more than my life's worth to take any more risks."

Charlie blows out his cheeks. "I'm sorry. You're right. I just don't want to share you with anyone else yet."

My stomach knots up. I've got to tell Charlie that it's over – that our brief one-afternoon fling was just that. I like Charlie a lot – and yes, I did fancy him – but seeing Stefan again has changed everything. Even if Stefan isn't interested in me, I still know that Charlie and I will never work. I wish

I could find a way to say it nicely, but I can't. Instead, I say nothing.

When we stop at traffic lights, he leans over and kisses me. I let him do it. Then I feel terrible. I wish I had someone I could talk to – someone who would tell me what to do. The journey home is painful.

In spite of it all, things are certainly brighter at Grandmother's house now Charlie's back. By Sunday morning, Sarah is her usual self and the old routine is back to normal. Even Grandmother's smiling. Better still, Stefan is coming this afternoon to play for her. Or I hope he is. He hasn't answered a single text since I left him yesterday.

"So, I hear you're playing in the Albert Hall soon," says Charlie over lunch.

"Not quite." I'm not that interested in conversation. I keep texting Stefan. He'll have to answer sooner or later. I've rung him about twenty times since yesterday but it keeps going to his voicemail. I'll kill myself if he doesn't come.

"So where?" Charlie persists.

"Royal College of Music," I say as I press the send button yet again.

If this is what falling in love feels like, then I'm

right there. Everything I do has a crazy intensity. I've had a complete breakthrough with my music in the last few days and I know it's Stefan who's inspired me. And now I want him to hear me; I want to do this with him. He has to come.

Charlie scrapes his chair back from the table. "You're great company," he says.

"Sorry." I get up and carry my plate towards the dishwasher, hardly taking my eyes off my phone.

"Oh, give it to me," says Charlie grumpily and grabs my plate off me.

I go straight back down to the music room. I've spent most of the day in here. It's been one of those slow-fast days. I don't quite have enough time to do all the practice I want, yet every time I look at the clock it doesn't seem any closer to four. The last half hour drags so slowly I almost give up.

"That's sounding good," says Sarah as she comes in with a cup of tea. I'm relieved it's her and not Charlie. "I hope your friend knows not to be late. That wouldn't be a good way to start with your grandmother."

"I've told him. I've been trying to call him but he's not answering any of my messages."

"Oh dear."

I text one more time. **Where the hell are you?**

"Charlie's gone to pick up Mr Ritchie," says Sarah. "They should be back any minute. Did you know he was coming to join you?"

"I had a fair idea," I say, "but it won't be much good if Stefan doesn't turn up."

Coming flashes up on my phone and I punch the air.

"Good news?" says Sarah.

"I hope so. He's on his way."

"Good. Perhaps you can calm down now. You've been like a coiled spring all day."

From the basement window, I see Grandmother's car pull up outside the house. I run up the stairs two at a time to catch Mr Ritchie before Grandmother gets to him.

"Hello, Jessica. How are you getting on?" He straightens his tie.

"Better than a week ago."

He chuckles. "Brute of a thing, that concerto — don't envy you one bit."

"I'm taming it — slowly!"

"Good girl. Don't tame it too much."

Mr Ritchie makes slow progress towards the

drawing room and I stay beside him, glad of the time.

"Now," he says, wheezing slightly, "I want to hear all about this accompanist of yours."

"Stefan?"

"Yes, Stefan Montgomery."

"Has Grandmother told you anything about him?"

"Not much. Anyway, I'd prefer your version."

"Well, he's a big fan of yours. Apparently he's studied you in great detail."

"Oh dear. How terribly dull for the poor boy. He probably knows things about me that I don't know myself."

"Probably, knowing Stefan. And he loves Blüthner pianos, so you have something in common."

"Interesting. I like him already. What else?"

"He's eighteen – comes from near Manchester – not near me, though. I met him a couple of years ago when we started playing together. We didn't get on that well at first. We're very different."

"That's sometimes a good thing."

"Maybe. We definitely cleaned up a few prizes. Now he's studying at the RCM, which came as a surprise, to be honest. I thought he was going to study in Manchester."

"A nice surprise, I hope?"

Grandmother is waiting for us at the door to the drawing room.

"Jessica's been telling me about Mr Montgomery," he says to her as we walk in. "She was just saying she was surprised that he was studying at the RCM."

Grandmother raises her eyebrows. "I would have thought it was the logical place for him to study," she says.

"There *are* other music colleges," says Mr Ritchie. He turns to me. "Your grandmother tells me he's very good, but I want to know what you think. Do you enjoy playing together? Do you have a strong connection?"

"I'm sure that will become obvious when we hear them play," Grandmother snaps. Her sharp voice makes me nervous; her mood seems tense. Not good.

Smack on four, the doorbell rings. Stefan's timed it to the second. He must've been waiting down the road, hiding behind a tree or something. I run out to meet him before Grandmother can stop me. Sarah's taking his coat. Charlie is leaning in the doorway of the kitchen, watching, his face fixed into hard angles. He glances towards me, goes back into the kitchen and closes the door.

Stefan walks into the light and I'm immediately shocked. He looks as though he hasn't slept for days.

"Are you OK?" I whisper. "You look awful."

"Thanks."

"Why the hell didn't you reply to me? I must've sent you a hundred messages."

"I was trying to practise. You weren't helping."

"Well, so-rree. Anyway, I have a surprise for you."

"What?" He sounds completely uninterested.

"George Ritchie is here."

"I'm not in the mood, Jess."

"I'm not joking. He's in there with Grandmother." I nod towards the door.

"Really?" Stefan's face brightens for a moment, then fades again, and he covers his face with his hands.

"What's the matter? I thought you'd be pleased."

"I'm exhausted, to be honest."

"I can see that. You'd better buck up a bit before we go in and meet them."

"Right." He doesn't move.

"Come on."

He looks at me almost desperately.

"Hey, it's OK." I give him an encouraging shove. "Come *on*."

This is not starting well, but the way Mr Ritchie greets Stefan, you'd think they'd known each other for years. He doesn't stop talking. I watch as he coaxes Stefan back to life. In contrast, Grandmother's face creases with irritation and, though it's quite funny, I wish Mr Ritchie would shut up. Eventually Grandmother orders us down to the music room.

Getting Mr Ritchie on and off the stairlift is a palaver. At the bottom Stefan takes his arm and helps him into the music room. Mr Ritchie rests against the piano, his hand gently patting the wood.

"Lovely instrument," he says.

Stefan lifts the lid and gazes at the piano, smiling. The smile isn't forced, but I can tell he's not relaxed.

"I'll sit with Stefan, if that's all right," says Mr Ritchie, making his way round the back of the piano.

I can feel Stefan's nerves as if they're my own. I watch him sit down, fumble with the seat adjustment, then rub his hands together. It's the same old routine but today there's an edge to it. I smile at him but he doesn't respond.

He plays some scales and arpeggios, his fingers running up and down the piano. I do the same, but it's Stefan's fingers I'm watching, reminding myself, trying to regain the connection. It's been months since we've played.

Mr Ritchie is listening intently, his head cocked to one side.

"I think we will go straight into the first movement of the Sibelius," barks Grandmother through the noise. "I take it you've prepared?" she says to Stefan.

"I haven't had much time. . ."

"Obviously," says Grandmother, cutting him off. "I realize that you have had no chance to rehearse together. I am not expecting performance standard."

"Don't take it too fast," I say to him, "but don't let it drag either, or it'll sound too heavy." I give him the tempo, slightly slower than ideal, then nod for him to begin.

It's the first time I've played this with accompaniment and I know how I want it to sound. I want Stefan to remember how good we can be and, more than that, we need to show Grandmother and Mr Ritchie what we can do. We begin and it's sort of OK. I try to lead Stefan through, but he's not getting it at all. His playing is distracted, dull. It's pulling me away from the music. In fact, it's hopeless. There's no point in carrying on. I drop my violin to my hip.

Stefan stops and looks at me, questioning.

"What are you doing?" I say.

He spreads his hands.

"I thought I said *don't* let it drag." I snap the words out angrily, and everyone is looking at me.

"I think you are being a little harsh, Jessica," says Mr Ritchie. "Stefan hasn't accompanied you for a while and he isn't as familiar with this music as you are."

"It's not that hard," I reply.

I see a look pass between Mr Ritchie and Grandmother. "Perhaps," he says to Stefan, softening his voice, "I could give you a short demonstration. I think it might help."

Stefan seems more than happy to get up from the piano stool and allow Mr Ritchie to take his place. This is not what was supposed to happen.

"I don't need to hear you play this music, George," says Grandmother. "It's Stefan I want to hear."

"You will," says Mr Ritchie, "later."

I'm surprised Grandmother doesn't argue.

"Ready?" says Mr Ritchie, looking at me. I lift my violin. Part of me is glad Stefan will get to hear Mr Ritchie play.

We begin again. Mr Ritchie murmurs instructions to Stefan. "This bit, like this . . . and then hold here . . . and on. . ." I lose his words, hear only the music. At the end, Mr Ritchie nods at me slowly.

"Bravo, Jessica," he says, "it is coming on very well." But there's no warmth in his voice and I know he's angry with me.

Grandmother has her eyes closed and her lips pressed tightly together. It's obviously not come on well enough for her liking.

"Now, Tara," says Mr Ritchie, "perhaps we could both do with a drink and we'll leave these two to work on the music for a short while." He turns to me. "We'll be back in, say, an hour?"

I nod. With any luck a large gin will sort them both out.

Stefan is busy thanking Mr Ritchie and he helps him back to the stairs. Finally we are alone. Now we can get our heads wrapped round this.

"That was a disaster," he says. "Thanks for your support, by the way."

"No need to be sarcastic. What were you doing?"

"I was doing my best. What did you expect first time round?"

"Don't be lame. You can play better than that."

"What if I can't? Perhaps you're right. Perhaps I am *lame*. We obviously can't work together any more."

"Oh, grow up. You know me and my big mouth. I just wanted it to be perfect, that's all. I wanted to impress them."

"That's not what I mean."

"What, then?" "I'm so far behind. I'll never catch up."

"That's rubbish. We need time to get the feel of playing together again and then we'll be fine."

Stefan shakes his head. "Forget it, Jess."

I sigh. "I've only got the hang of this in the last few days. It's taken me weeks. You'll get a hold on it soon."

"I feel like an amateur. It's hopeless."

"Hey, come on. You can't compare yourself to Mr Ritchie. He's a master. He's been doing this for about a hundred years."

"I'm not comparing myself to Mr Ritchie. Have

you listened to yourself recently? Like really listened? Your playing is unrecognizable. It's brilliant. You're a genius – way out of my league."

"You don't need to flatter me. It evidently wasn't good enough for Her Majesty."

Stefan stretches out his arms along the length of the keyboard and drops his head on to the piano, making the notes clash together. I've never seen him like this before. I move behind him, put my hands on his shoulders, then gently massage his neck. The muscles relax a little.

"Are you going to tell me what's really wrong? I've never seen you so tense."

"I've just told you."

"I don't believe you. There's something else."

"And you're honestly going to tell me you don't know?"

"Know what?"

I feel his muscles bunch again and he shakes me off. Stands up.

"Oh for goodness' sake. This is stupid. I've had enough."

"Chill out. There's no need to get in such a stress."

He slams his music into his case, snaps the case shut and bolts up the stairs. It takes me a moment to register what's happening. I can't believe he's being serious. By the time I decide to chase after him, it's too late. He's out of the front door and off down the street.

"Come back!" I yell after him, but he keeps running. "Idiot," I shout and slam the door. I'm not sure if I mean him or me. I turn around to find Charlie standing at my shoulder.

"Do you want me to run after him?" he asks. "I'll catch him up pretty quickly."

I barge straight past him without even answering and storm into the drawing room.

"He's gone," I say.

"Are you surprised?" asks Mr Ritchie. "You weren't kind to him. Not kind at all. I would have left a lot earlier if I were him."

"Yes, you would," says Grandmother. She looks as though she has more to say but she must think better of it because she smiles instead.

"Does Stefan always have such an artistic temperament?" she asks me.

"No. Not at all. Please, you have to do something, I don't want to work with anyone else."

"You should have thought of before denting his pride so badly," says Mr Ritchie.

"My granddaughter is nothing if not impetuous," says Grandmother. "I think we all know that by now."

I fling myself into a chair.

"I'm not sure he's up to it anyway," she says. "Whatever spark of connection there was between him and Jessica seems to have gone, even at the most basic level."

"Come now, Tara. I've heard enough of his playing to know he's perfectly up to it. A touch of nerves, that's all. Which puts him and Jess on an even footing. I suspect that spark can be rekindled."

"Not according to Stefan," I say. "He's got it in his head that I'm too good for him – which is rubbish. And he says he doesn't want to work with me any more. He's such an arrogant. . ." I kick the table leg hard. Grandmother scowls at me.

"He'll come round," says Mr Ritchie. "He'll go away and do some hard work and then he'll be back when he's ready. That's what I'd do if I were Stefan."

"But you are *not* Stefan, are you?" says Grandmother.

"As an accompanist, I can relate to Mr Montgomery. Now I suggest the two of you leave

Stefan to me. I don't want either of you to contact him for a few days. Do you understand? He needs some peace to sort a few things out."

"I can't sit here and do nothing," I say. "I'll have to ring him at least."

"Take some advice for once, young lady. Let him be."

"What, not contact him at all? And if you're wrong?"

"If I'm wrong, I'm wrong. We'll deal with that outcome if we have to."

"I hope you're right then."

Mr Ritchie looks at me over the top of his glasses. "I have to tell you, Jessica, I am disappointed in your behaviour today. You should never criticize a friend's musicianship in front of others."

"Well, Stefan's done it to me," I say, "so it won't hurt him to have a taste of his own medicine."

"Personally I think it was Stefan who behaved badly today," says Grandmother. "He was poorly prepared and he left without a word of thanks."

Mr Ritchie glares at Grandmother. "I trust you will let him return when he is ready?"

"That will be Jessica's decision." I look from one to the other. It's the first time that Grandmother has ever openly supported me. The trouble is, it doesn't solve anything.

"Unfortunately," I say, "there is only one person who will decide if Stefan will come back, and that person is Stefan."

"Exactly," says Mr Ritchie. "Give him time, Jessica. Give him time."

Chapter 19

Three days pass and there's no word from Stefan. Nothing. I've used up every bit of self-control to stop myself from calling. I knew Mr Ritchie was wrong. He doesn't know Stefan like I do. If Stefan doesn't call me by Friday evening, I'm calling him – whatever.

At four o'clock on Friday there's still nothing. I close my theory books and put my head on my desk. What if Stefan thinks I've given up on him? What if he's waiting for me to call? I'll give him till six.

The hands of the clock move slower than slow while I sit on my hands, staring at my phone. There's no one home except Sarah and me. Charlie's taken Grandmother to some concert, as usual. I'm glad he's out of the house. I've been trying to avoid him and he knows it. I can tell by his eyes. I tell him it's Grandmother's rules and he can't argue with that. But it's still awkward.

Don't contact him. I hear Mr Ritchie's words over and over as the minutes count down towards six.

OK, one more day. Maybe I'll give him one more day. Maybe he's waiting to see me at the RCM tomorrow. But what if he's not? I don't even care if he never wants to play for me again; I want to see him.

I have to do something or I'll go out of my mind thinking about him. I go down to the music room, switch on my iPod, put the headphones on and crank up the third movement of the Sibelius to full volume. I lie on the floor, close my eyes and let the music take over. It suits my mood. I drift between the real world and the world of the music.

∫ ∫

It's funny how you know someone is there, even with your eyes closed. I pray it's not Charlie. I don't know what time he's due home. The last thing I need is some confrontation. It'll have to come sometime but not now – please not now. I keep my eyes tight shut. There is still someone there. I can feel them near me now.

"Go away," I say, and open one eye.

I sit up fast. It's him – hair everywhere, dark lines around his eyes, crumpled clothes. He looks worse than last time.

"Stefan? What are you doing here? Why didn't you tell me you were coming?" I scramble to my feet. I'm looking equally horrible in a hideous baggy old tracksuit. I turn off the music.

"Can I ask you something?" he says. "You must answer truthfully." His intensity is slightly unnerving. He's almost manic.

"What?"

"Are you and Charlie – you know – is something going on between you and Charlie?"

"Me and Charlie? No!"

"Are you sure?"

"Sure I'm sure. I mean, we're close. But he's more like a brother. He's twenty-three. Much too old for me." I hate myself for the lie – but it's not really a lie. There is nothing going on between us – not any more.

Stefan takes a step towards me and gently puts

his hands on either side of my face. "Good. I just needed to check before I did this."

Before I can blink, his mouth is on mine and he's kissing me so passionately I can hardly breathe. I don't want to breathe. I could die happy like this. It's hard to smile and kiss at the same time.

He stops. "Sorry," he says. "I've been waiting to do that for nearly two years."

I'm looking into his eyes and seeing all the uncertainty and I'm trying to catch up with myself. I can still taste his lips on mine and I want him to kiss me again, just in case it wasn't real the first time. He takes a step back.

"Don't go," I say.

"I thought you might hit me." He's smiling, and I kiss him again.

"You never said anything."

"You must've known."

I shake my head.

"I could never work you out," he says. "I didn't know what you thought. I've never met anyone like you before."

"What, someone common, you mean?" I laugh. "All that wasted time when I convinced myself you didn't like me."

"We can make up for it." He slides his arms around my waist and pulls me towards him. We stand in the absolute silence of the room and let our bodies melt together, my forehead on his chest, his chin on the top of my head. I breathe him in.

"I've been working on the Sibelius all week," he says. "I know this is going to sound stupid, but would you mind if we played it? Now?"

"Now?" I tilt my face up towards him and he kisses me gently, and then not so gently, and I'm still trying to convince myself it's real. "I can think of things I'd rather do."

"Me too, but I need to prove something to myself."

He looks serious and I immediately understand. That suffocating insecurity. I thought it was just me. I hold him tighter.

"Please?" he says. He pushes me back so he can look at me and I can almost hear words pouring from those troubled eyes.

"Come on, then," I smile, "but don't expect me to play well – I'm not even sure I can hold my violin after what you've just done!"

"Good, that'll make me sound better."

He sits at the piano and plays the opening bars.

I watch him as I begin but his focus is on the piano. He's disappeared into the music. Every note wraps itself around my heart and that's where I want to keep it. And I do play well, and so does he, and we both know that we have found what was lost.

The end is sudden and the silence is full. He doesn't need me to tell him he can do it. He's proved everything he needs to prove. I wish I could say what I really feel. I wish I could tell him he's brilliant, that I love him for going away and getting this perfect, that I love him full stop. But I'd only make a fool of myself. So I just smile.

He beckons me over to him and pulls me down on to his lap. My back rests against his chest and I can feel his heart beating.

"I've hardly slept all week," he whispers. His lips are close to my neck and I lean back into his shoulder.

"I can tell. You must have been working on the Sibelius non-stop. How did you get it so perfect so quickly?"

"It's not perfect. Nowhere near. But daily visits from George Ritchie helped a lot."

"Oh." I suppose I should've guessed. I shake my head. I should've known Mr Ritchie had a plan. That he was on our side.

"I didn't ask him to come." Stefan idly plays a few notes on the piano. "It was his idea. He's amazing. I don't know what I would have done without him. I couldn't bear the thought of letting you down."

I give him a gentle nudge. "You couldn't bear the thought of letting yourself down, more like."

"OK. That too."

I stroke his forearm, trace the thin blue veins down to his wrist and back up again. "Play me something," I say.

"I can't, not with you sitting there."

"Try."

He stretches round me and rests his chin on my shoulder. I'm happy to watch his hands and his fingers move over the notes. The tune is simple but sad. I don't recognize it. It's beautiful.

"I've never heard that before," I say. "What is it?"

"I wrote it for you when I was in Italy, when I thought I'd never see you again."

I don't trust myself to speak.

"That probably sounds pathetic," he says.

"Totally." We laugh.

He runs his hand along the piano keys again. "It's his," he says.

"What's whose?"

"This piano. It's George Ritchie's."

"Is it? What's it doing here?"

"He didn't say, but this might have something to do with it." He stretches down and pulls something out of his music case. It's an old book. "Mr Ritchie gave this to me yesterday. It's about his early life. It's not in print any more so it's quite special."

I take it, flick through, stop at a photo I recognize.

"Grandmother's got this photo of him upstairs."

"Has she? That's interesting."

Stefan's voice makes me curious. He puts the book down on the keyboard and starts flicking through the pages until he stops at an appendix that gives a long list of Mr Ritchie's performances.

"Look," he says.

"Wow." I run my eyes over the dates and places. "And this is only his early career."

"You're not looking."

I pick up the book. Stefan points. I read.

1956, Royal College of Music. Tara Chamberlain
(violin – debut performance).
Sibelius Violin Concerto in D Minor, Op. 47.

I frown at the words, not believing what I'm seeing, not making sense of what this is telling me.

"Grandmother playing the violin?"

"It looks that way."

"The Sibelius?" I shake my head. "It's not possible. It must be a mistake."

"I don't think so. It's unlikely they would get it wrong."

"Not as unlikely as Grandmother performing a violin concerto with George Ritchie."

"You think?"

"She would've said something, wouldn't she? I mean, why would she keep it secret that she's a violinist? Particularly if she's performed this wretched concerto."

"It might explain why she chose it."

"No. You're wrong. She'd have told me."

"Perhaps she thought it would put too much pressure on you."

"Pressure? She loves putting pressure on me. Thrives on it." I look at the book again. Stefan slowly rubs his hands up and down my arms.

"It makes no sense," I say, still staring at the words. "I was talking about it to Mum on the phone only the other day. She said Grandmother didn't play an instrument. Mum would know after living with her for thirty-six years."

"Look, I'm not saying your mum isn't telling the truth, but it does make it slightly hard to explain the fact your grandmother did a concert with Mr Ritchie."

"If it is a fact." I turn the pages, skimming through the long list of concerts and performances. "Did Mr Ritchie say anything to you when he gave you this book?"

"No, not really; said he thought I might enjoy reading about his early experiences. I only spotted the bit about your grandmother because I was interested to know how many times he'd performed the Sibelius."

"But do you think that's why he gave you the book – because he knew you'd find it?"

"Possibly."

"Anyway, why did he give it to *you*? She's *my* grandmother."

Stefan pushes me up gently and turns me round so we're sitting face to face. "I'll tell you what I think, as long as you promise not to laugh."

His hands press gently on my back. He doesn't start speaking immediately and I wait, enjoying our physical closeness.

"I wasn't in a great space last week. I spent a lot of time with George: playing the piano, talking, drinking."

"Drinking? With Mr Ritchie?" I try to make it sound jokey but I feel left out.

Stefan looks away from me. "I had stuff I needed to deal with. But that's not the point. He knows how I feel about you, Jess. I suppose it's pretty obvious. He knows I was desperate not to let you down. And he told me about a girl he'd been in love with when he was young. He thought it would help."

"Help what?"

"Help convince me that I could work with you again. He told me not to give up until I'd won you back. Or I think that's what he said." He laughs nervously. "Sounds silly now."

I rest my forehead against his.

"The thing is . . . he gave me the strong impression that this girl was your grandmother."

This takes a few seconds to sink in. "Mr Ritchie and Grandmother?"

"He didn't admit it as such, but it's not such a crazy idea, is it?"

"It's completely crazy."

He tilts my chin up with his fingers and his lips

are on mine, briefly, as if trying to convince me. "I think Mr Ritchie was in love with your grandmother and I think he still is."

I stand up, pace across the room and back. I can't think at all being this close to Stefan. "Well, if Mr Ritchie was in love with her, it must've been one-sided."

"Why?"

I'm pleased I know something that Stefan doesn't.

"Mum was born in 1957, July the twelfth. This concert was in 1956. You see: Tara *Chamberlain*. Grandmother was already married and she can only have been – what – twenty? Doesn't exactly give Mr Ritchie much of a look-in, does it?"

"Who was she married to?"

"Mr Chamberlain, I suppose. He died before Mum was born. Grandmother obviously loved him very much because she can't talk about him at all, even now, not even to Mum."

"Mrs Chamberlain." Stefan's tapping the book with his fingers. "What was her maiden name?"

"No idea."

"Don't you know anything about your family?"

"Not much."

x

335

"You'll have to ask your mum, she'll know. Then we might be able to find out more about your grandmother's early career."

"There's a lot about my family I haven't told you," I say.

"I haven't told you much about mine either – not that there's much to tell. We haven't had any time together, that's the problem. I don't even know how you came to be in London." Stefan comes over and wraps me in his arms, then pulls me down so we're sitting on the floor, cross-legged, backs against the wall. Our knees just touch.

"So go on," he says. "Tell me."

Where do I start? I tell him, as simply as I can, about what happened after my scholarship performance, about running away to London and about Mum's upbringing with Grandmother and how she ran off with Dad.

Stefan pushes his hair back with both hands. "Phew," he says. "Some story. I suppose that might explain why your grandmother and Mr Ritchie only played together once. Imagine losing your husband and having a baby." Stefan shakes his head as if he's trying to get his brain wrapped round the idea. "Perhaps it also explains why Mr Ritchie didn't marry until very late. Maybe he hoped he could win your grandmother over. Wasn't going to happen, though, was it? Not from what you've told me. Sounds like your grandmother has never managed to let go."

"Does Mr Ritchie have any children?" I don't know why I've never asked him.

"No. He told me he was sad about that."

"Mum said he was always very kind to her."

I lean over and rest against Stefan's shoulder, both of us silently thinking.

"And what about Charlie?" he asks.

"What do you mean?" It comes out sounding defensive. I don't want to talk about Charlie.

"Well, something must have happened. I'm not so stupid. You told me you'd been in trouble with your grandmother. From what I overheard of your conversation, Charlie was in trouble too. So what happened?"

"Oh, it was nothing, really." I keep my voice bright as I tell Stefan about Ciaran and the band and how Charlie and I visited them in Ealing instead of going to museums and how Grandmother found out.

"So she sent Charlie away and gated you just for that? Sounds a little unreasonable."

I know I have to tell him. "Stefan – when I said that there is nothing going on between Charlie and me, I wasn't lying. There isn't. But there was one afternoon in the park – on my birthday. I'd drunk too much champagne and . . . you know how it is. And then when we got back here Charlie came down to the music room and Grandmother walked in when he was kissing me. . ."

Stefan puts his finger against my lips and smiles. "It doesn't matter," he whispers, "and I guess Hattie and I . . . these things happen, but it doesn't mean anything. In fact, I'd rather not think about it!"

I shake my head and we both laugh.

"Come here," says Stefan and kisses me again. Then he groans. "I'm going to have to go soon." He glances at his watch. "Shit, is that the time? I had no idea it was that late. I'm meeting my parents for dinner." He's already on his feet.

"Don't go." I'm desperate for him not to leave.

"I have to."

"When am I going to see you? Can we meet on Saturday after my ensemble?"

"Can't. My parents are staying."

"So when?"

"Phone me. I can't think now. The following

Saturday, for sure. I'll come over in the afternoon so we can rehearse."

"That's ages away."

"Ring me!" He flies out of the door. About ten seconds later he runs back in again, grabs me, kisses me, then rushes out again.

I laugh.

"You're amazing!" he shouts as he runs towards the stairs.

"I love you!" he yells from halfway up. "But don't tell anyone!"

As if the whole street doesn't know by now! I'm glad it's only Sarah home.

I let everything fizz for a while. Finally I sit at the piano and rest my hands on the keys. I close my eyes and feel Stefan's fingers on mine, his lips on my neck. And I think of Grandmother and George Ritchie. It makes no sense, and I know I'm missing something important. I go through everything again, searching for threads that might help. Everything leads nowhere.

I think about the Sibelius violin concerto and I'm certain, somewhere in that passionate tangle of music, I will find the answer.

Chapter 20

I have no idea what Mum does or doesn't know about Grandmother and I don't want to upset her. There are questions I want answered, but I'll have to think carefully about how I ask them. I practise a few ideas; try not to sound too probing. Once I'm ready, I ring, but she doesn't pick up. I suppose she'll be at work. Impatient, I send her a text.

Ring me when you can chat.

Next morning, at the RCM, rehearsal drags on and on.

Charlie comes to pick me up and he's in a filthy mood. I ignore it for a while but then it starts bugging me.

"What's up?" It comes out more unfriendly than I'd intended.

"You tell me."

I stare out of the car window. I don't know what he's expecting me to say so I say nothing. He turns off into a side street and stops the car. I know this means trouble.

"Saturdays aren't the same any more without our trips to Ealing," he says.

"Well, there's not much we can do about that. They're away in Ireland and you and I aren't supposed to spend time alone together. In fact, I'm amazed Grandmother's allowed you to pick me up today."

"She hasn't. Sarah was supposed to come."

"Charlie, that's the second time you've done that. She'll throw you out again if she discovers."

"She won't – discover, I mean."

"That's what we said last time."

"Anyway, what's it to you if she does throw me out? You seem to have moved on pretty quickly."

"Meaning what, exactly?" My heart is beating fast.

"You know what I mean."

"No, I don't. And for your information, I would care if Grandmother gave you the sack."

"I'm talking about Stefan." Charlie says his name with such aggression it makes me shrink back in my seat.

"Stefan?"

"Sarah told me. She thought it was funny. That shaggy-haired drip running up the stairs shouting about being in love with you."

"He is not a shaggy-haired drip."

"So it's true, then."

I cover my face with my hands. I don't know what I can say.

"Jess?" Charlie pulls my hands away from my face and holds them. "I know we can't afford to get into any more trouble with your grandmother, but that doesn't change the way I feel about you."

I try to meet his eyes. Whatever I say, it's going to come out sounding cheesy. "Charlie, I really like you. I mean that. But I'm too young for you. You're twenty-three. I'm seventeen. And there's too much at stake for both of us."

"So you prefer Stefan. That's what you're saying."

"Stefan is . . . I didn't know he was going to be in London. It was pure chance we met up. I've known Stefan for years — we've worked together for years. I've told you that."

"But you're not just working together now. There's more, isn't there? Or was there always more?"

"I don't know. Maybe there was. But neither of quite realized how the other one felt."

"You seem to have realized pretty quick since meeting up again. You haven't exactly wasted much time."

"That's none of your business."

Charlie gives a loud laugh. "None of my business? You've got no idea, have you? Have you thought, at all, about how I feel? You're right. You are too young for me." He starts the car and hits the accelerator. "Oh, and don't expect me to come running round after you any more. I've wasted enough of my time trying to stick up for you with Mrs Chamberlain. I don't know why I bothered. You can fight your own battles now."

"Don't be like that, Charlie. Can't we at least. . ."

"If you're going to ask if we can be friends, no, we can't. Forget it."

We drive home in silence. My phone rings. I'm desperate to answer it but I don't. Even I can see that it wouldn't be fair to start talking to Stefan now with Charlie sitting there. So we both listen to the ringtone as it cuts through the silence.

As soon as we're home, Charlie heads straight off up the stairs. I check my messages. It wasn't Stefan; it was Mum. I ring her straight away.

"Hello, stranger," she says.

"Sorry. I know I haven't called for ages. There's been a lot going on."

"Good things, I hope."

"Some."

Mum tells me about Dad's new job as handyman at the rest home. Apparently he's much better now he's back working again. And Aunt Molly's got her leg in plaster.

"And how are you?" she asks. "Recovered?"

"Yeah. Eventually. Tired. A lot of rehearsal."

"And how is my mother?"

"All right. Same as usual."

"No surprises there, then."

If only she knew.

"I was wondering," I say. "What was her maiden name – before Chamberlain?"

"Chamberlain is her maiden name."

"But she's *Mrs* Chamberlain."

"Yes, I know. She once told me her married name was unpronounceable, so she kept her maiden name for professional reasons. And with my father dead, well, I suppose it made sense. My grandfather was Colonel Chamberlain. Not that I ever met him. The first time I went to his house was for the funeral. He lived in Dorset. I don't think my mother got on with him very well."

"What is it with our family? Doesn't anyone get on?"

Mum doesn't answer. I can hear the TV going in the background.

"So you never took your father's name," I say.

"No."

"And you don't know what it was?"

"What is this? Twenty questions? No, I don't."

"Isn't it on your birth certificate or something?" I realize I'm not doing a good job of not probing, but I can't hold myself back.

"No. I was registered as Susan Chamberlain."

"Isn't that odd?"

Mum sighs. "Not really. I had no father. My mother was working as Tara Chamberlain and it would've been confusing for me to be something different."

"Didn't you ever want to know more about him? Weren't you curious?"

Mum sighs again. "I've told you before – Mother

couldn't stand me talking about Father. If I even mentioned the word she got angry. When I was a teenager, I was desperate to know more, and I nagged on and on. Mother said if I mentioned the word *Father* one more time, she'd lock me in the boiler room. I didn't believe her – which was a mistake. The first time she only locked me down there for about ten minutes. That was bad enough. The next time it was for an hour. I stopped asking after that."

I'm so shocked I don't know what to say. Even over the phone I think I can hear a slight quaver in her voice.

"I'm sorry. You should've told me."

"No, I shouldn't. It's not something I like to talk about."

"There's a lot our family doesn't like to talk about."

"Anyway, perhaps now you understand why we didn't want you to go to London."

"Well, you needn't worry. The only time I spend in the basement is in the music room."

"The music room? Which room is that?"

"On the left at the bottom of the stairs. It looks as though it's been done up quite recently. It's freshly painted. New carpets and all."

"That used to be the old storeroom. The boiler room was the one at the end on the right. It's probably been done up as well. A gym or something."

"Who for? Grandmother?" I laugh. It's a chance to break the tension. "If it was a gym, she would've had me in there for sure – with Rosie making me do endless weights. So I think we can rule that out. In fact, I've never taken any notice of what's at the far end. No one seems to go down there. I'll check it out." I say it flippantly but I'm curious. The idea of Mum being locked in some room in the basement is horrible, but I can't help wanting to see for myself now she's told me.

"It wasn't all bad in the end," says Mum.

"How can being locked in a basement be not bad?"

"I'll let you in on a secret if you like."

"Go on then." This'll be a first, Mum letting me in on a secret. How many secrets can one family have?

"Your dad and I used to meet in the boiler room when we were courting."

"Courting! That makes you sound about a hundred."

"Dating, then, or whatever you say now. Once my mother was in bed, Dad used to sneak down the stone steps behind the railings and climb in the basement window. My mother kept the room locked, but I'd seen her hide the key behind the radiator. It was the easiest way your dad and me could find to meet without Mother knowing or getting suspicious, and it saved me finding excuses to go out. She always wanted to know where I was going, what I was doing, when I'd be back . . . it was so hard."

Mum's sounding really upset now and it's my fault, but it's interesting hearing her talk. Some of it sounds so familiar. A pattern. Not so bad now, but still a pattern.

Mum clears her throat and immediately brightens. "It was a tiny window," she says. "God knows how he got through." She gives a deep sigh, loud enough for me to hear clearly. "Anyway, why the endless questions?"

"I'm trying to fill in a few gaps; trying to get to know my grandmother better."

"Good luck." She doesn't sound optimistic and I don't know why I don't tell her the truth. Except I'm not sure what the truth is. Something tells me to keep my mouth shut.

"Are you sure you're all right?" asks Mum.

"Yeah. I'm fine."

"Not long till you're home."

We witter on for a few more minutes, but I'm not paying much attention. She's given me too much to think about. My mind is full of pictures of Grandmother and Mum. I imagine Grandmother dragging her down to the basement like some witch in a fairy tale. It makes me feel ill. Then I imagine Dad squeezing through some tiny window to secretly meet with Mum. Was I the result of them meeting in that room? I don't think about that for too long. And if Chamberlain is Grandmother's maiden name, how do I find out her married name if Mum doesn't know? I blow a stream of air out through my lips, breaking it into a staccato rhythm.

That night I lie in bed listening to the night-time noises. Distant sirens, the occasional car. I try to ring Stefan but it switches to voicemail. He must be rehearsing or asleep.

As the night drags on, the house becomes silent, but my brain is buzzing. I'm never going to get to sleep. At two a.m. I sneak downstairs and try the door to Grandmother's office. Perhaps I can find something. It's locked, of course. I look around for obvious places to hide a key, but there's nothing. I give up and go back to bed. How can I find more information? Was Mr Ritchie really in love with Grandmother? Did they really perform together? I hope it will all become clear in my dreams.

It doesn't. Instead, when I finally drift off into a restless sleep, I dream of Stefan – and Charlie.

Chapter 21

Stefan, Stefan, Stefan. Life in London is so complicated. Every time I think about him I get that strange swirling feeling inside and it bugs me because I can't control it. I want so much to be with him but we never get any time alone together and the air between us almost hums with frustration. With each rehearsal it gets worse. I can't be this close to him without going mad. I don't want to look at him because I'm frightened I'll lose control – but how can we play together if we don't look at each other?

Grandmother's promise to help me has resulted in her sitting in on every rehearsal with Stefan. Just when I want her to leave me alone, she is always there. But I'm convinced now that Stefan is right. She's played all this stuff. I can't understand why I didn't put two and two together before. She never touches my violin or tries to demonstrate, but it's the comments she makes. They're not a critic's comments, they're a violinist's comments: insightful, sharp, condescending.

I'm bursting to ask her about her time as a musician, but I can't. And as for the rest? I've told Stefan about Grandmother locking Mum in the boiler room and he agrees we need to keep everything we've discovered under wraps until December. I need to survive until my concert is over, and that means staying out of trouble.

"Be patient," Stefan says dismally over the phone. "It's not long until Christmas and then we'll both be back in Manchester."

"Christmas is months away."

"You think I don't feel the same? But whatever we do, we can't risk getting into trouble with your grandmother. So, we do nothing wrong, and we say nothing to her about what we know. Don't blow it, Jess, not now. There's too much at stake."

"There's always too much at stake where Grandmother's concerned. How can you be so bloody sensible all the time?"

And if it's not Grandmother rehearsing with us, it's Dr McNair or Mr Ritchie and Helena. We're bound together in this incredible music, every moment of eye contact held for a breath too long, the effort of keeping my emotions under control spreading tension all the way through my body, through every nerve and muscle and all the way to my bow. I can't work like this. It's affecting every aspect of my playing. Which is probably why Grandmother wants to speak to me in her office. I slump my way up the stairs, scuffing my toes on the carpet.

I find her at her desk, as usual. She looks tired — very tired.

"Come in, Jessica. I need to talk to you."

This doesn't sound like the beginning of one of her lectures. I wait.

"I know it is getting close to your performance, but I am afraid I have to go away. It is unexpected, urgent."

"Where are you going?" I'm both intrigued and excited. I try not to show either.

"The Czech Republic. Prague. George and I go sometimes for the music." She trails off.

It hardly sounds unexpected or urgent. I wonder if she's lying. It makes no difference to me. The fact is, she's going away, and as far as I'm concerned, that's brilliant news.

"We will be leaving on Friday. Charles will accompany us. George can't manage by himself any more." She shuffles papers on her desk.

"How long are you going for?"

"About a week. But you and Stefan mustn't worry. I will leave detailed notes for your rehearsals."

"Thank you," I say, and smile.

A whole week without Grandmother. I'm so excited that I have to scrunch my toes up and down to stop myself from leaping up and dancing round the room. I want to run and tell Stefan straight away.

"You must promise me that you and Stefan will adhere to your rehearsal schedule."

"Of course we will."

"And you won't do anything stupid while I'm away."

I wonder what she defines as stupid. I promise her anyway. She narrows her eyes.

"Sarah will be responsible for you. You wouldn't want to get her into trouble, would you?"

"No."

"I needn't remind you what happened last time?"

"I've promised – OK?"

She holds up her hand, almost as an apology. "I feel very bad about the timing of this trip," she says. "I want you to know that I think you and Stefan are doing very well. Though the tempo of the third movement is too slow."

This is a different Grandmother. Gentler. It's too much all at once. She's being nice to me and she's going away. I look down trying to hide my emotions.

"Don't doubt yourself, Jessica. I think you can do it." She takes both my hands and her eyes are soft. For a moment I can't move. I think I'm the first to step away and she immediately turns and busies herself with papers on her desk.

I escape from her office and close the door, leaning against it for a few seconds. Then I leap up the stairs to my room and ring Stefan.

For the rest of the week, I barely see Grandmother. On Friday morning, I sit with Charlie and Sarah in the kitchen and swirl the dregs of my tea in the bottom of my cup. The suitcases are lined up in the hall.

My phone is on the table and it keeps buzzing as Stefan texts every few minutes.

"He's a bit keen, isn't he?" says Charlie.

"How d'you know who it is?"

"A wild guess," he says sarcastically. He gets up and storms out, slamming the door behind him.

Sarah looks at me and frowns.

"A holiday will do him good," I say.

"Hardly a holiday – looking after your grandmother and Mr Ritchie."

"OK, well, a break, then."

"A break from what?"

I look at Sarah, try to size up what she knows. "From me."

"Ah. I thought as much."

"Has he said anything to you?"

"He didn't need to. It's been obvious for a while that he's had a crush on you."

"A crush – that's a quaint way of putting it."

"Well, whatever you call it nowadays."

"It's a disaster," I say. "I'm not proud of the way I've treated Charlie." I stare miserably into my teacup. "I mean, if Stefan hadn't come back, then who knows? But still, it wasn't right. I knew that."

"It wasn't very fair to lead him on then, was it?"

"I didn't. It was fun having Charlie as a friend. Now everything's wrecked. I wish he hadn't changed everything."

"So he gets all the blame, does he?"

"Anyway, why would he fancy me? He's way older. What about Rosie – she's more his age and she's pretty and fun and they could go on romantic runs together. She'd be far better than some scrawny, spotty, violin-obsessed teenager."

"Is that really what you think? Have you looked at yourself recently? You're beautiful, Jess. You're interesting, unusual, talented, fun – well, fun most of the time."

I blush. "I'm no fun. I'm grumpy and knackered most of the time. And no one could ever call me beautiful."

Sarah folds her arms and shakes her head. "You've no idea, have you?"

"So people keep telling me." I go back to examining the tea in the bottom of my mug. "How was I supposed to know Stefan was going to reappear? I knew as soon as I saw him at the RCM. I've known for ages, if I'm honest. It's not something you can control, is it."

"No, it's not. However, you can control the way you deal with Stefan in front of Charlie."

"Like how?"

"What I'm trying to say is that I think it would be a good idea if you could be a little more sensitive as far as Charlie is concerned. Don't sit there texting Stefan every two seconds in front of him. You're hurting him, and he doesn't deserve to be hurt."

"What can I do if Stefan keeps texting me?"

Sarah gives me an exasperated look.

"OK, I'll try. I really didn't mean for all this to happen. Charlie needs to find a nice girlfriend – someone nicer than me, at any rate."

Sarah laughs. "I don't think he's short of admirers. But you know his story. It takes him a while to trust anybody."

"Don't make me feel worse."

"Anyway," says Sarah as she searches through a cupboard for something, "talking of Rosie, are you running this morning?"

"Nope. It's her cousin's wedding tomorrow. She's gone to Newcastle."

"Wow. A day off for you."

I smile. I'm hardly going to admit that I quite like running these days.

I wander out into the hallway. The front door is open and Charlie is loading the luggage into the car. Guilt makes my stomach sink. Grandmother hurries out of her office and locks the door. She opens and closes her handbag about three times, checking, searching, checking. She needs to stop faffing around and get going. She looks up and sees me watching.

"Now, Jessica," she says, "you remember what you promised. You will continue to work hard while we are away. I have left rehearsal notes with Dr McNair. There's not much time left. You have to make the most of every lesson and rehearsal."

I don't need to be told – again.

Charlie comes back in and picks up the last of the cases and Grandmother follows him towards the door. I'm caught up in farewells. At the top of the steps, Grandmother turns and gives me a small kiss on my cheek. My first kiss from my grandmother. Now that's something I wasn't expecting. I watch her elegant figure descend the steps, wrapped in a long coat with a fur collar.

Charlie's hanging back, pretending to make sure he's got everything.

"Bye," I say. "Have a good time."

"Bye," he replies. His voice is flat. "Don't do anything I wouldn't do." He gives a dry laugh and lopes down the steps.

Sarah and I stand and watch as the car drives off down the street. Then she pushes the door closed and we both breathe a sigh of relief.

Chapter 22

Next morning, I have breakfast in my pyjamas. Sarah's padding around wearing jeans and no shoes. I wish it could be like this every Saturday.

"I'll drop you at college for your ensemble, and then Dr NcNair is going to drive you and Stefan home. Grandmother has asked her to sit in on your rehearsal."

"Why? We don't need Dr McNair."

Sarah shakes her head.

"We just need time together."

"Time for what?" says Sarah.

"To practise." I look daggers at her and she shrugs.

"Well, I'm sure you'll have plenty of time for that – even with Dr McNair."

"Doesn't Grandmother trust us at all?" I bang my head on the kitchen table a few times. I want to cry.

In ensemble I make a mess of everything and snarl every time any of the others make a comment. We're all in a bad mood by the end. On the way home, Stefan and I sit in the back of Dr McNair's car, as close as we dare. Our arms touch, our legs touch, and Stefan winds his little finger round mine as we politely discuss the weather.

Sarah's put a plate of sandwiches and some drinks down in the music room. I keep pouring more and more juice for Dr McNair in the hope that she'll have to go to the toilet and leave us alone, even for a few minutes. She doesn't.

After we play the whole way through the third movement, Dr McNair reaches into her briefcase and pulls out a yellow folder.

"Prepare yourselves," she says. "There's enough in this blessed folder to keep us going for months."

I recognize Grandmother's handwriting at once. The three of us sit together and study the pages of notes. Some of the instructions are written in black. They're technically specific and the detail is mind-blowing. Others are written in blue and are more performance-related. We discuss, evaluate, experiment.

"Your grandmother should stick to her job as

a critic," huffs Dr McNair as she thumps the notes down on the table.

Stefan and I look at each other. Surely Dr McNair can see that these are the notes of a musician who knows this concerto inside out – probably better than Dr McNair herself.

The rest of the afternoon is intense, furious and frustrating. We go way over time.

At the end, Dr McNair tosses the yellow folder at me. "For you," she says. "Enjoy."

"Thanks."

"Get your things together, Stefan, I promised Mrs Chamberlain I would drive you home."

"It's fine," says Stefan, "I'll stay and do a bit more practice with Jess. I think we could do with going over that third movement again."

"You certainly could," says Dr McNair, "but I gave Mrs Chamberlain my word. She told me to drive you back to your front door. Don't worry, it's on my way home."

Stefan hangs back as Dr McNair leaves. He grabs my hand, holds it tight.

"What are we going to do?" he whispers.

"I'll think of something," I say.

He kisses me fast and I cling to him.

"Hurry up," shouts Dr McNair.

I prop myself in the door frame of the music room and let myself be miserable. As I stare blankly down the corridor, the greyness at the far end swims into focus and a tiny spark of an idea begins to form. I stand up straight as it takes shape. I leave the music room and walk towards the radiator at the far end of the passage. I don't know what I expect to find. I keep checking over my shoulder, as if I'm doing something wrong. The door at the end is pressed back into a little alcove. The white paint is peeling off, leaving some areas of scratched bare wood and some slivers of green. There's a heavy bolt on the door, held closed by a padlock and a thick mesh of spiders' webs. This room was obviously ignored when the rest of the basement was renovated. I rattle the padlock but it's locked. So this is the boiler room.

The radiator is one of those heavy, old-fashioned things, curved at the top with individual pipes. I slide my hand down the back and feel around, pulling away quickly when the spiders' webs get the better of me. Maybe it's just my desperation, but I feel certain that I'm going to find that key. I keep searching. I feel the hook first and then my fingers touch something string-like. I work my fingers down the string until they close on a key. I knew it. I remove it carefully. It's not rusty but it's dirty. I wipe it on my jeans and slip it into the padlock. It turns surprisingly easily.

I wish I could say the same for the bolt. It's rusted and stiff. I work it up and down, up and down, trying to coax it to move. The metal rasps and clunks and the noise is loud in the quiet of the basement. At first the bolt moves very slowly, and then it suddenly gives up its grip and jolts back, catching my finger. I nearly fall over and I swear as I shake away the pain, then suck at the expanding droplet of blood. I push the door open.

Inside it smells old and ignored. When I try the dinky old-fashioned switch, nothing happens. I'm not surprised. I wait for my eyes to adjust, running my fingers over the dusty surfaces of cardboard boxes and old suitcases. I wouldn't like to be locked in here, that's for sure.

"Jess?" Sarah's voice calls me from upstairs. "Can you come and give me a hand with these sheets?"

"Coming," I say, and quickly pull the door closed. I don't bother with the lock.

We fold sheets, then cook supper and eat it in front of the telly.

"Well, I might get an early night," says Sarah. "This week's been frantic."

"Fine by me."

"Are you going to bed or back down to the music room?"

"Music. Dr McNair wasn't impressed with my harmonics in the third movement. I need to do more work on them."

"I'm surprised you've got any fingers left. I'll do the external alarms before I go up, so don't throw open any windows. I'll leave the rest off tonight."

I have no idea how the alarm system works, but I sometimes wonder what Grandmother is so afraid of. I suppose she might have stuff worth stealing – if you know what you're looking for. I've only heard the alarm go off once, when the engineer was here testing it. It was enough to scare the living daylights out of anyone.

"Turn out the lights when you come up," she says, "and for heaven's sake, get some rest."

"Yes, Grandmother!"

Sarah wags her finger at me, smiling. I wait for her to go upstairs and then I run straight back down to the boiler room. I want to take a closer look. A smudgy orange glow from the street lights makes its way through the dirty windows and I wedge the door open to give me as much light from the corridor as possible. I don't think anyone's been in here for years.

Slowly, things begin to take form as my eyes adapt. The windows are high and small. Dad never would've got in through one of them. Mum must've made it up. The room is stacked with shadowy boxes. In the semi-darkness, I choose the one closest to me and heave it over towards the window. It's heavy, maybe full of books or something. At least it's good and solid, so I clamber up on it, and now my nose is level with the window. It opens out to a small area below the level of the road, accessed by some narrow stone steps. It's protected by railings at street level. I've noticed them before, of course, from the outside, but it looks different down here.

I check for alarm sensors but there's no sign of them, though it looks as if the window has been sealed up. I grapple with the latch. It won't budge. It hasn't been sealed, exactly, but the gap between the window and the frame is filled with lumpy paint. I hop down and go back to the music room, where I grab scissors and the fine knife I sometimes use when I'm re-stringing. Back on my box, I edge the knife down into the crack, scraping away the paint. Then I go at the latch again and manage to open it. Eventually, the window begins to give, and after a good hefty thump on each side of the frame, it opens.

The night air rushes in, cool and damp. I stick my head out. Mum's right; this is a small window. But Stefan might get through. I try to pull myself up, but the window is at an awkward angle. I slide back down and the small window shelf grazes my skin as my jersey slides up. It hurts. With me helping, Stefan could get back out, I'm sure.

I shiver as I sit on a box and dial Stefan's number. It's not warm down here. He's slow to answer and he sounds croaky.

"Did I interrupt something?" I ask.

"Jess?" Stefan laughs. "No, I was asleep."

"Well, wake up and get over here."

"It's after eleven."

"I'm going to sneak you in. I mean it. Please come. Bring a torch if you've got one."

"What is this, Jess – a joke?" He sounds uncertain.

"Stop asking questions, get your kit on and get over here."

It takes forever for him to arrive. I close the door

to the boiler room and wait in the semi-darkness, listening and listening for his footsteps amongst the general city noise. I imagine Mum locked in here in the dark, the sound of that bolt closing. Finally I hear sounds coming to a stop outside and I hop up and poke my head out of the window.

"Pssst. Down here."

Stefan stares through the railings, confusion all over his face.

"You'll have to jump the gate," I whisper.

He looks around quickly to make sure no one's about. "She hasn't got a security camera, has she?"

I shake my head.

He leaps the iron gate and tiptoes down the steps. He's breathing loudly.

"OK, get down on your stomach – feet first," I say.

He hands me a small bag, then lowers himself to the ground.

"It's wet," he moans.

"Stop complaining."

He wriggles through and slides into the basement. I shut the window behind him.

"Burglar's heaven," he says, brushing himself down.

"Hardly. They'd have to get through that door there. It's bolted and padlocked from the outside. They'd wake the whole house."

We laugh, then stand in silence. Neither of us moves. I haven't thought this through at all. I'm holding my breath, unsure of what happens next.

Stefan steps forward and wraps his arms around me. "So what gave you this idea?"

"Just something Mum said."

"Are you going to tell me?"

I look up at him and shake my head and he laughs. He holds me loosely at first and I put my cheek on his chest. I press his back so we're closer and I can feel the tension in both our bodies. The uncertainty. His face nuzzles mine, wanting me to look up. He kisses me and kisses me. I touch his hair, his ears, feel his neck, then his shoulders. And I know that this is it – that we're not going to stop. I don't want to stop.

His hands slide up under my sweater. Touching, exploring, making me gasp for breath. Everything is happening so fast, yet I'm aware of each and every moment. There are blankets on the boxes and he's pulling them to the floor. Pulling me to the floor. Clothes jumbled and disappearing. Stretching out our arms and our hands so that every part of us touches. Wrapping ourselves around each other.

Afterwards we hold each other quietly. I can't let go of him. I want to stay on this dusty floor for ever, listening to his breathing.

Eventually he laughs. "You're covered in bits of fluff from that old blanket."

"You too."

He puts the palm of his hand flat against mine, holding our hands in the air where we can both see them. He plays the tips of my fingers with the tips of his fingers. I lie and watch.

Then he runs his hand down my arm. "You're getting cold," he says. He pulls my sweater back over my head and we dress quietly. I feel self-conscious, glad there's not too much light. He doesn't stop looking at me.

"What?" I say.

"Nothing. Just you."

He pins me in the beam of his torch and laughs some more. I've never felt this happy. He puts his arms around me again so my back is to him, his chin resting on the top of my head, his hands still clasping the torch as he shines it around the room. Cardboard boxes everywhere, taped up, and then, just in front of us, an old trunk. It must have been covered by the blankets. He lets the beam rest on the faded white lettering.

T P M CHAMBERLAIN

"That brings back memories of boarding school," he says.

"Grandmother's old school uniform, perhaps? Shall we look?"

We kneel in front of it and open the lid. Lying across the surface is an old shawl, thin and ragged and patterned with a bluish-green mould. I pull it back carefully and it crumbles in my fingers. I sneeze.

When I open my eyes again, Stefan's shining his torch on an old leather violin case. We look at each other.

"Well, well," he says, "I think we should take a closer look at this."

It opens like my suitcase: press a small button and the catch pops out. I smile at Stefan before I lift the lid. Inside is the most beautiful violin I've ever seen. I run my fingers over the grain of the wood. One string is missing altogether; the others are broken. Two bows are stretched across the lid, threads of horsehair hanging loosely. The rosin has hardened to a tough orange lump. Stefan picks it up and it glows in the torchlight.

"Pine sap," I say, "plus a few other things. It's almost fossilized."

I reach into the box and lift the violin like a baby from its cot. It is fragile, extraordinary. I feel the weight of it in my hands. Turn it over. On the back are two delicately carved cherubs. I lift the violin to the playing position and it tucks neatly under my jawline. As it touches my collarbone, a thrill rushes through me.

"I wish I could try it," I whisper.

"It doesn't look very playable," says Stefan.

"It just needs cleaning up and the strings replacing." I shine the torch on it and examine it for cracks. None that I can see, but the light isn't great.

"Jess?"

There's something in Stefan's voice that makes me look up. He's holding up a clipping from an old newspaper. Yellowed and jagged round the edges.

"Look," he says. His voice is urgent.

I look closely at the photo in the torchlight.

"Isn't that your grandmother?"

She's young, but unmistakable. I look more closely, squinting.

"Crap," I say. Even in this faded photo, the horseshoe brooch is clear on her dress and the impact of what I've done hits me. I haven't mentioned the brooch to Stefan and I'm not about to admit to it now.

Stefan misunderstands. "No, it is her, I'm sure." He moves the torch to my face. "It could be you. That's incredible."

"I do not look like my grandmother, thank you very much."

We turn back to the article. The yellowed paper glows dimly in the light.

"'*Tara Chamberlain disappoints on her return to London*,'" Stefan reads aloud. "'*Twenty-year-old Tara Chamberlain's return to London after two years in Prague. . .*'"

"Prague? What was she doing there?"

"More to the point, what's she doing there now?" He reads on. "'. . .*after two years in Prague failed to excite the audience. Miss Chamberlain played the Sibelius Violin Concerto in D Minor, and though the first movement was well-executed, it lacked conviction. If the audience hoped for more as the evening progressed, they were to be disappointed. Her playing was technically sound, even brilliant at times, but she failed to connect with the audience on any level, leaving them feeling cheated and unimpressed.'"*

"Oh God," I say. My hand is over my mouth.

"Wait," says Stefan. "Listen to the end." He reads it out loud. "*'Her young accompanist, George Ritchie, gave his usual virtuoso performance. He tried hard to lift Miss Chamberlain's playing, but with little success. We will be seeing much more of this young man.'"*

Stefan shines the torch close-up on the photo. In the background is what looks to be a dark-haired man seated at the piano. He's not in focus.

"Mr Ritchie," I say.

Stefan nods. "Date?"

"There's no date."

"Turn it over. Check the other side. It'll be in the top corner."

"Fifteenth of December, 1956." My voice trails off as this information registers.

"The fifteenth of December? The same date as our concert," says Stefan. "That's a strange coincidence."

"No," I say. "I don't think it's a coincidence at all." My brain is racing. "She's planned all this on purpose. Everything. I know it. What I don't know is why."

"Jess . . . you know when you were telling me about your family? When did you say your mum was born?"

"Nineteen fifty-seven. July."

"Correct me if my maths is wrong, but that means your grandmother must have been pregnant when she gave this concert."

I count with my fingers and nod. He's right.

"She doesn't look it," says Stefan.

"She wouldn't. Not that early on."

"But they refer to her as Miss Chamberlain."

"That doesn't necessarily mean anything."

"It might."

"A lot of performers use their maiden name." I start searching deeper in the trunk. Scores and scores of violin music. It's like treasure. I want to look at every one. They're all annotated. Pencil marks everywhere.

"What about these?" Stefan's holding up a bundle of letters tied with string. "These look more interesting."

I take them. They're arranged neatly, all exactly the same size. They burn into my hand.

"We shouldn't look," I say, dropping them to my

lap. "Letters are private." But my fingers move back towards them, curious.

"They can't be that precious stored away in this old trunk. We can put them all back, just as they are. No one need know."

"OK, we'll look at just one. Then we'll decide."

Holding the envelope with my fingertips, I extract the first letter. Stefan holds the torch while I read aloud.

12th January 1954

My dearest Tara,

I am so glad to hear you and Mother have arrived safely in Prague and that there was no problem with your visas. It is a beautiful city, particularly in the snow.

It fills me with happiness to know that your violin studies are now in hand. I am certain your time in Prague will serve you well. You are fortunate to be learning with such a master.

Your many friends ask after you. George and Helena particularly.

Look after your mother for me.

With all my love,

Father

"Nineteen fifty-four," says Stefan. "So she was in Prague studying the violin two years before her concert and her mother was with her. A chaperone?"

"And she must have been friends with George and Helena before leaving. They've known her all these years."

I fold the letter with great care. Replace it. Take out the next letter.

21st February 1954

Dear Tara,

It is quite natural for you and your mother to feel a little homesick from time to time. You will soon get over it. I am sorry your mother has been unwell.

Jelinec has sent me good reports of your playing. I know you say he is very demanding, but surely you wouldn't want him to settle for anything less than perfect? I only hope that you are not being too wilful. It will not help your mother's health, or your teacher's temper.

It is raining here in London and my business is keeping me well-occupied. Hard work is the only route to success. I suggest you remember that.

With love,
Father

"Hmmm," says Stefan, smiling. "Wilful! So that's where you get it from."

He pinches me on the arm. I pinch him back. He kisses me. For a few minutes we are lost, again, in our own world. Finally we turn back to the letters.

"It's a weird name," says Stefan, pointing at it. "Jelly-neck? Probably Yel-i-nec or Yel-i-nech."

We try out the possibilities. Something is pulling at my memory. Jelinec.

"I've seen that name before," I say.

"Jelinec?"

"Yes. Or something like it. On a letter in Grandmother's office." I tell Stefan about it, about Grandmother swiping it away. We read over this letter again.

"Your grandmother doesn't sound happy, does she?"

"Not at all."

"Let's look at one of the letters further down; they'll be the most recent."

He strokes my finger as I pull out the bottom letter. It's dated 1956.

"This could be more helpful," I say.

1st November 1956

Tara,

    Your last letter was most distressing.

    I cannot describe how angry I am. Your behaviour has been a great embarrassment to me. I had hoped that you might learn to keep that temper of yours under control.

    Jelinec is seeking recompense for the bite you gave him. Furthermore, he has threatened to send word of your appalling behaviour to London. Even you must recognize that it is within his grasp to ruin your career. I have had to agree to a generous settlement of money in return for his silence. I cannot believe your foolishness.

    I have arranged for your earliest return.

    As to your performance, it will go ahead in December whether you like it or not. It is the least you can do under the circumstances. George has kindly agreed to accompany you. I trust you will treat him with more respect than you do your teacher. He is making a good name for himself, which is more than you will ever do unless you learn to behave like a lady.

    Father

We stare at the letter in silence. I read it again.

"She bit her teacher? You'd have to be pretty angry to do that." I try to imagine biting Dr McNair. Not a nice thought.

"What did your grandmother do that was so appalling? Surely it wasn't just the bite? This Jelinec bloke – it sounds like he's blackmailing them."

It's frustrating having only one side of the correspondence. Gradually we read through all the letters and try to piece together Grandmother's side of the story from the replies she received. One thing is clear: Grandmother seems more and more desperate. It's horrible to read. I find myself feeling sorry for her. She was so young and she hated her violin teacher. Her mother was sick. All she wanted to do was go home. And he wouldn't let her. What kind of father won't let his daughter and sick wife come home?

"Poor Grandmother," I say. Yet, in the back of my mind, I can't help thinking of how Grandmother has treated Mum. It makes me feel strange. I keep my thoughts to myself.

"I'm glad I haven't got her father," says Stefan. "He doesn't sound like a good person at all."

"Nor does her violin teacher. Mum said her

grandfather was a colonel or something. I don't think she ever met him, but she told me she went to his funeral."

"You're not exactly a close family, are you?"

"Don't criticize my family." I bite my bottom lip. It's easy for Stefan. He's not having to piece together who he is. I don't want to be part of a useless, dysfunctional family. I want to be normal.

"The strange thing is —" Stefan fans the letters "— if your grandmother says her husband died before your mother was born, and if she was pregnant by the time she gave the concert, then when did she marry — and who? There's no mention in any of these letters about a boyfriend or a wedding or anything."

I flop forward and lean my head against the edge of the trunk. I'm suddenly tired of all this.

"I don't know," I say. "I just don't know. But whatever happened, it seems to have affected Grandmother for the rest of her life. And Mum. And now me. And I don't think it was anything good."

We search to the very bottom. More music, a couple of newspaper clippings in a foreign language with photos of Grandmother. I sigh and push back the empty trunk. There's nothing more.

Stefan reaches out and takes my hand and I slump against him.

"We'll work it out," he says. "We've got more information now."

His lips are on mine again and I want to respond but I'm exhausted.

"I'm sorry, Stefan. I think I need to sleep."

He gives me a look so desolate it makes me smile. It makes me feel more wanted than ever.

"Do you know what time it is?" he laughs. "It's four-thirty in the morning! You're right, we need to sleep, and I need to get out of here before the world starts to wake up."

We put everything back in the trunk and cover it with the blankets, just as it was.

"I don't want to leave you," he says.

"You can come back – every night, if you like."

"I might. Can you make the place a bit more comfortable next time? Bed, duvet, that kind of thing."

"Go home, Stefan." I'm almost too tired to smile.

It's much harder getting Stefan back out of the window and I have to give him a foot-up. He sticks his head back through and kisses me again. I watch as he disappears up the little steps and scrambles over the gate.

I close the window, shine the torch around the room one more time and wonder what other secrets are waiting to be discovered.

Chapter 23

I wake up to a laser beam of sunlight coming through a crack in the curtains and almost straight into my eyes. It hurts. It's nearly midday. I smile and stretch out across my bed as the memory of Stefan fills my body.

As for the rest, it all seems less real in daylight.

I'm awake, I text.

I'm in library, see you two-ish for rehearsal. X

That's two whole hours. I want him here now. I try to do some work but I'm not in the mood.

Sarah comes up and knocks on my door to check if I'm still alive.

"You must be tired," she says. "You slept for hours."

"I practised until late."

"Good grief, what have you been doing?" Sarah has picked up my sweater and is shaking it. Bits of moth-eaten blanket fall on to the carpet. I can't think of an answer. "Dr McNair is not coming to rehearsal today. She says you know what to do."

"Thank God for that," I say.

"Actually, you can thank me." Sarah smiles. "I thought you two needed a break."

"You genius!"

∫ ʔ

Stefan doesn't turn up until nearly three and I've never seen anyone looking so smug.

"You were supposed to start at two," Sarah says. "Just because Dr McNair isn't coming doesn't mean you can slack off. Now straight to work or you'll get us all into trouble."

She shoos us down to the music room, pretending to be angry, mumbling about Grandmother being right not to trust us.

"You're looking pleased with yourself," I say.

"I am." He slides his hand up under my shirt and I think about dragging him straight back to the boiler room.

"Stop it!" I say, giggling. "Sarah could come in at any moment. Anyway, we need to work."

"In a minute."

Finally, reluctantly, we pull away from each other. He raises his eyes to the ceiling. "OK, agreed, we'll have to set some rules round here or we'll never get anything done. But first I've got something to show you." He pulls out an envelope. "I've found out a bit more about this Jelinec character. I've even got a photo."

He hands me the envelope and I pull out a photocopy of an old picture.

Stefan is still smiling. "I've been in the library all morning searching. I never thought I'd find anything, but persistence paid off in the end."

I am not smiling. I'm hardly breathing. I close my eyes tight, open them again. But the photo doesn't change.

"Jess?"

It's the nose. It's unmistakable. And the little V-shaped veins in the forehead; the straight, lank hair.

"What is it?" says Stefan. He's got his arm round me.

"This photo. I know who it is."

"I've just told you who it is. That's the point. It's Miklos Jelinec; your grandmother's violin teacher."

"It's my frickin' grandfather!" I shout it through clamped teeth.

Stefan backs off from my anger. "How can you know that just from a photo?"

"It's Mum. Mum's nose, Mum's hair, Mum's veins in her forehead."

"You can't be sure. That's a big leap."

I race up to my room, grab the photo by my bed and run back down again. Stefan looks. Compares.

"Maybe," he says.

"Oh come on. There's no *maybe* about it."

"Your mother is much prettier."

"Is that supposed to make me feel better? I don't want *this* as a grandfather." I wave the photo at Stefan, then thrust it back in the envelope. "Not after reading those letters."

"You could be wrong."

I stuff the envelope in the back of the yellow music folder where it's out of sight.

"Do you want to know what I found out about him?" Stefan asks.

"No."

"I'm going to tell you anyway. It might cheer you

up." He reads from a slip of paper. "'*Miklos Jelinec was an outstanding Czech violinist who trained many young virtuosos. He was heir to one of the great estates in Prague and inherited a fortune when his parents died. He was purported to be a communist sympathizer during occupation.*'"

"Fine."

"According to the article, he became a recluse. It says he has no known offspring. So maybe he isn't your grandfather after all. Maybe your imagination is working overtime."

"It is not my imagination," I say, my jaw still clenched.

"Well, even if he is your grandfather, it's not so bad, is it? This is all ancient history."

"How can you be so insensitive? No, it is not all right. When did he die? Can you tell me that? Exact date?"

"Doesn't say."

I know, without any shadow of doubt, that the man in the photo is my grandfather, but I wish I didn't. I turn my back to Stefan, get out my violin and start my warm-ups.

"Don't shoot the messenger," says Stefan, and sits down at the piano. "I thought you'd be interested. I thought you wanted to find out more."

I don't trust myself to speak. Even I'm surprised by the strength of my feeling. This burning fury. I take out my anger on the music, throwing all my pent-up frustration at the violence of the third movement. By six o'clock I'm done. Exhausted.

"Is it safe to come out now?" asks Stefan.

"I'm sorry," I say. I sit on the floor and cradle my violin on my knees. Stefan comes and sits beside me. "I just want to get this performance over and done with and go home to Manchester. I wish we'd left everything alone. I wish I'd never come here."

"You can't go back to Manchester, not now I'm in London. You need to stay here. You have to study here. So you'd better make sure you nail this performance."

"Dad and Mum will never let me stay in London. Anyway, where would I live? I doubt Grandmother wants to put up with me for a minute longer than she has to. Anyway, I don't know if I'd want to stay in this house – not with all this." I wave my hand vaguely towards I'm not sure what.

"It's not just about *you*, Jess. What about me? We're in this together, and if we're going to stand a hope in hell of making it in this world of music, we need to stick together. I'm not going to stand here and let us throw it all away. We've done that once and we're not doing it again."

He puts his arm around my shoulders and pulls me in protectively. I close my eyes and try to blank out everything. Right now, the past seems more important than the future.

Chapter 24

On Tuesday the rain begins. It makes little difference to me except that I can hear it hammering on the pavement outside the music room window. My dark mood gets even darker.

Time plays its tricks. So much has happened in the last week and yet it doesn't seem a moment since Grandmother left. Now she's coming back. Sarah's rushing around making sure the house is immaculate. I'm practising harder than ever – trying to lose myself in the music. At least Grandmother can't accuse me of slacking while she's been away.

I'm not sure what I'll feel when she walks back through the door. In my mind, my grandmother has become a different person. I know things about her. Things she doesn't know I know. It changes everything.

And there's guilt too. It hangs over me, black as black. We had no business reading those letters.

They arrive home slightly earlier than we expected. Charlie helps Grandmother from the car; holds an umbrella over her head. She's unsteady coming up the steps and Sarah and I make way for her. Her face is grey. Grey like the sky. She looks tired, so tired.

"Welcome home," says Sarah.

"Thank you. Hello, Jessica." Her voice is small. "Sarah, would you mind helping me to my room. I'm not feeling at all well."

Sarah and Charlie exchange worried looks. Sarah hooks her arm through Grandmother's and they walk slowly towards the stairs. I'm left behind with Charlie.

"Hi," I say awkwardly.

"You look different," he says.

"I do?"

"I suppose he's got what he wants from you now, has he?"

"What!" I can't believe Charlie just said that.

"I thought so."

I'm ready to storm off but Charlie grabs me by the hand. "I'm sorry," he says. "I shouldn't have said that."

I close my eyes. Breathe.

"I am sorry, really. Come on, come and have a cup of tea." He pushes me gently towards the kitchen.

I sit at the kitchen table while he gets out the mugs. Pours tea over tea bags. It feels almost normal.

"I wanted to talk to you. I thought I'd let you know that I've worked things out now," he says.

"Oh?"

"You're right. You and me. It wasn't going to happen. Not really."

"No."

"You like this Stefan bloke, don't you?"

I nod.

"I hope you're being careful."

"Charlie!" I must be blushing from my head to my toes.

"Well, that's OK, then. That's good."

Charlie takes my hand and holds it too tight. I look at him. And I can see it's not OK. It's not good. He puts my hand on the table and pats it slowly, then sits back in his chair.

"It's nice to have a proper cup of tea," he says. "I didn't like the stuff in Prague."

"Is Grandmother OK?"

He gets up, shuts the door and talks in a low

voice. "She's not great. It was busy in Prague. Lots of meetings." He talks quietly, as if he's worried someone might hear.

"Who was she meeting with? I thought she was going to some music festival."

Charlie shakes his head. "Lawyers, business people – no music. Nightmare city for driving. So many people. I'm not surprised she's tired. Mr Ritchie too. I've never seen him look so worn out."

"They're getting a bit old for all that rushing about."

"They're both pretty amazing, considering. They're made of tough stuff, that generation."

"Talking of rushing about, have you heard from the boys?" I ask.

"Yep. They've extended their tour in Ireland. They'll be back in a couple of weeks."

"I miss them," I say. "I've tried to talk to Ciaran a couple of times but the signal's so bad it's not worth it."

"How's it going – the stuff you're rehearsing?"

"Hard. Good. I think we'll be ready."

Grandmother doesn't come out of her room for the rest of the week and I find myself hanging around outside her door, listening. I'm worried and it surprises me that I care so much. I want to go in but Sarah says we must let her rest.

"Does she need a doctor?" I ask. "She's not dying or anything?"

"No. She needs peace and quiet."

"Is she depressed?"

Sarah hesitates before she answers. "No. No, I don't think so. She says she'll be up tomorrow. She wants to join you and Stefan for your Saturday rehearsal."

"Hopefully we can cheer her up. I think she'll be pleased with us."

Grandmother is as good as her word. By the time I'm back from my quartet at the RCM on Saturday morning, she's up and seems entirely normal. If I was expecting a different person, I was wrong.

"You didn't go to the college dressed like that, did you, Jessica?" I'm wearing a very short skirt and ripped tights. We're standing in the hallway where she's caught me on my way back in.

"No, I went dressed as a Roman centurion, but I thought I'd change for lunch."

I expect her to ignore my sarcasm, but she smiles.

"We'll have to find you something more twenty-first century and, of course, a suitable dress for the concert. I will telephone Selina. Now, how are you and Stefan getting along?"

I follow her into her office. Her last question almost makes me laugh. I'll give her the censored version.

"Yeah, we're good, thanks. Still plenty to do."

"There's always plenty to do. You haven't missed any rehearsal time?"

"No."

She closes the door and we sit down. "And he's not letting you down?"

"Definitely no. Not in any way."

"Good. It's an important performance, Jessica. You know that, don't you?"

The shadows of our discovery are pressing on me and I want something from her – though I'm not sure what. "Important for who?" I say.

Grandmother pats her hair at the back, as if a strand might be out of place.

"As you know, there will be people there who need to hear you play," she says. "We have to think about your future. We have to think about applying to music college. We want to be sure you are ready."

This much I'd expected. She's already told me about her list of invited guests. But now my performance has taken on a much greater significance. Grandmother's voice is calm and composed – if I thought she might react to my question, I was wrong. And perhaps it could be a coincidence after all, that December fifteenth just happens to be a convenient day, that she thinks the concerto is a good choice as an audition piece? But it isn't a good choice and it isn't a coincidence.

Grandmother taps her fingertips together.

"I was wondering if you might be missing something?" she says. I sit up, believing for a moment that she may be about to tell me something. Then I see her pick up a box from her desk.

"Did you know you had lost the brooch I gave you?" she asks. She doesn't seem angry.

She holds out the old blue leather box. I squirm with guilt as I think of her photo in the old newspaper clipping. The shadows of the past get darker.

"My brooch?" I say, trying to sound shocked. "Where did you find it?"

"One of our neighbours picked it up off the street

outside your window. Did you take it out with you in your bag? You must have dropped it." Her voice is distant, almost dreamy.

I shake my head as if I can't imagine. She's given me my excuse and I'm not going to add anything else. I try to meet her eyes. She stares down at the brooch with such a look of sadness that I have to look away. I fight with my own feelings.

Grandmother gives a little shudder, as if she's pulling herself from her thoughts. "Perhaps I should keep it safe for you for the time being?"

I nod. "Thank you. I think that would be better."

"You can wear it for your performance."

"No!" I say sharply. "I mean, I never wear jewellery when I perform."

"We'll see," says Grandmother.

I don't want the brooch back. Not ever. There's something about it – but I can hardly tell her that. She puts it in the drawer of her desk. I hope she's put it the right way up.

She looks at her little gold watch. "Stefan should be here shortly. Perhaps you had better go and start your warm-ups."

I nod and flee from the room.

When Stefan arrives, he's made an effort and is

looking very smart, except for his hair, which has a mind of its own. My chest tightens as he comes through the door, and I have to tell myself to be professional and keep a lid on everything but the music.

"Is everything OK?" he whispers, giving me a quick hug.

"Not really."

Stefan raises his eyebrows questioningly. "No word of what she was doing in Prague?"

I shake my head. "Lawyers, is all Charlie said. She looked dreadful when she came back."

We get to work. Grandmother joins us and says she'd like to hear the third movement. Suits me. She sets the metronome. Its rhythmical click, click, click is terrifyingly fast. I widen my eyes at Stefan and he smiles. He hasn't got to do the hard stuff. Grandmother gets out her notebook.

At this speed the third movement is fiendish. I feel I'm fighting for survival, clinging to a cliff with my fingernails. With each slip the panic rises. It's excruciating but I get to the end. Stefan turns down his mouth at the corners. It wasn't as good as we wanted.

"You've worked hard, but not hard enough," says

Grandmother, looking only at me. Then she turns to Stefan. "Your accompaniment is exemplary, if I may say so. I am impressed. It seems George's faith in you was not misplaced. So now I would like to do some work alone with Jessica. I will ask Charles to take you home."

"Stefan can walk," I say quickly. Stefan and Charlie alone in a car together is *not* a good idea.

"But it's raining," says Grandmother.

"I'd rather walk," says Stefan, catching my warning. He piles up his music and leaves me to my fate.

Grandmother sits and drums her fingers on the yellow folder. "What did I say to you about those double stops?" she asks. "Did you read any of my notes?"

"All of them."

"Precision is key. I was quite specific. Let's see." She opens the folder and begins leafing through her notes.

Suddenly my stomach disappears and the world flips. This is panic like I've never felt panic before. It's still there in the back of the folder. The photo of Miklos Jelinec is right under Grandmother's fingertips.

"What's this?" she says, as she finds the brown envelope.

"J-just some extra notes from Dr McNair," I splutter out.

"Interesting. What did she have to say?" Grandmother's fingers are already edging open the flap.

"Oh, nothing useful, really." I try to sound offhand. "That's why we've left them in the envelope."

She's reaching inside.

"Honestly," I say, "they're not worth looking at."

"I shall be the judge of that." She looks at me over the top of her glasses and I seize the moment and try to grab the envelope away from her.

She's not letting go. We're locked in a tug of war.

"I want to see what she's written," says Grandmother. "Why do you have a problem with that?" She pulls the envelope away from me and slips out the sheet of photo paper.

I hold my breath.

She goes pale. A tiny muscle moves in her jaw.

"Where did you get it?" she whispers.

"It's just a photo Stefan found," I stammer.

"Don't lie. Where would he have found this photo – lying around on some park bench?"

"He was doing some research, I think. A project?" I'm not sounding convincing.

"Research? I don't think so. You have been prying. Delving into my past. Interfering in things in which you have no business."

"It's my past too."

"How dare you!" She rips the photo in two and lets it drop to the floor.

"If he's my grandfather then I want to know."

Grandmother freezes, statue-like. What colour she had has drained away.

"So I'm right. That *is* your husband." I point at the torn picture.

"Husband?" Grandmother hisses the word and takes a step towards me. "Husband!" she screams. "Why couldn't you just leave things alone? I thought you could help me move on from the past. But no. You're just like your mother. A constant reminder."

Grandmother is so close to me now that I can feel her spit on my face.

"I think I have a right to know," I shout back. "I think my mother has a right to know."

"Right? You have no right to dredge up all this misery; no right to throw my generosity back in my face. None. You don't even have a *right* to play this instrument." She grabs my violin and waves it in the air.

"Give that back," I yell. I reach for it but Grandmother smashes it down on the back of the chair. She smashes it again and again and again.

"Stop it!" I shout. I fight to wrestle it from her but her anger has given her unbelievable strength. "That's my violin – what are you doing – *stop it*!"

I get a hold on her arms but it's too late. She lets my precious instrument drop to the floor. We stare at the contorted shape, the shards of wood, the slack strings. Bruised, broken, irreparably damaged.

"That's how easy it is to destroy a dream," says Grandmother, her voice barely above a whisper. "And I should know." Her chest is heaving, her legs not quite supporting her. "God knows, I should know."

Her last word disappears as her body crumples. I just manage to catch her as she passes out but I can't support her and we both end up on the floor in a tangled mess. I can't move. Grandmother's face is grey. My own breath comes in quick snatches. It's loud in my ears.

I try to think what I need to do. I manage to get my fingers on her wrist to check her pulse. I can't feel anything. She's dead. I've killed her. It's all my fault. I try to shout for help but nothing comes out of my mouth. I stare at her in desperation, my tears falling on her pale face.

"Wake up," I say. "Don't die. Please don't die."

She gives a little cough and her body twitches. She's not dead! She's breathing. Her eyes flicker open.

"You're OK," I say to her. "You're OK." I repeat it over and over. "I'm going to lie you down so I can get you some help."

Her eyes flash on to mine. She grips my hand.

"No!" Her voice is weak but clear. "Just give me a moment. I'll be all right in a moment."

Neither of us moves. Then she begins to shifts her weight slightly so I can wriggle out from under her.

"Now help me up. I'll be all right."

Very carefully, and with some difficulty, I help her to her feet and on to a chair.

"Some water, please."

I pour half a glass of water from the jug on the side. My hands are shaking so much I know I'll spill it if I pour more. Grandmother struggles to get a grip on the glass and I attempt to steady it for her as she raises it to her lips.

She seems to be gaining strength now and she raises her eyes to mine. The look on her face is desperate.

"Why?" I say.

I pick up the shattered heap of wood and strings and hold it up in front of my face. Splinters snag at my skin. I toss it back on to the ground. Her gaze drifts away to the far wall.

"I hope you're satisfied," I say.

"Miklos was my violin teacher," Grandmother whispers.

I can barely hear her. I move closer.

"In Prague."

She has my full attention now.

"I was a good violinist. A prodigy, some called me. But that wasn't why my father sent me away to study. He was having an affair with an actress. He wanted Mother and me out of the way."

I sink to my knees in front of her so my face is level with hers. Her eyes are still on the wall.

"Prague is a beautiful city now, but then it was under communist control. Mother and I hated it. I was homesick. I missed my friends. I missed George."

She trails off. I can hear her uneven breath.

"Miklos was demanding. He wanted perfection at all times. I tried my best. If I did anything wrong he would make me – do things."

The words sink into the silence of the room.

"It wasn't much at first. Just undoing the top button of my shirt – his hand deep in the pocket of his trousers." Grandmother's hand flies to her mouth as if the thought of it is too shocking to bear. It *is* too shocking to bear.

"You don't have to tell me," I say.

She shakes her head quickly and violently and locks her eyes on to mine.

"I begged Father to let us come home. He wouldn't listen. I couldn't tell him. Miklos said if I breathed a word he would ruin my career. I'd always wanted to be a concert violinist. I was prepared to do anything."

I know that feeling. I know what she's saying.

"I practised until my fingers bled. If it was perfect then he would leave me alone. But he'd usually find something. It was a vicious circle. The more scared I became, the more mistakes I made." She screws her eyes tight shut.

I take Grandmother's hands. She doesn't resist. I stare at the hands, the little ridges of loose skin, the thin blue veins. I imagine the blood on her fingers.

"I tried to fight him off. He was a big man. Much bigger than me. And strong. I think he enjoyed the fight. When he pressed himself against me I thought I would suffocate. Sometimes I prayed I would suffocate."

I can't look at her. I keep staring at her hands.

"I was twenty – but I was so innocent. It was different then."

The rain beats down. Cars rumble by.

"Finally he went too far and I bit him on the arm. I drew blood. His anger." She pulls her hands from mine and clasps them together. I force myself to look at her but her eyes are closed again. "He said he'd make me pay for it."

Her breath catches in her throat.

"And he did . . . he raped me . . . on the floor of his music room . . . my mother in the sitting room next door."

The words come out, simply, starkly, quietly. Distilled moments of pure horror.

Suddenly the hatred goes and her eyes are full of tears. "No, Jess, he was not my husband. But yes, I am sad to say he was your grandfather. And for that I am truly sorry."

I swallow. Not wanting to understand or believe. So much worse than my worst nightmares.

She raises her shoulders towards her ears and then drops them again. She seems to be trying to regain some composure. "How did you find out about him?" she asks.

"We found some things." My voice is tiny. "In the boiler room. We know about your concert with Mr Ritchie."

"Oh. I was going to tell you – before your own performance – not about Miklos, but about George and me. I owed you that much."

"Tell me now," I say. "Please."

She smiles gently and puts her hand on my face. "Father forced me to play that concert in London. It was to launch my music career. Dear George tried his best. We were in love, you see, before I went to Prague. We planned to marry when I came home." She smiles the saddest smile. "But it was too late by then. I was damaged goods. I vowed never to let another man touch me after what had happened with Miklos. I didn't want to pass on his filth. I couldn't bring myself to tell George so he, of course, assumed I was no longer in love with him. He was devastated."

I try to imagine how it would have been. Grandmother's agonizing secret and Mr Ritchie not knowing. It's all so sad.

"Our performance of the Sibelius was faultless. I had learned never, ever to make mistakes. But I was emotionally dead. Raped by a man I hated and barred from the man I loved. I knew I could never be a violin player. I packed up my violin and all my music. And I never played again."

My insides twist harder and harder. Everything is too close. Her pain is filling every inch of my body.

"Did you ever tell Mr Ritchie?"

"I thought I could hide it from him for ever, but I was wrong. I didn't discover I was pregnant until after the concert." Grandmother gives a bitter laugh. "That was Miklos's final punishment. The ultimate price for failure."

"No, you can't think that," I say. "It wasn't your fault."

"I owed George an explanation. I told him everything. He told me he would take care of me. He begged me to marry him. He said it didn't matter that I was pregnant, that we would pretend the baby was ours. When I refused, he said he'd wait. He said I'd change my mind in the end. But I knew

I wouldn't; not after what had happened to me. George waited for sixteen years. When he finally gave up and married someone else, it destroyed me."

Grandmother's depression, her isolation; it all begins to make sense.

"And you never told Mum?"

"How could I? What good could it have done? When Miklos heard about the baby, he begged for me to go back to Prague, promised me he would look after me. I knew what that meant. He offered my father a lot of money. Miklos enjoyed many privileges. He must have been a good friend to the communists."

"He tried to buy you? That's disgusting."

"My father expected me to go. Imagine! To become Miklos's wife and make everything respectable." She laughs drily. "But I wouldn't go and they couldn't make me because I'd lost everything already. My father was implicated almost as much as Miklos. There were, without doubt, underhanded dealings of a politically sensitive nature, let alone the issue of Father's mistress and what had happened to me. I threatened to tell Father's friends everything. Mother would have backed me up. She only had months to live. Nothing mattered any more. There was nothing more they could do to hurt me. My life was over."

I put my hand on her arm. I want her to know I understand.

"Miklos was a coward underneath it all. A weak, pathetic coward. He gave me this house, limitless money and anything else I wanted in return for my silence."

"So that's where all your money came from?"

"Yes, and I was happy to take it at the time. It gave me independence from my father. I was estranged from my family and I had a baby to bring up, so I had little option but to allow myself to be kept by Miklos. I thought the money would give me power. I was wrong."

"But you didn't marry him?"

"No, I did not. That was my father's story. He couldn't cope with the scandal of an illegitimate grandchild, so he told everyone that my husband had died before Susan was born. In some ways it helped. I made it clear that I was unable to talk about my husband and I was accepted back into the music world with sympathy. I thought I could bury the past. I thought I could find happiness again."

"But you couldn't?"

"I had Susan. As a small baby, it wasn't so hard. The bond between a mother and her baby is powerful.

But as she grew, she became more and more like Miklos. Her face was his face — a reminder every day and night of what he did to me. I tried to be a good mother, I tried to love her unconditionally, but I couldn't, and I will never forgive myself for that. Then, when George's wife died, he dedicated himself to convincing me that it was time to start afresh and to try to leave the past behind. I was a sick woman, Jessica, but I made a huge effort. I cleared out all my old papers, redecorated the house and decided I was going to do everything I could to make it up to your mother. But she never gave me the chance. She ran away from me be with that . . . to be with your father. She left me alone. And she was pregnant. I couldn't forgive her for that. I resented her happiness."

"If only you'd told her. You never gave her the chance to understand," I say.

"I swore I wouldn't tell her until after Miklos was dead. What if she'd tried to find him?"

I've been so taken in by the story that my grandfather had died before Mum was born that I hadn't considered anything different. Now I can see this is even worse than I'd thought.

"But he must've died years ago," I say.

"Oh no. He lived and lived, until the age of one hundred and one, until March this year."

Suddenly the time frame has narrowed, intensified. The past has marched straight back into the present. And I begin to understand.

"But with Miklos gone, things changed. I was no longer living a lie. Your mother's father was now, truthfully, dead. Suddenly my life was my own again. I had followed your progress as a violinist – it wasn't difficult with my contacts and your mother's letters. I knew you had a gift. I knew it was in your blood. I was expecting you to get the scholarship, and when I saw you and Stefan on that stage, you reminded me so much of George and me as young musicians. It was terrible to see you fail. I lived every moment of it with you and I had to give you a second chance; the chance I never had. I thought, perhaps, you could finally make things right again. I think you are the only one who can truly understand. You are my only hope. And you deserve a place at the RCM. That is where you belong. With Stefan."

"Our concert on December fifteenth," I say as the final pieces fall into place.

Chapter 25

Friday, December fourteenth. It's so cold you can almost feel it cutting through the glass in the windows of the drawing room. I scrunch up my legs and pull my sweater over my knees, hugging them into my body. I've persuaded Dad to go to the Science Museum. He'll love it there. I'd have gone with him but Mum wanted me here. I've had to lie a fair bit to set up this meeting. I've said nothing to Mum about Grandmother's story. It's not for me to tell her. Now they're sitting at opposite ends of the sofa, a large box file perched like a wall between them. I've played out this scene in a thousand different ways. I doubt any of them are right.

Grandmother asks Mum if the hotel is comfortable and Mum asks about the arrangements for the concert tomorrow. There are no fireworks, it's all very polite, but conversation quickly stutters to a halt.

Sarah brings in tea and they sip it carefully, almost in time with each other. My cup sits unused. I hate drinking tea out of a cup and saucer. That dainty clink of china puts my teeth on edge and makes me nervous and I'm nervous enough as it is. All this and one day to go until my performance. I look at my chewed fingernails, my ragged cuticles.

"Take your feet off the chair, Jessica," says Grandmother.

Reluctantly, I unfold my legs and slip my shoes back on. Mum raises her eyebrows as if amazed I'm doing what I'm told. A lot has changed in six months. Everything has changed.

Mum puts down her cup and Grandmother says, "I think Jessica has told you that I have something important to discuss with you."

"Yes, she has – and as I assume it concerns Jess, I thought she should be here with us."

"It concerns all of us," says Grandmother. "However, Jessica already has full knowledge of what I am about to tell you and I think she would agree that this is a conversation that you and I should have alone."

Mum fiddles with the button on her shirt. I wonder if she has any idea what all this is about. The silence seems to stretch and stretch.

Grandmother signals with her eyes and I stand up to leave. Panic flashes across Mum's face and her body seems to fold. Surely she can't still be afraid of being alone with her own mother?

"I'll be downstairs in the music room," I say. I try to make it sound reassuring.

Mum nods. The air feels almost sick with tension. I get out of the room as fast as I can and put some distance between myself and the door before doubling up as a heavy blackness swims over me. Before I know it, Charlie's by my side, hand under my arm, sitting me on the stairs. He kneels in front of me, his face full of worry.

"What's going on?" he asks.

I shake my head. He moves to sit beside me and puts his arm rather awkwardly round my shoulders.

"Come on, you can tell me," he says gently.

"I can't."

We sit in silence for a few minutes.

"Is this something to do with Stefan?" Charlie sounds almost hopeful. "Because if it is then he'd better know I won't have him hurting you — not ever. If he so much as. . ."

"It's got nothing to do with Stefan."

"Oh." He drops his arm and we both sit with our hands clasped between our knees.

"So is it the concert tomorrow? Ciaran and the boys are coming. I told you that, didn't I?"

"Yes, you did."

"Is it. . ."

"Charlie, I can't tell you. I'm sorry."

"You can. You can tell me anything, you know that, Jess. I will always, always be here for you. Whatever happens."

I glance towards him and he's staring down at the stair below. I bite the inside of my cheek. I know he means it.

"Thanks, Charlie. Really thanks."

I look upwards, trace the line of the stairs that I've run up and down so many times. My life here could be about to come to an end. Whatever happens, I'll be back in Manchester for Christmas. After that, I've got no idea. But the reality is, I don't want to leave. I don't want to leave London or this house or Grandmother or Sarah or Charlie. I need Dr McNair and Professor Jenniston and my ancient friends at Harris House. I need Ciaran. But most of all, I need to be where Stefan is. And that is here, in London.

The door to the drawing room opens and Mum walks fast across the hall. I don't think she even notices us on the stairs. I stand up, block her path.

"It wasn't my fault!" she shouts straight into my face. "It wasn't my fault she was raped. I didn't ask to be born. I didn't choose to look like my father. I didn't mean to wreck her precious musical career." Mum is near hysterical. "Why didn't she tell me? All those years I tired so hard. I blamed myself. My whole life." She's gulping for air. "How was I supposed to know?" She barges past me towards the door. Grabs her coat.

"Mum! Mum, wait."

She flings open the door, then turns to me. "My whole life – I've hated myself. I thought it was me. But it wasn't. It was *him*. And she didn't tell me. And it's such a *waste*."

"Mum, please." I try to take her hand but she pulls it away.

She staggers down the steps and I follow her. Her mobile phone is in her hand. She stops and looks at me properly.

"I need time alone," she says. "I need to think straight. Stay here. Please don't try. . ." She tails off. "I'll call you later."

I watch her leave. I don't know what to do. My legs won't move. My thoughts roll like thick fog through my head. As she disappears around the corner, Stefan swings into view, striding down the street, briefcase in hand, ready for our final rehearsal. As he gets closer, he begins to run. He knows everything. He knows about the meeting between Mum and Grandmother today. He knows I'm in bits.

"It's OK," he says as I collapse against him. He drops his briefcase, scoops me into his arms and carries me up the steps. Charlie holds open the front door. His face is a mask. Grandmother is disappearing into her office. I see it all in black and white, like stills from an old movie. It's all up to me now. I'm the only person who can make things right. I have to pull myself together. A voice threads its way into my consciousness. It's a voice I recognize – or a mixture of voices.

Use it, Jess. Don't fight your emotion. Pour it into the music.

The shadows roll away and the passion begins to burn once more.

Chapter 26

I take a deep breath, push back my shoulders and begin the lonely walk to the centre of the stage. It is exactly fifteen steps. I know. I've counted.

The audience clap and murmur quietly. I wait until I've reached my position, then turn to face them. One performance. That is all. The rest can wait.

My grandmother and George Ritchie sit at the front. Mum sits next to Grandmother, back stiff, body angled slightly away from her. Dad is on the other side of Mum. The hall is packed with people: friends, teachers and "invited guests" from Grandmother's extensive connections in the music world. But I'm not performing for them.

I'm performing for Grandmother, for Mum and for me. This is our chance; this is more important to me than anything else and I will not let them down.

I wait for the applause to die away. My left hand holds the neck of my grandmother's violin. My right hand grips the bow, just a little too tightly. I loosen it. Breathe.

The auditorium lights fade to darkness and I'm isolated in the spotlight. My dress is wickedly short, laced down the back. My heels are high, my make-up dark. I am not my grandmother. I will not fail.

I tuck the beautiful old violin under my cheek and feel the cherubs on my shoulder. I smile at Stefan. There is a brief pause. Someone coughs.

The notes of Stefan's introduction float into the air and, as I lift my bow, a silver-white heat spreads through my body. My fingers fly up and down the strings as my bow caresses, flutters and flies through the music. Deep inside the passion burns, reality disappears and the dream lives.

At the end I keep my eyes closed and listen to the silence. Listen to my heart pounding against my ribs.

The audience erupts into deafening applause. They stamp, they whistle and they whoop. Everyone is on their feet. Now I allow myself to look: Mum and Dad and all my friends from Harris House. Dr McNair, Professor Jenniston, Mr Noble. Harriet, Su-lin and Flora. Clapping, waving, smiling.

I bite my knuckles, stunned at the warmth and enthusiasm of the reception. Sarah's jumping up and down. Charlie's punching the air and hugging Rosie. I spot Grandmother's hairdresser, Michael, and he waves. Ciaran and the boys are going wild.

I turn to look at Stefan. He is standing as well, applauding. I put out my hand to him and he joins me.

We face Grandmother and Mr Ritchie. They remain seated in the centre of the front row. Grandmother's eyes are shining. Without taking his eyes off us, Mr Ritchie takes Grandmother's hand and raises it to his lips.

Stefan takes mine and does the same, and for a second the four of us are suspended in a parcel of time that will never be forgotten.

We leave the stage and return again as the stamping gets louder. I begin to relax, begin to enjoy myself. On our fourth return to the stage I see Grandmother lean towards Mum and say something. Mum smiles.

I dare to hope.

The applause finally dies away.

And reality returns.

I place Grandmother's violin in its case and run my fingers slowly along the strings. I pick up the little horseshoe brooch that I'd carefully tucked into one of the compartments and I put it back on my dress where Grandmother had pinned it before my performance.

Then, slowly, I close the lid.

This is just the beginning.

Acknowledgements

Thank you to my editor, Helen Thomas, for the enthusiasm, patience and charm with which she approached my manuscript and, likewise, to all the team at Scholastic. To my agent, Juliet Mushens, for her guidance, professionalism and fun. And to my tutors and fellow MA students at Bath Spa University, whose insights, expertise and continued support have made so much difference. Particular thanks to Julia Green and Steve Voake for their willingness to share their time and their knowledge, and to Janine Amos and John McLay, whose gritty advice on the business of publishing will stay with me for ever. I am also grateful to those with whom I have discussed music, musicianship and the legacy of abuse. Finally to my husband, daughters and sisters – for their inspiration and for making sure that life is never dull. And to my (long-deceased) grandmother, whose violin we discovered in the attic.